CADENCE

Also by B. J. Hoff
in Large Print:

Prelude
Song of the Silent Harp
Land of a Thousand Dreams
Heart of the Lonely Exile
Masquerade
Sons of an Ancient Glory
Dawn of the Golden Promise
Dark River Legacy
Vow of Silence
The Tangled Web
Storm at Daybreak
The Captive Voice

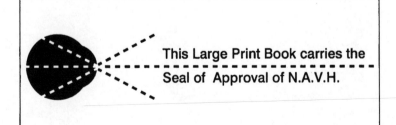

This Large Print Book carries the
Seal of Approval of N.A.V.H.

CADENCE

AMERICAN ANTHEM
BOOK TWO

B. J. HOFF

Thorndike Press • Waterville, Maine

Published in 2004 by arrangement with Thomas Nelson, Inc.

Thorndike Press® Large Print Christian Fiction.

The tree indicium is a trademark of Thorndike Press.

The text of this Large Print edition is unabridged.
Other aspects of the book may vary from the original edition.

Set in 16 pt. Plantin by Liana Walker.

Printed in the United States on permanent paper.

Library of Congress Cataloging-in-Publication Data

Hoff, B. J., 1940–
    Cadence / B.J. Hoff.
      p. cm. — (American anthem ; bk. 2)
    ISBN 0-7862-6023-8 (lg. print : hc : alk. paper)
    1. Italian Americans — Fiction. 2. Immigrants — Fiction. 3. Singers — Fiction. 4. Opera — Fiction. 5. Blind — Fiction. 6. Large type books. I. Title.
PS3558.O34395C33 2003b
    813′.54—dc22   2003061347

CADENCE

As the Founder/CEO of NAVH, the only national health agency solely devoted to those who, although not totally blind, have an eye disease which could lead to serious visual impairment, I am pleased to recognize Thorndike Press* as one of the leading publishers in the large print field.

Founded in 1954 in San Francisco to prepare large print textbooks for partially seeing children, NAVH became the pioneer and standard setting agency in the preparation of large type.

Today, those publishers who meet our standards carry the prestigious "Seal of Approval" indicating high quality large print. We are delighted that Thorndike Press is one of the publishers whose titles meet these standards. We are also pleased to recognize the significant contribution Thorndike Press is making in this important and growing field.

Lorraine H. Marchi, L.H.D.
Founder/CEO
NAVH

* Thorndike Press encompasses the following imprints: Thorndike, Wheeler, Walker and Large Print Press.

CONTENTS

CADENCE

*It matters not
If the world has heard
Or approves or understands. . . .
The only applause
We're meant to seek
Is that of nail-scarred hands.*

— B. J. Hoff

AMERICAN ANTHEM

Characters

Michael Emmanuel
Blind conductor-composer. Formerly an internationally acclaimed tenor.

Susanna Fallon
Sister of Michael Emmanuel's deceased wife. Emigrated from Ireland to help care for Michael's daughter (her niece).

Caterina Emmanuel
Michael Emmanuel's four-year-old daughter.

Paul Santi
Michael Emmanuel's cousin, assistant, and concertmaster of the orchestra.

Liam and Moira Dempsey
Husband and wife. Caretaker and housekeeper at the Hudson River Valley estate of Michael Emmanuel.

Rosa Navaro
Reowned opera *diva*, friend and neighbor of Michael Emmanuel.

∾:∾

Conn and Vangie MacGovern
Husband and wife. Irish emigrants eventually employed at the Hudson River Valley estate of Michael Emmanuel.

The MacGovern children
Aidan, Nell Grace, twins James (Seamus) and John (Sean), and Baby Emma.

Renny Magee
Orphaned street busker who emigrates from Ireland with the MacGoverns.

Andrew Carmichael
Physician from Scotland who devotes most of his medical practice to the impoverished of New York City.

Bethany Cole
One of the first woman physicians in America and Andrew Carmichael's associate.

∾:∾

Frank Donovan
Irish police sergeant and close friend to Andrew Carmichael.

Maylee
Abandoned child afflicted with premature aging disease.

Mary Lambert
Single mother of three children. Opium addict.

By Mention or Brief Appearance:

Fanny J. Crosby
Hymn writer and poet.

D. L. Moody
Evangelist.

Ira Sankey
Singer, songwriter, and partner of D. L. Moody.

The Mahers
Susanna's former employers and sponsors in Ireiand.

Robert Warburton
Prominent, influential clergyman and lecturer.

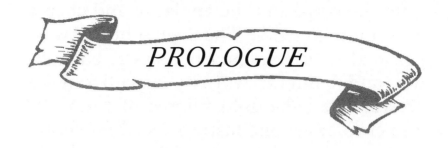

THE TROUBADOUR'S QUESTION

'Tis past; 'tis gone. That fairy dream
Of happiness is o'er;
And we the music of thy voice
Perhaps may hear no more.

FANNY CROSBY, from a tribute written
for Jenny Lind, the "Swedish Nightingale,"
upon her visit to the New York Institution
for the Blind

New York City, 1869

"Bravo! Magnìfico!" The curtain fell on the
final act of *Il Trovatore* to a deafening ovation,
and the auditorium quaked under the riotous
explosion.

Michael Emmanuel made yet another
deep, sweeping bow as bouquets were flung

onto the stage and the applause and cheers grew more frenzied. The theater blazed with prismed light refracted by crystal chandeliers and diamonds worn by the ladies in the crowd. Even the gold filigree of the walls and cornices shone lustrous, as if reflecting back the fire and passion of the enthusiastic crowd.

Michael had performed the part of *Manrico* the troubadour on many stages, in many countries, to much acclaim. But never had he been lavished with more adulation and fervor than here in America's greatest city.

The crowd began to chant *"Trovatore, Trovatore!"* calling out the name like a mantra until he obligingly took another bow. Twice more the curtain rose and fell, but this exuberant audience seemed to have no intention of letting him go. As he stood at center stage taking his bows, the cries of the crowd washing over him like a flood, he struggled to recapture even the slightest semblance of the elation that once would have accompanied such a triumphant performance. Instead, another feeling, all too familiar, drew in on him, engulfing him with a suffocating closeness. A wound in some dark hidden place, torn wider with each performance, had become

16

a deep, aching pit of yearning — a yearning for some nameless, indescribable . . . *something.*

The critics and the international press often spoke of Michael as having "the music world at his feet," but lately it had come to feel more like a predator at his back. His joy had abandoned him, leaving in its place only a gnawing emptiness. The crowds, the acclaim, the glitter, the fame, even the music itself — none of it seemed to matter any longer. It held no meaning for him, no value.

In that moment, a wildly irrational thought seized him. What would happen if, this very night, he were to take his final bow, turn, and simply walk away from it all — the years of study and preparation, the relentless discipline and drill, the never-ending rehearsals and performances and unceasing demands on his time and energy?

The adulation of the crowds. The sense of power. The celebrity. The glory.

Could he leave it all behind? What would it do to him? How would it change him?

Would he be a different man? A lesser man?

Or would he somehow become a *better* man?

His mind reeled with the idea, and he found it impossible to recapture reason, to return to himself. The sea of faces dimmed; the clamor of applause receded. His throat tightened. Scarcely breathing, he waited for some cold touch of dread to descend on him, or at least some sense of impending loss and grief. But nothing happened. He felt nothing but the nagging weight of fatigue, the exhausting aimlessness that had plagued him for months now.

Suddenly he thought of Deirdre. He had been questioning what such a radical change might do to *him*. Now he could not help but wonder what it might do to his wife.

Instinctively, he glanced toward the wings, but Deirdre wasn't there. She still blamed Michael for her failure to secure the role of *Leonora*. Incensed by his "betrayal" of her — his refusal, for the first time, to use his influence on her behalf — she hadn't shown up at the theater since the day he had told her that Annabella Antolini had been signed for the coveted soprano's role.

If he were to quit, to leave the world of opera altogether, Deirdre would never forgive him. Never. There would be no end to her fury. She would believe — and perhaps rightly so — that his defection would strike the final blow to her already downward-spiraling career.

He was suddenly jerked back to his surroundings as a young assistant placed a bouquet of roses in his arms. Michael stared at the flowers, then at the boy. Finally, he managed a forced smile and gave another brief, wooden bow to the audience.

When the curtain came down once again, he stumbled from the stage. Ignoring his manager and the others milling about in the wings, he raced to his dressing room, closed the door with a firm thud, and turned the key.

A STIRRING IN THE HEART

There is a murmur in my heart. . . .

EDWARD DOWDEN

Bantry Hill Estate, Hudson River Valley
Late November 1875

"No, no! *Assolutamente non!* I cannot do this, Michael!"

"Pauli, listen to me! I told you, Dempsey will be with you the entire time. He and the handler will see to the horse. You will have nothing to do except to sign the papers."

"I do not like the horses, Michael! You know I do not like the horses!"

"You need not *like* the horse, Pauli! The handler has been paid to bring him from the ship to the stables. You will simply go with

20

Dempsey in case he should need your help."

"What *help?* I would be of no help!"

Susanna, on her way down the hall in search of some clean sketch paper for Caterina, stopped short at the sound of raised voices coming from Michael's office. She wasn't intentionally eavesdropping, but it would have been impossible not to over-hear the boisterous dialogue taking place between Michael and Paul Santi.

Neither of the two men sounded angry, merely persistent. Some of their exchange was in English, some in Italian, but Susanna understood enough to gather that Michael had a new horse arriving at the harbor and was insisting that Paul accompany Dempsey to claim the animal.

Clearly, Paul had other ideas.

"You know I am no good with the horses, Michael."

"I know you are *afraid* of the horses, Pauli."

"No, not afraid. *Terrified.* I am terrified of the nasty beasts! You know this — and the horses know it also!"

"I am not asking you to *ride* the horse, Pauli, merely to go with Dempsey."

"Why does Dempsey need *anyone* to go with him? Why can he not go alone?"

"I *told* you. There will be papers to sign."

Michael lowered his voice. "Have you forgotten that Liam cannot read?"

Silence. Then, "Oh, all right, all right! I will go! But you remember, *cugino:* if your precious horse ends up in the ocean and me with him, my death will be on your head!"

Susanna smiled. She was used to these impassioned outbursts by the lively young Italian. Paul and Michael frequently sparred, but seldom about anything of real importance. She suspected that some of their disputes were deliberately instigated — sometimes by Paul, sometimes by Michael — simply because both of them enjoyed the verbal fencing. Michael often sounded amused during their contests, and it was common to see them both laughing and pounding each other good-naturedly on the back only minutes later, like schoolboys pleased with their own cleverness.

Just then Paul emerged from Michael's office, caught sight of her, and threw up his hands. "Why do I bother, I wonder? Always he wins!"

"What have you gotten yourself into this time?"

Paul rolled his eyes, giving a palms-up gesture of futility. "This is not *my* idea, you can be sure! It's all Michael's doing. He insists that I go with Dempsey to the harbor to fetch one of his ill-tempered beasts!"

Michael appeared in the doorway, dressed in a dark wool jacket and white shirt — more businesslike apparel than he usually wore at home. Was he going away again? Susanna tried to suppress a pang of disappointment at the thought.

He wore his dark glasses, too, and she wondered whether he had put them on for her benefit. He seldom wore the glasses except in her presence, a fact that she found increasingly puzzling — and annoying.

"Paul would have me believe I endanger his life by sending him to the docks," Michael said. "The truth is, I suspect he's eager to go, to avoid working this afternoon."

Paul feigned an injured look. "Susanna," he said solemnly, "if I do not return, I would like you to have my violin."

"But I don't *play* the violin, Paul."

"All the same, I want you to have it. In my memory."

"Well, that's very kind of you, Paul." She imitated his grave tone. "You can be sure I'll pray for your safe return."

"You see," Paul said to Michael, "even Susanna knows you have placed my life at great risk."

One eyebrow went up as Michael crossed

his arms over his chest. "I believe Dempsey is waiting for you."

"You are a hard man, Michael."

"So you have said. Many times. Now go."

"*Sì*, I go." Paul shot an impish smile at Susanna, then hurried off down the hall.

Susanna watched him go, relieved that Michael and his cousin were obviously back to normal in their relationship. She had developed a genuine fondness for Paul Santi, a bond forged the day Paul had finally divulged to Susanna what Michael had refused to reveal about her sister.

It had been Paul who explained about Deirdre's alcoholism, her turbulent and disastrous marriage to Michael, and the events that had led up to her death on the treacherous mountain road after a violent argument. Convinced that by withholding the truth from Susanna, Michael would only inflict more pain on her and, ultimately, on himself, Paul had told Susanna what Michael would not, risking his own relationship with the cousin he revered.

When he learned that Paul had broken his confidence about Deirdre and their marriage, Michael had been furious, bitterly denouncing Paul for a deliberate betrayal of trust. Only after much explanation and persuasion on Susanna's part had Michael finally moved past his anger and accepted that Paul had acted with honorable intentions. Paul had seen what Michael could not: that in his efforts to keep Susanna's memories of her sister untarnished, Michael was actually hurting her, fostering a distorted image of Deirdre, and encouraging Susanna's increasing suspicion of himself.

To Susanna's vast relief, the two had finally reconciled. There seemed to be no lingering evidence of the rift between them.

She suddenly realized that Michael was still standing in the doorway, waiting.

"I . . . I was looking for some fresh drawing paper for Caterina," she said, embarrassed by her own woolgathering. "She seems to have used up her entire stock."

"In here." He motioned Susanna into his office. "Cati likes very much to draw, no? Does she have any particular ability, do you think?"

"Actually, I think she shows quite a lot of skill for one so young. But, then, Caterina seems to do extremely well in whatever she attempts," Susanna said. "Except perhaps for her sewing."

"So I have heard," he said dryly. "Just so you'll know, Rosa, too, has tried to interest Cati in the sewing, also with no success."

Susanna smiled to herself. Rosa Navaro,

the famed opera star, had long been a close friend of the family — a neighbor and a surrogate aunt to Michael's daughter. Caterina adored her; if even Rosa could not interest Caterina in sewing, it might well be a hopeless cause.

Susanna waited as he crossed the room and opened the door of a floor-to-ceiling storage cabinet. As deftly as if he could see the shelves, he retrieved a thick pad of paper and handed it to her. "She likes best to draw the animals, no?"

"Yes. Horses are her favorite subject."

"*Sì,* she loves the horses. Already she rides well." He paused. "And you, Susanna? Do you ride?"

"Oh, no! No, I've never ridden. I'm afraid I share Paul's apprehension about horses. I've always been rather frightened of them."

"Ah, but there is nothing to be afraid of," he said, coming around to his desk and resting his hands on the back of the chair. "We must respect them, of course. But there is no need for fear."

He paused. "You think it strange that I would say such a thing."

It was a statement, not a question. And indeed, Susanna had been thinking exactly that, given the riding accident that had caused his blindness. Deirdre had written only the sketchiest of details about the incident: apparently Michael had been jumping his favorite horse when a pheasant flew out of a hedge and startled him. The horse's forelegs had become tangled in the hedge, and he failed to clear the jump. Michael was thrown, striking his head against a rock. According to the doctors, the blow caused irreparable damage to his optic nerve, blinding him for life.

Michael nodded as if he had read her thoughts. "What happened to me is most likely the reason for Paul's fear. But it wasn't the horse's fault. It was simply an accident."

He indicated that Susanna should sit down, and he lowered himself into the chair behind the desk and shuffled some papers out of his way. Although the dark glasses tended to put her off, his blindness evoked no feelings of pity for him. Sympathy, perhaps — after all, life must be much more difficult for him than for those who could see. But not pity. To the contrary, she felt admiration that he could live so fully, so *generously*, in spite of the obvious difficulties his disability presented.

But, then, Michael defied just about every preconceived notion she'd ever held of him. He was a man of many facets, a different kind of man entirely from what she once feared he might be.

He was also a man who could, with absolutely no warning, kindle feelings that confused and agitated her. She was attracted to him. Strongly attracted, in a way she had never before experienced. Consequently, she found herself torn between trying to avoid him and wanting to be near him.

According to Paul, the attraction wasn't entirely one-sided. Michael, he insisted, was coming to have "much affection" for Susanna. So far, Susanna had managed not to delve too deeply into the implications of this remark. Nevertheless, she couldn't entirely dismiss the quick dart of excitement that grazed her heart. Could Paul possibly be right? And if so . . .

She realized with a start where her thoughts were leading her and felt a sudden urgency to distance herself from the man across the desk. She stood so abruptly that her chair almost tipped over. "Well . . . ," she stammered, "I expect I should be getting back upstairs to Caterina. She'll be wondering what's become of me."

Michael got to his feet, his expression puzzled as he lifted a hand to delay her. "I was about to ask you if you would mind working with me this afternoon. Paul will be away, and I'd like to follow the Braille through the new sections of the *Anthem*. It would help me very much if you would play the piano so I can concentrate on the score."

Susanna's old uncertainty, the familiar feelings of ineptness, surfaced immediately, and she hesitated.

"If you'd rather not —"

"No . . . no, it's not that. I'll be glad to help. If I can, that is."

He smiled a little. "When will you ever dismiss this foolish sense of inadequacy, Susanna? You are much more accomplished than you're willing to credit yourself. Indeed, I suspect if I could ever catch you unawares, I would discover that you are a most gifted pianist. But every time I enter the room you stop playing."

Susanna couldn't think how to reply. Michael's incomparable musicianship intimidated her to the point that whatever ability she *might* possess invariably froze in his presence. It was one thing to accompany him and Caterina during one of their lighthearted evening songfests, but quite another to perform music of a more serious nature for Michael alone — especially one of his own compositions.

"I'll be in the music room most of the afternoon. Why don't you come down after

Caterina is settled in for her nap?"

For a moment, Susanna found herself staring, caught up in the warmth of his smile, the stubborn wave of dark hair that tumbled over his forehead, the breadth of his shoulders, the strength of his features that could soften when least expected —

She blinked, forcing herself to answer. "That won't be too late? I mean — aren't you going away?"

He frowned. "Going away?"

"I thought perhaps you were going downriver . . ."

He passed a hand over the sleeve of his coat, shaking his head. "No, not tonight. I'll be at home tonight."

Susanna's earlier disappointment vanished. "Well . . . all right then." She paused to clear her throat. "I'll just take this paper up to Caterina, and come down later."

"*Grazie,* Susanna."

It was impossible, of course, no more than a fanciful notion. But Susanna almost felt as though he were watching her as she left his office and started down the hall.

TWO

A LOVE BRUISED BY PAIN

Many days you have lingered
around my cabin door!
Oh! Hard Times,
come again no more!

STEPHEN FOSTER

New York City

Conn MacGovern got up and pulled back the blanket between the sleeping quarters and the other half of the room that served as the kitchen. Vangie was already at her work, even though it wasn't yet daylight.

She sat at the table, bent low over the sewing, her hair falling free as she worked by the flickering light of an oil lamp. Conn stood watching her for a moment, his throat

31

tight, his mouth sour with bitterness.

Whatever had possessed him to bring her here? This "house" was nothing but a hovel, a dilapidated shack of board and tin and tarpaper, squeezed among dozens of others just like it, or worse. The golden streets of America had turned out to be paths of mud and garbage, and the promise of a "job for every man" nothing but a lie.

Close on two months now they had been here, and so far he had found no work. Nothing more than an occasional odd job to help pay the rent. Were it not for Vangie's sewing and the pittance Nell Grace earned making artificial flowers, they wouldn't even have a roof over their heads.

Had his dreams of America been nothing more than folly after all? There sat his wife, crooking her spine and straining her eyes over piecework that paid a pitiful poor wage. His children were sleeping in broken-down beds in a cold and drafty room where, come winter, they would surely be taken with the rheumatism or even pneumonia.

Nell Grace was actually thinking of hiring herself out as a servant at one of the big houses uptown, though he would hear none of that foolishness. There was never enough to manage anything more than mere survival, not even with Renny Magee's meager findings from the discards in the alleys or the occasional coin she earned from entertaining a paltry audience on the street.

A worm of self-pity twisted in his gut. What more had he ever wanted, after all, than a patch of good land, a few animals, and a free man's sun on his back? And just see where his foolish dreaming had landed them all: in the heart of a godforsaken slum where people piled their waste in the streets like animals and drank water that tasted as if it had been drawn from a poisoned well.

Better they had stayed in Ireland than this! At least in Dublin they hadn't feared for their lives every time they stepped out of the house.

He sighed. Vangie turned and saw him watching her.

Conn tried to smile but failed. "You ought not be working in the dark, love." He buckled his belt and made an effort to smooth his hair with his hands before crossing the room to her. "Won't you be ruining your eyesight altogether?"

She lifted her face for his kiss. "I could do this in my sleep," she said. "And what are you about today?"

Conn heard the note of caution in her voice. She knew him so well, knew how it seared his pride, this going out in search of a job day after day only to return home empty-handed. "I'll be going back to the docks," he said, forcing a cheerful tone. "Sooner or later I'm bound to get on if I show up every day."

"You have the right of it there. As soon as they get a look at you, they'll see that you can do the work of three men, and won't they be hiring you on the spot?"

Leave it to Vangie to put a good face on things, he thought with a rush of gratitude. Her unfaltering faith in him was all that kept him going at times, and that was the truth.

"Your breakfast is ready," she said. "You go and wash, and I'll dish it up."

When Conn returned to the table, she had set a bowl of stirabout and a chunk of yesterday's soda bread at his place.

"I heard Nell Grace getting dressed, but the boys are still asleep," she said. "Renny has already gone off on one of her excursions. I do wish she wouldn't venture out on her own so, in the dark. Who knows what might become of the girl out in the streets by herself?"

"That one can take care of herself well enough. Only a fool would go and tangle with the likes of Renny Magee."

He adopted a gruff tone, but in fact he felt a certain peculiar pride in the girl's cheeky resourcefulness. Even so, he hoped he was right about her fending for herself. She was a rascal, she was, but though she fancied herself fierce enough to stand off a battalion of Brits, she was but a slip of a girl and hardly a match for some of the vile bounders afoot on the streets of New York.

Just then Baby Emma appeared in the gap between the curtains, her rag dolly tucked under her arm. She came trundling over to Conn to be picked up, and he swept her into his arms, tousling the mop of golden red curls as she nuzzled her head under his chin. She was warm and sweet, her skin still flushed from sleep, and in spite of his earlier dour mood, love spread over him like a soft cloak.

As he sat there, dandling his baby girl on his lap and watching his beauty of a wife, Conn thought about his two sons sleeping healthy and whole in their bed and the grown daughter who was an incredible gift to them all. How could he forget, even for a moment, the undeserved goodness of his life?

But directly on the heels of his remorse came the grievous thought of the lad they had left behind: Aidan, his eldest son.

Well, that had not been *his* doing, now had it? He'd had his passage, bought and paid for. But as the boy himself was wont to remind them with his bold tongue, he was a man grown, he was, and could live his life the way he wanted. His ticket to America had meant so little to him he'd been willing to give it up to Renny Magee, a total stranger, an itinerant street busker.

And hadn't they all tried to make him see the foolhardiness of his action?

Aye, but perhaps there was something more a father could have done, had he not lost his temper and washed his hands of his own son . . .

Conn clenched his jaw, recalling Aidan's warning that they might meet with more trouble in America than anything they had ever known in Ireland. What a bitter thing it would be if his son turned out to be right.

Vangie still held it against him that he had not been able to coax Aidan into coming with them. No doubt she thought if he had tried harder, he might have changed the boy's mind. But Aidan had made his choice, and that was the end of it. There was no purpose in dredging up the pain time and again. They had enough to worry over as it was.

Vangie was keen on reminding him that worry was a sin, that the answer to their prayers might not come quickly, but it would come *eventually* if they maintained their faith. Conn wanted to believe, as his wife did, that it was only a matter of time before something good found its way to them. But he had never been a patient man, and it was a hard thing entirely to have patience in the face of his family's growing need.

"In God's time," Vangie would say. "It will happen in God's time."

He could only hope that God's time would come soon, for he did not see how they could go on as they were much longer.

With Baby Emma in her arms, Vangie cracked the door enough to watch Conn trudge off down the street, his hands in his pockets, his cap pushed back on his head. Love for him welled up in her, but it was a love bruised by pain. The pain of watching her husband's pride drain away, day after day, like the lifeblood trickling from a mortal wound.

Conn was a proud man. Too proud, some might say. But he was also a good man, a man who looked after his family and took seriously his responsibilities as a husband and father. He had never been one for the drink, nor had she ever known him to cast a roving eye, although the women were quick enough to eye *him.* Gambling held no appeal for him, and he routinely handed his pay over to her before it had so much as warmed his palm. Back home, he had been known for his honesty and his willingness to lend a hand to his neighbors. By any account, he was a man to respect.

He was not, however, a man meant to be idle. It was bitter enough for a man like Conn to be unemployed, but to see his wife and daughter working when he could not must chafe his very soul. Vangie had seen the anger — and the anguish — that flared in his eyes when he walked into the room and saw her and Nell Grace at their respective tasks, and him with nothing to do. She knew all too well the toll this was wreaking on him, and the knowing wrenched her heart.

If only Aidan had come with them, perhaps things would have been different . . .

Impatiently, she shook off the thought. What would have been different? Then *both* of them would have been looking for work. A lot of help that would be to Conn.

But at least she would have had the comfort of her son. If Conn's temper hadn't been so quick that last day in the harbor, perhaps he might have been able to talk some sense into Aidan and persuade him to come with them after all.

The nails of both hands dug into her palms until she wondered that she didn't draw blood. She had to stop this puzzling over what they might have done — what *Conn* might have done — to keep Aidan from staying behind. Had to stop wishing for what might have been.

Had to stop blaming Conn for their son's willfulness.

She turned away from the door and set the baby to the floor beside the table, giving her a tin cup and spoon to play with. Nell Grace came into the room, her dark red hair tied neatly back with a piece of ribbon. "Morning, Mum. I'll dress Emma if you like."

"There's no hurry. You have your breakfast first so you can get on with your work. The boys will be up soon, and we'll need to clear a place for them to eat."

As if she could read the worry in Vangie's face, Nell Grace came to put a hand to her arm. "Da will find a job any day now, I'm sure. He just needs to find the right place, is all. A place where someone can recognize a man's worth for what it is."

Vangie turned to look at her, surprised but grateful for this thinly veiled attempt to lift her spirits. "Aye, the both of us know that, now don't we? 'Tis himself we need to convince."

Nell Grace smiled a little as she sat down

to her bowl of stirabout. "You could convince Da of just about anything, I expect."

Vangie looked at her. "Is that so?"

"It is," Nell Grace said, not looking up.
"Doesn't he dote on your every word? I only
hope the man I marry will be as taken with
my opinions as Da is yours."

"And aren't you a bit too young just yet,
miss, to be thinking about the man you will
one day marry?"

Nell Grace lifted one delicate eyebrow.
"Tell me again, Mum, for I forget — how
old were you when you married Da?"

Vangie's attempted frown crumbled
under her daughter's mischievous grin.
"You know very well I was exactly the age
you are now. Seventeen years. But didn't it
only make things harder for us, being wed so
young? I want better for you."

Nell Grace regarded her with a long, unsettling look. "Then you want more for me
than I want for myself. I couldn't imagine
anything much better than being married to
a man who would look at me the way Da
looks at you, and after twenty years at that."

Vangie felt herself flush. "*Fuist!* Such
foolish talk, and to your mother! You'd best
finish your breakfast and tend to your
flowers, miss."

She went to start the dishes, but after a

moment stole a glance at Nell Grace, who already seemed to have forgotten their exchange and now sat eating, absorbed in her own thoughts.

Vangie smiled as she turned back to the dishes. Nell Grace was right. Despite the struggles and drudgery that had filled so many of their years together, what she had with Conn MacGovern was something other women could search for a lifetime over and never find.

In truth, she wouldn't have traded even the hardest times for a different life with someone else. She was blessed even when burdened. The thought both shamed her and quickened the struggling hope within her heart. And suddenly even the chill that clung to the cabin walls seemed to give way to an unfamiliar warmth, a warmth that had nothing to do with the stingy bit of fire fighting to stay alive in the aged stove.

Vangie felt a tug on her skirts and looked down to see Baby Emma reaching up for her. Quickly she dried her hands and lifted the toddler into her arms, burying her face in the cloud of red-gold curls that so distinctly marked the offspring of Conn MacGovern.

THREE

Toward Home

Let others delight mid
   new pleasures to roam,
But give me, oh, give me,
   the pleasures of home!

JOHN HOWARD PAYNE

By midmorning, Renny Magee was hotfooting it back toward the house. Already she had dodged two drunken reprobates, a filthy old woman with not a tooth in her head, and a gaggle of swaggering bullies too young for whiskers, but who clearly fancied themselves men to be reckoned with.

Of course, they hadn't counted on Renny Magee. Just because she was slight and thin

42

as a whip, their type almost always made the mistake of assuming she was also frail and weak — and perhaps simpleminded as well.

She grinned to herself at the thought of how she had easily showed them up for the great lumpheads they were. Like most of the other tomfools who lurked about Bottle Alley, the boyos she'd met up with this morning had been neither clever enough nor quick enough to so much as give her a good chase. She'd outrun the lot of them in a shake without ever losing a breath.

Her morning foraging had not been a colossal success, but at least she had more to show for her efforts than what she'd started out with. She had crammed her pockets with some sizable scraps of material salvaged from the bins behind the German tailor's shop on Broadway. As clever as Vangie was with a needle, she would put the colorful pieces to good use.

The best of her booty was a perfectly good wooden chair, which someone had discarded in back of one of the row houses. A coat of paint, and it would look as good as new. She had also come across one of yesterday's papers, clean as could be, which the MacGovern would appreciate. He enjoyed his newspapers, he did.

Today she had gone as far as East Fourteenth Street, scouting for open parks and other sites where a busker might attract a crowd. Renny had gotten to know this end of the city fairly well by now, venturing into a new neighborhood every chance she got. Based on what she'd seen so far, she figured the district called the Bowery would be one of the more likely areas where a street performer could attract a crowd.

For now, however, she needed to get back to the house and help Vangie with the boys and Emma. Mornings were devoted to exploring; afternoons for helping out with the children and doing chores about the house. Then in the evening, depending on whether Vangie needed her or not, she would go back to the streets.

Renny had already figured out that if she were ever to turn a profit as a busker in New York, she had a great deal more to learn. Folks here seemed to mostly want songs and stories about the lands from which they'd come and this new land where they'd settled.

Not so in Ireland. There they hankered for the old tales, the legends of the ancient heroes and fairies and favorite saints. Back home, it had been as easy as chasing a hare out of the bushes to entertain a crowd on the street. A tune, a tale, and dancing feet had enabled Renny to make out just fine. Why, she could have gone anywhere in Dublin — in the entire surrounding countryside, for that matter — and earned a respectable wage for her efforts.

This place, though, was a city of foreigners. These people were strangers, with sundry origins and varied histories. How was she to learn such a jumbled mix of stories and legends, not to mention the different songs each clan boasted as their own? In two months of roaming about the littered streets and fetid alleys, Renny had taken in all she could, but in truth she was woefully ignorant of the different sects that made up this sprawling city.

New York was a stewpot of foreign faces and foreign tongues. The music was strange, the food even stranger. She was coming to recognize some of the more distinctive features of the Italian peddlers, or the small Oriental folk who hobbled down the lanes with their hands clasped as if in prayer, or the solemn-faced Hebrews who hurried along in pairs, always looking to and fro. But although she was learning her way about the city, she felt as if she'd only begun to scratch the surface. Why, the very sounds of New York — not to mention the astonishing sights and revolting smells — were enough to confuse a scholar. Such shrieking and screaming and cursing and cater-wauling the likes of which she had never heard! It seemed to Renny that, for the most part, these New Yorkers were a demented lot entirely.

Demented or not, she meant to soak up all she could about them. And she needed to do it as quickly as possible, if she were to earn her own keep and help out the MacGoverns. Things were hard for them right now, and Renny meant to do whatever she could to ease Vangie's worries and the needs of the children.

If only she could read . . .

Her mind raced as she hauled the chair along behind her, heading down Mulberry Street. If she could read, there would be no limit to what she could learn. If she could only access the newspapers — and perhaps even books — why then, she would surely find everything she needed to know and then some.

The MacGoverns could read, every one of them — except for Baby Emma, of course. Even the twins knew their letters and a number of words, and them only eight years old. Apparently, the MacGovern him-self, who claimed to have had an educated da, had taught his entire family, including Vangie.

So far Renny had been able to keep her inability to read a secret. None of her chums back home had been able to read, either, and such things hadn't mattered on the streets of Dublin. But she was beginning to realize that, here in America, a person who could not so much as read a newspaper was at a definite disadvantage.

She had briefly considered asking Vangie to teach her. Or perhaps Nell Grace. But they were always so busy, tending to their piecework and the household tasks and the children. She couldn't imagine presuming on them to spend time helping *her*. Why should they?

Besides, the very thought of revealing her *disadvantage* to anyone — even to Vangie — made Renny's skin heat with shame. No doubt it would make her even smaller, *poorer*, somehow, in their eyes, were they to know the truth.

It cut against the grain for Renny to ask for help. With few exceptions, she depended on no one but herself.

She despised admitting that there was anything — anything at all — that she could not manage quite well on her own. But when it came to the reading, if she didn't make her problem known to someone, then how could she ever hope to learn? No matter how resourceful she happened to be, she couldn't fathom how she could teach herself to *read*.

She slowed her steps, hefting the chair onto her shoulders as she turned the corner to Baxter Street and home.

Home. Was that really how she thought of her present situation, then? The rickety shack with the tarpaper roof, perched in the midst of all the other shanties just like it. Had this really become *home* to her?

In truth, Renny had never had a real home, so it was difficult for her to understand exactly *what* she felt, or was supposed to feel, about the place she shared with the MacGoverns. Yet she did like the sound of the word. *Home.* She liked the snug feeling that came whenever she said it aloud. Sometimes she would repeat it over and over to herself, savoring it as if it had a taste all its own.

But she was hard-pressed to find the right words to define it. A roof over her head. A mattress on the floor alongside the baby's cradle. Food on the table, no matter how plain the fare or how scanty the portions. A place where she didn't have to fear the shadows that moved about in the night, where she could sleep without a brick clutched in her hand for protection.

And yet it was more than that. Home, for Renny, was the MacGoverns.

But only, she reminded herself, as long as she was under her pledge to them.

Six months. That's what she had committed, to stay with them for six months in exchange for her passage to America.

She considered six months quite a long enough period of time to be obligated to anyone. She had her own life to live, her own future to see to. She had not come to America just to fetch and carry for the MacGoverns, no matter how decent to her they might be. Renny Magee was not meant to be anyone's *property*.

Indeed not. And that being the case, she would do well not to attach too much importance to her present circumstances. In a relatively short time, having kept her commitment, she would be free to go her own way. No doubt the MacGoverns would be as pleased to see the last of her as she would be to leave them behind.

And yet the thought of her eventual freedom failed to kindle in her the sense of anticipation and excitement it once had. Still, she had four months left to go before she could reclaim her independence — a considerable length of time. It was only natural she wouldn't yet feel any real eagerness at the prospect. For now, she would simply do the work expected of her and bide her time. When the day finally arrived that she could once again be responsible to no one but herself, she expected she would scarcely be able to contain her enthusiasm.

The house was in sight now, and as the morning fog lifted to reveal the small, leaning shack at the edge of the row, Renny stepped up her pace. Vangie would have saved her a bowl of stirabout, and there would be water heating on the stove for the dark tea the MacGoverns fancied.

All in all, Renny decided, the day was looking fine.

FOUR

SOMETHING OF GENIUS, SOMETHING OF GOD

Sweet blind singer over the sea,
Tuneful and jubilant, how can it be,
That the songs of gladness,
   which float so far,
As if they fell from an evening star,
Are the notes of one
   who may never see
"visible music" of flower and tree.

FRANCES RIDLEY HAVERGAL

Every day for weeks now, Caterina had taken to coaxing the old Irish tales from Susanna. Today was no exception. So, after lunch, with Gus the wolfhound dozing at the foot of the bed, Susanna spun yet another of the mythic

51

tales, this one about the lazy princess and her three aunts.

". . . And although the girl was lovely as the day itself and had three mysterious helpers to aid her in winning the prince, she was lazy to the point of despair. No doubt when she grew older and was no longer so fair, she would pay a dear price for her slothfulness . . ."

By the time the story was finished, Caterina was asleep. Susanna watched her for a moment. For the most part, the little girl seemed to have regained her strength, but two successive bouts of croup had left their mark. There were still times when the child seemed to tire too easily, times when her color wasn't quite as it ought to be. Susanna thought it was probably a good thing that Dr. Carmichael would be stopping by later in the week to check on her.

Finally, she went to her own bedroom to freshen up before going downstairs. She had barely managed to brush her hair and smooth her collar when she heard the sound of the piano coming from the music room. Apparently, Michael was already at work.

She hurried down the steps, anchoring her hair clasp as she went. By the time she reached the end of the hallway, the music of the piano had changed to that of the mandolin. With it came Michael's voice, honeyed and light.

Susanna stopped to listen just outside the music room, marveling at the tones that seemed to flow with such ease, such perfection. He was singing what sounded like an Italian folk song, a tune infused with sunlight and rolling hills and peaceful pastures.

Through the doorway, Susanna studied him. He sat on the window seat, the late afternoon sun casting a dappled glow on his features. He had changed to a scarlet-colored shirt of soft wool, which only intensified his dark good looks. With his eyes closed, his strong profile haloed by the light streaming through the window, he appeared younger, less formidable. Perhaps even vulnerable. And undeniably handsome.

At almost the exact moment she walked into the room, he stopped playing, unfolded himself from the window seat, and stood, smiling. "Ah, Susanna, you are here." He laid the mandolin on the window seat. *"Buono."*

There seemed to be no such thing as sneaking up on Michael, despite his blindness. And yet it both pleased Susanna and unsettled her that he always seemed to know the instant she entered a room.

"I'm sorry it took me so long. Caterina wanted a story."

He waved off her apology. As he reached for the dark glasses in his shirt pocket and slipped them on, Susanna felt a familiar sting of irritation. Why was it he never seemed compelled to wear the glasses in the presence of others, only with her? It was almost as if he felt a need to *shield* himself from her.

Susanna suddenly felt awkward and uncertain. "Michael . . . I don't know how much help I can be —"

Before she could finish, he motioned her to the piano stool. Susanna eyed the Bösendorfer's keyboard with a mixture of anxiety and anticipation. She loved to play this magnificent instrument, yet she was so tense that for a moment she could only sit and stare at the smooth ivory keys before her.

Michael, of course, could not see her agitation. He leaned over her shoulder to place a pad of manuscript against the music rack, and Susanna gave an involuntary shiver.

"If you would play this for me and then make notation, please? Paul will render the Braille later."

The section he pointed to was several pages into the score and barely legible.

Susanna did the best she could, disconcerted as she was by his voice.

And his nearness.

After she'd finished the notation in a shaky hand, he asked her to go back and play from the beginning. Susanna looked at him, then turned back to the manuscript, flipping through the first few pages. The first part had already been roughly scored for orchestra, but soon melded into a primary melody line with just some harmony and miscellaneous notes.

She eased her shoulders, flexed her fingers, and willed herself to relax. This was no concert hall, she reminded herself, and she was not a performer. She was merely helping Michael through some initial stages of his own music.

"Remember, Michael, I'm no virtuoso —"

"I know, I know. So you have said. Just . . . ah . . . play it as you like for now. In parts or with accompaniment. However you like."

At first Susanna had no conception of what she was playing, no real awareness of anything except the cool smoothness of the ivory under her fingertips, the absolute purity of sound as she pressed each key. She did exactly as she was told, initially playing one part at a time while Michael, still standing directly behind her, hummed a little and occasionally uttered, "No, that's not it," or, "Ah, yes! That's exactly what I want there."

It took Susanna a few minutes to realize he wasn't commenting on her playing, but rather on his own composition. The first time she brought together all the parts, she both felt and heard the stiffness in her technique, the utter lack of color and emotion in her playing, and she cringed.

But Michael didn't seem to notice. He merely went on humming, occasionally murmuring to himself. Then he moved around and began to tap lightly on the side of the piano to spur her on to a brisker, more strident rhythm.

The longer she played, the more the music began to reach out to her, beckoning her, drawing her out of herself. She started, caught off guard when Michael moved behind her and began to tap her shoulders with both hands, urging her forward, driving her on. After a moment, however, she lost her self-consciousness, and her fingers seemed to fly over the keyboard, improvising, adding, drawing forth an extensive accompaniment to the notes on the pages. The force of the music infused her spirit, raising her to the level of performance such glorious music demanded. The sounds and rhythms marched and danced, filling Susanna's soul, transforming the room into a concert hall, the Bösendorfer into an entire orchestra.

This was Michael's newest work, the *American Anthem*. He rarely spoke of it to her, but she had heard him and Paul working on it together, knew he often labored over it long hours into the night. Twice he had incorporated excerpts from it into the orchestra's concert program.

A distinctly nationalistic flavor ran through the work, as if it had been woven by the people of many nations, striving to form a whole. Although symphonic in its structure and complexity, it was an *earthy* folk music.

But more than anything else, it was a music of the spirit. Triumphant and rejoicing, it proclaimed a mighty faith, yet in places it was imbued with such plaintive melodies and sweetness it brought a kind of yearning to the soul.

Too quickly, it ended.

Susanna reached the end of the pages in front of her, her hands clinging to the last chord as she sat in stunned disbelief. The work was not even half complete; obviously, it was destined to be a huge, expansive score. But even in its unfinished and preliminary state, it left her both exhausted and exhilarated, her pulse thundering, her mind racing.

On occasion, Susanna had caught such a strong sense of a composer through his music that she felt as if she *knew* him, or had at least caught a glimpse of his heart. So it was at this moment. She was convinced that she had heard the song of Michael's soul in his music. She had heard something of genius, certainly, but even more, she had heard something of God.

She felt acutely disappointed, even stricken, by the music's *incompleteness.* It was like being held captive by the power of a thundering, monumental story — only to find that it was a story without end.

Then she came to herself and realized that Michael's hands still rested on her shoulders.

The strength and warmth of his hands stole the breath from her, even as the *Anthem* had left her breathless. She tensed, and he dropped his hands away, leaving Susanna to wonder at the inexplicable feeling of abandonment that followed.

Michael heard her catch her breath, felt her stiffen beneath his touch. Immediately he released her, but too late. She jerked to her feet, made a hasty apology, and left the room.

He hadn't meant to offend her. In truth, he'd been so caught up in the music and her interpretation of it that his actions had been more instinctive than deliberate.

Yet more than once he'd been seized with a strong urge to touch her. Whenever she took his arm to guide him, or drew close enough that he caught the sunny scent of her hair, he would find himself over-whelmed by the desire to pull her closer. But always he stopped himself in time. He had no way of knowing whether she might wel-come the familiarity or shrink from it. Or slap his face.

Now, standing alone at the piano, he won-dered why he found it so difficult to sense Susanna's feelings. True, he was often frus-trated by his inability to assess facial expres-sions, but he considered himself reasonably intuitive. Despite the blindness, he believed he was capable — at least in most circum-stances — of gauging another person's re-sponse to him.

Not so with Susanna.

Just when he thought she might be warming to him, if only as a friend, he would hear a distance in her voice. He could never be quite certain whether she genuinely wanted to be with him, or simply tolerated him as she might have endured the attendance of a tiresome but unavoidable employer.

The very possibility made him cringe.

Michael found the idea of being *tolerated* just as abhorrent as being *pitied*. And to be tolerated by a woman who could make his head swim simply by entering a room was more than he could bring himself to face.

On the other hand, perhaps he was expecting too much. Given Susanna's earlier suspicion of him — induced in part by Deirdre's blatant lies, but also by his own attempts to conceal the truth — perhaps the fact that they had progressed as far as they had was no small achievement. At least she no longer seemed to mistrust him, no longer openly avoided him. At times, in fact, he could almost bring himself to believe that she was becoming . . . fond of him.

Of course, that might be nothing more than wishful thinking on his part. Or self-delusion.

Or abject foolishness.

Why should Susanna be even remotely attracted to him? He was blind. Years older than she. And as best he could recall his own shaggy reflection in the mirror, not exactly the stuff a young girl's romantic dreams were made of.

Worse, he had been her sister's husband, in a marriage that had been *disastrous*. When Susanna first arrived at Bantry Hill, Michael had attributed her coolness not only to her distrust of him, but also to the difficulty of her position. She was the sister of his deceased wife, yet she had been separated from Deirdre for years and had never even met him — her brother-in-law — until her arrival in America. Even her relationship with Caterina was complicated by the fact that she was not only the child's aunt and companion, but in addition functioned as a kind of nursemaid and governess.

Susanna had been thrust into a household of strangers in a foreign country, to live under the same roof with a man she didn't trust, a man who, for all she knew at the time, had made her sister's life one of unhappiness and tragedy. Such a situation would have strained the endurance of the most rugged, intractable personality, much less that of one so young and — unless he was badly mistaken — so unsophisticated and tender-hearted. And yet she *had* endured, and had come to trust him.

But even if she no longer suspected him of being the monster Deirdre had apparently made him out to be, Susanna might never be able to feel more than a passionless regard for him. A sisterly affection, at best.

The very idea brought up a swell of revulsion in Michael's throat. The role of elder brother might be more appealing than that of barbarian, but it was most definitely not the role he would choose to play in Susanna's life.

And what about Paul? Was it possible that Susanna and Paul might be attracted to each other? Paul could not speak of Susanna with anything less than admiration and warmth. And as for Susanna, even without the ability to see them together, he could sense that she held Paul in extremely high regard, that she genuinely liked him.

Everyone liked Paul, he reminded himself. How could they not? Pauli was lively, quick-witted, sensitive. What was there about him *not* to like?

Young girls seemed always to find Paul appealing, with his boyish charm and courtly manners, his zest for life. His youth . . .

Michael shook his head. *Santo cielo,* he himself was only thirty-seven! Not yet ready to be put out to pasture!

Then another thought occurred to him. Perhaps Susanna's awkwardness in his presence had nothing to do with him, and everything to do with her own background. Because of her steady nature, her considerable education, and the maturity that seemed to far outdistance her actual age, Michael tended to forget just how sheltered Susanna's life must have been. As the youngest daughter of parents who made their living from a small farm, she had no doubt lived a rustic existence — simple, quiet, and remote.

He had the impression — mostly from Deirdre — that their early lives had centered primarily around church and immediate family. The rebellious Deirdre apparently had broken out of that vacuum, managing to escape the isolation of the dairy farm.

Hadn't she often taunted him with tales of her various wild escapades, her many beaus, and the libertine company she'd kept, unbeknownst to her family? These stories might have been overblown, even fabricated, but Michael had no doubt that Deirdre would have found a way to create an active social life for herself.

The opposite was probably true of Susanna. He suspected she had stayed close to home, ill at ease with most people — especially men — and he doubted she had ever been romantically involved with anyone, at least not seriously.

If he was right, might that not account for at least some of the uneasiness he sensed in her when they were together? Granted, things were better between them now, but there were still times when she seemed uncomfortable, as if she couldn't wait to get away.

For his part, Michael sensed a major battle going on between his brain and his heart. He wanted to protect her, to shelter her. He wanted to know her better. He wanted to encourage her, to build her confidence, to help her realize her natural gift for music.

He wanted to hold her.

At various times, Susanna displayed the curiosity of a child, the idealism of a young girl, the reasoning of a scholar, and the bedrock steadiness of a saint. She had a way of laughing that made him wish for more, an enthusiasm that could strip away his well-placed defenses, a joy that lifted his heaviness of spirit, and a quiet faith that seemed to have been tried both by intellect and experience. She was guileless but not naive, agreeable but not complacent, practical but never predictable.

She could exasperate him one minute with a noncommittal remark about a piece of music, only to disarm him a moment later with an unsolicited but surprisingly insightful observation about the composer's intention for that music.

In spite of her youth, she was far more complex than any woman he had ever known. She was as fascinating as she was complicated, as frustrating as she was delightful.

The truth, rather than striking him like a thunderbolt, had been creeping in on him for weeks now, a stealthy but insistent shadow. He didn't know whether to moan with despair or sneer at his own foolishness.

For the first time in years — and against any common sense his infuriatingly romantic, Tuscan-Irish spirit might claim — he was falling in love.

In love with Susanna.

FIVE

BLACK BEAST OF BEAUTY

Opportunity often shows its face in an odd and most unlikely place. . . .

IRISH PROVERB

The wind blew raw with winter riding on it when the word came down once again: no jobs today.

Conn was cold and sore discouraged, yet could not bring himself to leave the harbor. The thought of the worry in Vangie's eyes kept him ambling about the docks long after he had an excuse for being there. She was doing her best to keep their spirits up, but Conn knew too well the look of desperation that would greet him when he walked through the door again with empty pockets.

Hands shoved inside his jacket, he stood staring at the big ships rocking in the water. Crewmen roamed the decks: laughing, shouting, cursing, herding passengers aboard, or slinging their gear over their shoulders as they prepared to disembark. Nearby, a raggedy child wailed, clinging to the skirts of a mother wasted from starvation or illness. At a blast from a ship's horn, the child squalled even louder, but the mother turned her face away, paying no heed.

The usual assortment of immigrants milled about, anxiously searching for a familiar face or someone who would show them where to go. A dozen different languages could be heard, but — Irish was the most prevalent — here a Kerryman's sharp accent, there a Donegal lilt.

Conn knew he ought to go into the city and try some of the factories again, but hopelessness settled over him like a sodden blanket, thwarting his intentions and draining his strength. After countless weeks of trudging the streets and haunting the warehouses, hadn't he tried every possible place where work might be found? And all in vain. There was simply nowhere else to go.

The sound of a loud commotion farther up the docks caught his attention. He looked, but could see only a raucous crowd gathered near the pier. He turned to go, but stopped again when he heard a sound that chilled his blood.

A horse, screaming wild with panic and pain. He had heard the sound too many times not to recognize it.

He shouldered his way through the crowd and saw two men trying to lead a big, powerful-looking stallion off a rusting, blistered ship. The great beast was savage in his resistance. He was a magnificent brute, midnight black and strongly muscled, but the fine, elegant head was encased in an iron muzzle, which the horse was fighting with a vengeance.

As Conn watched, the stallion reared, striking out with deadly hooves when one of the men attempted to restrain him. Conn looked around. Close-by — but not *too* close, he noticed — stood a slender young fellow seemingly intent on the goings-on. He had the dusky skin and features of an Italian, but was dressed too fine for any Italian immigrant Conn had ever met up with.

At the moment, the lad looked a mite pale. Once he opened his mouth as if to call out something to the men struggling with the stallion, but the words seemed to die in his throat as he stood gawking at the scene before him.

Conn turned his attention back to the horse. The crowd was heckling the two men, shouting and jeering at their lame efforts to subdue the stallion. The handler was about to lose control, while the other, a thickset, middle-aged fellow with a drooping mustache, was clearly out of his element as he attempted to calm the animal. The poor beast was crazy with fear, no mistake about it. He wanted nothing more than to free himself, and he would kill anyone who happened to get in his way.

The jibes and catcalls, the confinement of the muzzle, and the inept efforts of the men trying to handle him had obviously served to fire the stallion's madness. When the fool hauling on the lead rope turned to bring a whip crashing down on the animal's lathered flank, Conn felt the beast's primal rage explode inside himself.

Every muscle in the horse's body seemed to knot with the effort to break free. He reared and hammered the boards with his mighty hooves. Ears pinned flat against his head, he swung toward the man on his left, then the other.

Scarcely realizing what he was doing, Conn wedged his way to the front of the crowd, stopping when he saw the stallion throw the handler off balance with a furious shake of his head. The ferret-faced man bellowed a loud curse as he jumped sideways. "I'll have no more truck with that black devil!" he roared. "This is as far as I go!"

Turning, he flung the whip down and stomped away, leaving the older man nearly helpless to control the stallion. As if he sensed the man's fear, the horse exploded in fresh fury, giving a vicious scream, lunging and heaving as he tried to wrest himself free.

Conn didn't think, but merely reacted. He threw himself past the crowd, yanked the lead from the gray-haired man, and shoved him out of the way. Gleaming with sweat, the stallion lashed out with his powerful hooves at this new adversary. But Conn gamboled around him, staying out of his way, giving him no target as he continued to grip the lead rope.

The stallion shook his head, spraying saliva through the muzzle, but in spite of the animal's resistance, Conn managed to keep a firm grasp on the rope. The great black beast eyed him with raw malice as Conn began to speak in broken fragments of the old Irish tongue. He kept his voice quiet but

70

steady, dropping it lower still as he coaxed and murmured to the enraged animal. When the horse dipped his head toward Conn as if to threaten him, Conn drew a step nearer to let the stallion catch his scent.

The sight of such a magnificent beast in that cruel iron contraption was a grief in itself, and Conn burned to free the animal from its confines. But for the moment, he had no choice. Trying to remove the muzzle would likely cost him a hand or an arm.

His shoulders ached from the strain, but he managed to retain his hold. By now the two were engaged in a deadly dance of power, each intent on forcing the other to capitulate. And all the while, Conn continued his low Irish drone, his eyes locked with those of the stallion.

Finally, the horse's wildness began to cool. Conn breathed a little easier as he saw the bunched muscles relax a bit. But those malevolent eyes followed his every move as he slowly and ever so carefully moved one hand to the horse's crest.

Immediately, the stallion froze, ears flattened, eyes glinting.

Conn stopped, then tried again. And again. On his third attempt the horse, though still guarded, seemed to realize this man meant him no harm, that he could tolerate his touch. For several minutes, Conn stroked him, first one side and then the other.

With his hand resting on the horse's withers, he stood, quietly waiting, until the stallion's skin ceased rippling and the dark eyes lost their wildness. Slowly, then, Conn unlocked the muzzle and carefully peeled it away, groaning to see the damage that had been done to that elegant head.

Ugly, seeping sores had formed from weeks of constant chafing. The animal had to be in absolute misery.

Conn felt the blood rush to his own head, pain hammering at his temples as he beheld what had been done to this noble beast. He could almost feel the animal's relief, to be finally shed of his torment.

Keeping a firm hold on the rope, he turned to the middle-aged man and his younger companion. "This horse needs attention right away. Those sores are infected."

The older man nodded and stood regarding Conn with a speculative expression. "We've lost the handler, as you saw for yourself," he said in a gravelly voice. "I've no idea how we'll get the animal upriver."

Another Irishman, Conn realized the moment the man opened his mouth. But, then, was there anyone in New York City who was *not* Irish?

He continued to stroke the stallion's back. Though still guarded and tense, the animal was at least standing quietly enough for now and no longer seemed bent on killing him.

"You work on the docks, do you?" asked the Irishman.

Conn shook his head. "There's no work to be had on the docks of late. At least, that's what we're told."

"So you're needing work then, are you?"

"Aye, that I am. Needing it in a bad way," Conn admitted. "I've found no job since we arrived, other than a bit of day labor, nothing that lasts."

"Dublin born, are you?"

"Not at all," Conn replied. "We're from the country — at least we were, until we had to move into Dublin City to survive. The wife and I were both born and raised in County Kildare."

The man nodded. From under his heavy eyebrows, his gaze traveled from Conn to the stallion, and then back to Conn. "You know horses."

It was a statement of fact, not a question. Conn nodded. "I do. I was a stable hand for a time, when I was a boy, and later I handled and took care of the stables for a fine trainer.

One of Ireland's best." He glanced at the stallion. "This, now, is surely a magnificent beast."

The other man turned to look at his younger companion, who raised his eyebrows.

The Irishman turned back to Conn. "You would be well paid if you were to go along with us upriver and handle the horse."

Conn stared at the man. "Now, d'you mean? Today?"

The older man nodded. "We need to be leaving right away. And this lad and myself are no match for that devil."

Conn's hand must have tightened on the stallion's back. The animal snorted, head lifting as his ears flattened again.

Instantly Conn gentled his touch, and the horse settled down again.

Conn looked from the stallion to the Irishman. "I expect I could go," he finally said. "But I'd have to be letting the wife know. She'll fret something terrible if I don't turn up before dark."

"Send one of the boyos with a message," the other man suggested, jerking his head toward a group of young boys playing along the pier. "I'll pay."

The Irishman watched Conn with an expression that seemed to indicate he had more to say. After a moment, he tipped his cap forward a little and crossed his sturdy arms over his chest. " 'Tis not for me to be offering anything for certain, you understand, but you might give a thought to talking with my employer when we arrive. We lost our trainer and stableman some time back, and he's in need of a man he can count on." He stopped. "He wants a good man with the horses as soon as possible, especially with this spawn of the devil arriving. There might be a job for you if you're interested."

Conn's heart leaped to his throat. "Is that so now?"

" 'Tis. As I said, I can't make any promises, but after seeing the way you handled this ill-tempered beast, I'd be willing to vouch for you."

He paused, eyeing Conn for another second or two, then added, "My employer won't stand for a drinker or a scrapper."

"Man, I am neither."

The older man's eyes held Conn's for a moment more. Then he raised a hand and gave a sharp whistle to hail one of the boys at the pier. Three came running, and he dispatched the quickest of them with a coin and the message Conn repeated for Vangie.

"All right, then," the man said, turning

back to Conn. "Do what you must with that black *pooka* and let us be on our way."

"How do I call you?" Conn asked.

"The name is Dempsey. And this here is Paul Santi. He's cousin to my employer, Mr. Emmanuel."

"And the horse, does he have a name?"

"Aye, as I was told, he's to be called 'Amerigo.' "

Conn turned away from the other two and looked at the stallion straight on, deliberately masking his sympathy for the animal, which was still a grand piece of horseflesh in spite of the evident abuse. The black beast eyed him in turn, his ears pricked.

"So, then — *Amerigo* —," Conn said, "will you come with me like a gentleman or must we be having it out again?"

The dark eyes shifted, and for a moment Conn braced himself for yet another skirmish. But finally the black stallion gave a princely toss of his head, snorted, then quieted, as if in concession to Conn's authority.

Conn watched him, strangely moved and even saddened to see the horse's grudging submission. "I know, big fella," he said softly in the stallion's ear. "I know how this must gall you. 'Tis a bitter thing to have no say in your own welfare, to be treated as nothing more than a piece of meat, your

76

only value the strength of your back and what you can earn for your greedy master."

He paused as the dark, world-weary gaze seemed to take his measure. "I promise you this, Amerigo," he said, his voice lower still. "You give me no grief, and you will get none from me. You will find that I am a fair man." He paused. "We will hope the same can be said of your new owner."

As they left the docks, Conn's mind played the Irishman's words over again. *"There might be a job for you if you're interested . . ."* He tried not to get his hopes too high, but how could he *not* hope? After all this time — all the disappointments and discouragement, the roads that seemed to lead to nowhere, the bitter taste of failure on his tongue from morning till night — what else did he have *but* hope?

Was it possible that this big, mean-looking beast might actually turn out to be more blessing than curse?

It was all he could do not to laugh aloud at such an unlikely idea.

Especially when he saw the hot-tempered *pooka* glaring at him as if he'd like nothing better than to dismantle Conn's head from his shoulders.

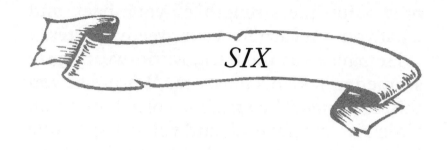

SIX

MEETING MAYLEE

Somewhere there waiteth
   in this world of ours
For one lone soul,
   another lonely soul —
Each chasing each
   through all the weary hours,
And meeting strangely
   at one sudden goal. . . .

EDWIN ARNOLD

After they closed the office for the afternoon,
Dr. Bethany Cole and Dr. Andrew
Carmichael settled themselves in the buggy,
pulled their lap robes snugly around them,
and set off for Mulberry Street.

The raw wind held a threat of sleet or snow, but Bethany had finally managed to convince Andrew that she didn't mind the cold. In fact, she actually enjoyed it — up to a point. What she really liked was the opportunity to study the busy city streets. New York was like an ongoing stage play, featuring new dramas with new actors and different scenes around every corner. Her fascination with the city never ceased.

At the moment she was following with great interest the progress of a pig and an extremely large black-and-tan dog as they made their way down Elizabeth Street. At first glance, she'd thought the pair seemed unlikely friends, but on closer inspection she saw that one was actually trying to muscle the other out of the street. When they reached the corner, the pig staked out a heap of garbage for his own, attacking it with zeal. When the dog pushed in as if to share a meal, Bethany assumed the pig, smaller by half, would simply leave the spoils and move on. Instead, the fierce little creature turned on the dog with such aggression that the startled hound took off as if he'd been attacked by a wild boar.

Bethany laughed, and Andrew, who had also been following the implausible scene, joined her. Once they were past, Bethany turned to him. "You said you'd tell me about the patients we're calling on this afternoon."

He nodded. "Have you heard of Michael Emmanuel?"

"The musician? Of course. He's a patient?"

"No, his little girl. She had a bad case of croup some time back. Had it twice, in fact — both very nasty bouts. She seems to be doing nicely now, but I stop in on occasion, just to check on her."

"But you actually *know* Michael Emmanuel? We're going to his *home?*"

Andrew shot her an amused look, and Bethany realized she must have sounded like an awe-struck schoolgirl. "Sorry. I suppose I'm something of a fan. I attended his opening concert this season. I also heard him sing once, in Philadelphia, before his accident. He was incredible! What a terrible thing to happen to him, losing his sight."

Andrew nodded. "I never had the opportunity to hear him sing, but I seldom miss one of the orchestra's concerts, if I can help it. Well — you'll meet him this afternoon, and I think you'll like him very much. He's quite a remarkable man. They live upriver, so we'll make that our final call of the day."

"I must say, I'm impressed, Andrew. I had no idea when I came to work with you that

I'd be meeting celebrities."

"Much as I covet your admiration," he said dryly, "I expect Michael Emmanuel is the only celebrity you'll be meeting through your association with me. As you've undoubtedly noticed by now, my patient list inclines toward a more modest social class. And in that regard, I should fill you in on our first call."

He reined in, allowing an omnibus to pass ahead of them. "Let's just say that while Caterina Emmanuel will no doubt *steal* your heart, I'm afraid our next patient will more than likely *break* your heart."

The orphanage was a bleak, three-story building on Mulberry Street with half a dozen sagging steps leading up to the front door. The windows were small and narrow, the roof in need of repair. Beneath a dull afternoon sky and devoid of any hint of color or greenery, the place reminded Bethany of every sorry-looking, grim institution she had ever encountered.

Inside, the long, uncarpeted hallways were cold and dim and quiet — too quiet for a place where children lived. The bare walls were relieved only by peeling paint and an occasional gouge in the plaster, and the few windows were narrow and uncurtained. But although the air was stale, it was noticeably free of the unpleasant mix of odors often associated with similar establishments.

"I suppose it *could* be more depressing, though it would take some doing," she said in a near-whisper. Something about the Cora Wylie Children's Home discouraged a normal tone of voice.

"I know." Andrew's voice was hushed as well. "But it's not really as bad as it looks. The place needs renovating, of course, but that takes money, and there's never enough for the essentials, much less a healthy infusion of light and color. Still, there's an excellent staff here: qualified and compassionate. I can assure you, that's not always the case among the metropolitan children's homes."

They passed three little girls who were being shepherded down the hall by an older companion. They all smiled at Andrew, and the older girl made a reply to his greeting. For Bethany, they had only curious looks.

At the end of the corridor, Andrew took her arm and guided her to the hallway on the left. "This way. Maylee is in a room to herself."

This was a shorter corridor, and as they approached the room at the very end on the right, Andrew pressed Bethany's arm to slow their progress.

"Just a reminder that Maylee is extremely bright and perceptive," he said. "She's not hard of hearing or slow-witted or any of the things people sometimes assume when they meet her for the first time."

With a quick glance in Bethany's direction, Andrew rapped lightly on the door, identifying himself but not waiting for a response before pushing the door open onto a small, neat room. Its corners were shadowed in the weak gray light seeping through a solitary window, but the bedding and curtains splashed color enough to dispel the gloom.

"Dr. Carmichael!"

"Well, Maylee, how are we today?"

Andrew motioned Bethany closer, and she went to stand beside him. "This is Dr. Cole, Maylee," he said, reaching to take the child's hand. "I told you about her last time I was here. Dr. Cole will be working with me from now on."

"Hello, Maylee. I'm very pleased to meet you." Bethany smiled and held the child's gaze. At this moment, she was thankful Andrew had taken the time to prepare her for this first meeting.

Maylee sat in the middle of a small iron bed, surrounded by pillows and a stack of books. She was even smaller than Bethany had expected — tiny and delicate, almost doll-like. Her face was thin and wrinkled, with small, sharp features and almost no eyebrows or lashes. Only a few wisps of snowy white hair dusted her scalp. Her elbows and knees appeared painfully swollen, and her hands exhibited the "liver spots" associated with the elderly.

She appeared to be an extremely small, wizened old lady.

She was eleven years old.

Bethany's heart wrenched in pity. She had never seen a disease like this before.

"You did it again, Dr. Carmichael!" Maylee exclaimed. "You asked me how *we* are doing today. Why do doctors and nurses always say 'we'? There's only one of me, after all."

Without waiting for a reply, Maylee turned her attention to Bethany. "Hello, Dr. Cole. How do you like working with Dr. Carmichael? Is he *very* difficult?"

The girl's voice was thin and high-pitched, but Bethany found herself immediately captivated by her smile and the distinct glint of humor dancing in her eyes. She reminded Bethany of a bright little bird, alert and eager.

"Well, I would say that Dr. Carmichael is actually quite easy to get along with," she replied. "*Most* of the time."

"And is he a *good* doctor?"

"Oh, he's an excellent doctor, I assure you," Bethany said with a straight face. "But hasn't he already told you that?"

Maylee threw her hands up and giggled. "Yes! Often!"

"That's just about enough from you two," said Andrew. He feigned an indignant look. "I would hope for a little more respect from my own associate and my favorite patient. Now then, Maylee — let's just have a look at you and listen to your heart, shall we?"

"See? You did it again! We can't *both* have a look at me and listen to my heart, now can we?"

Andrew summoned a stern expression as he removed the stethoscope from his medical case. "I was speaking of Dr. Cole and myself. Do you know what 'precocious' means, young lady?"

"Maturing early? Advanced for my age?" Maylee burst out laughing.

Bethany marveled that this child could find humor in her condition. That she could actually laugh at herself, given what she must endure, was nothing short of astonishing.

Apparently there was no research — at least none that Andrew had been able to come up with — dealing with a disorder such as Maylee's. He was at a complete loss as to any form of treatment. Two other physicians who had consulted on her condition leaned toward the influence of external agents, but Andrew strongly believed Maylee's disease to be the result of some sort of genetic mutation.

Bethany had seen the helplessness in his eyes when he told her about Maylee. Now, after meeting the child for herself, she understood his frustration. As physicians, there should be something they could do, some sort of treatment that would at least improve the quality of her life — a life that was certain to be woefully brief.

The painful reality was that the girl was aging at an incredible pace, and there was nothing anyone could do to stop it. Given her present rate of decline, Andrew projected that Maylee could not possibly live more than another year, if that.

At Andrew's suggestion, and with Maylee's consent, Bethany listened to the girl's heart and checked her pulse. The readings reflected the vitals of an elderly woman rather than those of an eleven-year-old child.

Andrew resumed his examination, this time concentrating on the girl's swollen and obviously tender joints. Maylee warmed to him — indeed, seemed to blossom under his attention. And Bethany remembered something else Andrew had told her about the unfortunate child: although she lived in an institution among dozens of other children, for all intents and purposes she lived alone.

It wasn't so much that the other children shunned her. To the contrary, Maylee was accepted and well-liked by the others. But given her physical limitations, especially the increasing stiffness of her joints and the fatigue that resulted from the slightest exertion, the girl found it all but impossible to participate in the normal activities of childhood.

She continued to study her lessons and played quietly by herself in her room. Sometimes, when she was strong enough, she would entertain one or two of the younger children by reading to them or telling them stories. What seemed to bring the girl more comfort and enjoyment than anything else were her books. Books, Andrew had told Bethany, were Maylee's best friends.

But how wretchedly unfair that books should be the child's *only* friends.

Later, after leaving the orphanage and starting for the ferry, Andrew seemed unusually pensive. Bethany was struggling with her own emotions, and neither spoke for several minutes.

The visit with Maylee had left her filled with a chafing pain that was anything but "professional." In fact, she couldn't remember that she had ever felt such a mixture of anguish — and anger — about a patient.

"Are you all right?" Andrew asked quietly.

Bethany cleared her throat. "It's so unfair! Isn't there *anything* we can do?"

He gave a long sigh. "Believe me, Bethany, I share your frustration. This is one of those times when I feel more like a failure than a physician."

Bethany looked at his swollen hands grasping the reins and saw that they were trembling.

"I've read every text, written to everyone I can think of, including some friends in Europe — anyone who might know something I don't. But not a one of them has ever seen a case like Maylee's. It's as if she's the only child ever to be afflicted in such a manner. The only thing I've found that helps at all, so far as the swelling and the discomfort, is what I take myself. Salicylic acid. That at least seems to give her some temporary relief."

Bethany's gaze traveled from his hands to his lean profile. His expression was uncommonly strained. "Do you ever get angry, Andrew?"

He nodded, not looking at her. "More often than you might think."

"But who do you get angry *with?*"

"With myself, I suppose. For not knowing enough, not being able to do enough. Or sometimes I suppose I simply get angry with *life* in general. For being so unfair."

"But not with God."

"God didn't do this to Maylee, Bethany."

"Then who did?" Outrage welled up in her and overflowed. It wasn't as if she hadn't attended critically ill or dying children before today. Even in the short time she'd been practicing medicine, she had encountered far too many cases that kept her awake nights.

But the disorder that would eventually claim Maylee's life seemed especially . . . cruel. A little girl shouldn't have to go through such an ordeal. She shouldn't have to watch herself turn into an old woman before she reached puberty. She shouldn't have to hear the doctor she obviously admired and trusted admit that he could do nothing — absolutely nothing — to help her.

A child should not have to die before she'd had a chance to live.

"Don't you ever question God, Andrew? Don't you ever wonder how to reconcile what we're taught about God's goodness, his compassion, when you see some of the terrible, ugly — *heartless* — things that happen to people? To innocent children?"

He turned to look at her. "Do I ever question why God allows these things? Yes, of course I do. How could any physician *not* question? But do I believe God is some sort of a vindictive spirit wielding his power on a whim — blessing some and cursing others? No. I don't for a minute believe he inflicted Maylee with this condition. He loves her more than that."

"He may not have caused it, but he *could* prevent it! If God loves her so much, then why doesn't he simply take it from her? Or at least provide a means of mitigating the symptoms and easing her misery?"

Andrew's reply was slow in coming. "He could have prevented the Cross, too," he said quietly, "but he didn't. I suppose if we could explain *that,* we could explain just about anything."

He turned to her again, his expression still solemn, but gentle. "I don't have an answer for you, Bethany. I can't even answer many

90

of my own questions. The only thing I know for certain is that God's love is beyond our comprehension. In fact, it seems to me that his love is as much a mystery as his will. As to why he does what he does or doesn't do what we think he should do — well, I suppose that's where faith comes in. Sometimes there's simply nothing else to do but trust him."

Bethany stared at him. One of the fundamental differences between Andrew's faith and her own was that his seemed to be inextricably woven into everything he did. He stepped boldly into the arena of life, went head to head with its injustices and evils, its challenges and struggles, securely armed with his faith. If he succeeded at what he attempted, then God was good and to be thanked. If he failed, well, God was *still* good and to be thanked. Simply because he was God.

Bethany, on the other hand, was more likely to leave her faith behind the lines for fear it wouldn't withstand the blows of battle. Her resolve, her own strength of will, and her stubborn refusal to concede defeat kept her going. Or so she had once believed.

Now she wasn't so sure. "I'm not like you, Andrew," she said hesitantly. "My faith is no match for yours. I have so many questions —"

He regarded her with a tilt of his head and a curious look. "Do you really think I don't? And how do we go about measuring faith, Bethany? That seems to me a futile effort altogether. We can't know very much about our faith at all until we find ourselves in a situation that tests it. Then, I expect we're often surprised by what we discover. About our faith — and ourselves."

His next words seemed carefully considered. "You asked me a moment ago if I ever question God. I think what I question is *life*, not God. It seems to me that life itself prompts continual questions. But the more I question, the more I find myself believing that the answer to all my questions is God. In fact, it seems to me that he's the *only* answer that can be trusted."

He shrugged and gave a self-conscious smile. "Sorry. I didn't mean to go on."

Bethany made no reply. She was reluctant to admit that she didn't quite understand what he was getting at. He had certainly given her something to think about. At the moment, however, the only thing that seemed to be registering was the realization that she no longer felt like shaking her fist at heaven and shouting *Why?*

Andrew reached to take her hand. "If it's any consolation, Bethany, I do understand. I'm not exactly a stranger to doubt or frustration."

"Andrew — you couldn't possibly understand how I feel. You're simply too good a man."

A look of dismay darted across his features.

"You've said that before, and it's not so." His tone was unnaturally sharp. "I'm not a 'good man,' Bethany. Not at all. Not like you think."

Bethany smiled to herself but kept silent. She had no intention of involving herself in a debate with Andrew about his character. For one thing, he was far too modest to admit to the admirable traits she saw in him. And for another, she wasn't ready to risk letting him see the strength of her feelings for him.

Although she wasn't at all sure how much longer she could manage to conceal those feelings.

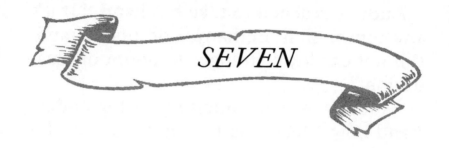

SEVEN

AFTERNOON ENCOUNTER

A copper-skinned six-footer,
Hewn out of the rock.

JOSEPH CAMPBELL

They were nearing the docks on the way to the ferry when they encountered Sergeant Frank Donovan. He was standing near the entrance to the harbor, stabbing the air with an index finger as he harangued a group of young boys.

Andrew drew the buggy to a stop and called out to him. The sergeant turned, his disagreeable expression clearing after a second or two. He made a gesture that they should wait, then turned and dispatched the youths huddled nearby with a chop of his hand.

"And it's a cell for the lot of you if I catch you bedevilin' old man Potkin again!" he shouted after them.

He approached the buggy, rapping his night stick against the palm of one hand. "And what would two of our city's most eminent physicians be doing in this part of town?" He doffed his hat to Bethany with a smile that made his dark eyes dance. "On a mission of mercy, are we?"

"Actually, we're on the way to the ferry, you rascal," said Andrew. "Dr. Cole and I are going upriver on a call."

The police sergeant fastened his full attention on Bethany, and she forced a smile in return. Donovan was tall, like Andrew. A big strapping Irishman, he gave off such an air of hardness and strength that he might have been hewn from a slab of granite.

And something about his eyes led Bethany to believe that he could be just as cold.

Andrew's friendship with this man puzzled her. She couldn't imagine how he and Frank Donovan could have possibly been more different. Andrew's strength and quiet masculinity seemed to derive from a deep inner peace — a *stillness* within himself —

95

while the Irish police sergeant struck her as a man burning with energy. Whether it was a fiery nature or raw power that fueled the flames, she couldn't have said. She knew only that Frank Donovan unsettled her.

He had a way of looking at her that bordered on impertinence but stopped just short of being downright offensive. On the other hand, his behavior toward Andrew appeared to be prompted by a genuine fondness, even though most of the time he tempered his respect with a biting edge of cynicism.

"Upriver, eh? Hobnobbing with the gentry, are we?"

The policeman was watching her, and Bethany felt her face flame at the realization that he'd caught her staring. She forced herself to meet his gaze straight on, and he lifted a dark eyebrow in an expression of wry amusement — as if he were completely aware of her discomfiture and enjoying it immensely.

"Not everyone up the river is gentry, Frank," Andrew was saying. "Actually, we're calling at the Emmanuel estate, up near West Point."

"Emmanuel? The blind man?"

For just an instant, Bethany detected a glint of irritation in Andrew's eyes. "Michael Emmanuel, yes," he said. "The *musician.*"

"How did you get mixed up with *him?*"

Andrew knitted his brows together in a dark frown. "His daughter is my patient, Frank. I'm not 'mixed up' with him."

Frank Donovan crossed his arms over his chest and tipped his hat farther back on his head. His gaze traveled to Bethany, then back to Andrew. "No need to get tetchy, Doc. You do seem to get yourself hooked up with some strange company at times, is all."

"I suppose I do, but you can be sure there's nothing in the least strange about Michael Emmanuel. He's an interesting man, and his daughter is quite a delightful child."

The policeman regarded him with a thoughtful look. "That may be, Doc, but there was a bit of talk at the time of the wife's accident, you might recall."

"There's always talk, Frank. And seldom much truth behind it."

Donovan shrugged. Turning to Bethany, he again lifted his hat to her. "Well, then, I won't be keeping you from your patients. You two have a care now."

Without another word, he turned and walked away.

Andrew shook his head, smiling a little.

"Have you been friends long?" Bethany said after a long silence.

"A few years now." He paused. "I know Frank can be aggravating at times. But he's a good man, really. A fine policeman, an *honest* one. And he has more courage than ten men — perhaps too much for his own good."

When Bethany made no reply, he added, "He doesn't mean any harm. It's just his way."

She shot him a dubious look.

"Really," he insisted. "Once you get to know him, you'll see what I mean. Frank just takes some getting used to."

Bethany had no intention of getting used to Frank Donovan. There was a *hardness* about the man that never failed to put her off. He always seemed to be darkly amused by his surroundings, but Bethany didn't for a minute believe he was as shallow as he pretended to be. To the contrary, she suspected that the Irish police sergeant possessed an intellect every bit as formidable as the courage Andrew had referred to — and a temper that could turn downright nasty if provoked.

And there was something else, something she couldn't quite define. The few times she had been around Frank Donovan, there had been a moment — albeit fleeting — when his behavior toward her seemed to reflect, not so much contempt or dislike, but *suspicion*. As if he didn't quite trust her.

Andrew, of course, hadn't noticed. Andrew seldom saw anything but the good in others. In fact, for a man of his intelligence and experience, he often seemed surprisingly *unworldly*, perhaps even a little naive.

An inexplicable trait, but one she found endearing. And also, at times, exasperating.

Andrew watched Bethany closely, secretly glad that she didn't seem to take to Frank Donovan. Perhaps he should have made more of an effort to point out his friend's good points.

But in truth, he was relieved. Frank, after all, did have a way with women. Andrew didn't really begrudge him the ease with which he attracted the ladies, although he *had* occasionally wondered what it would be like to have a dash of Frank's appeal.

Most of the time, however, Andrew actually found Frank's "Irish charm" rather amusing; he even enjoyed teasing him about it every now and then. But this was one time he was glad that Frank's charm hadn't worked its magic.

Andrew held no false illusions about himself. He knew he was a rather plain, decidedly awkward man. Awkward physically and, at least around women, awkward socially as well.

He hadn't minded all that much. Not until he'd met Bethany. Even then, he had been almost glad when she brought up the subject of his arthritis. After all, if she attributed his ungainliness to the disease, she might not realize that even if he didn't have an ache or a pain about him, he'd probably still be a bit of a dolt. At least around her.

He glanced at her again. She was studying the ships in the harbor, and he took advantage of the moment to indulge in an unhurried view of her profile — which to his way of thinking was nothing short of a work of art.

When she turned and favored him with an unexpectedly bright smile, he whipped his head around so hard he felt his neck crack.

Oh, he was in a fine fix, all right. A fine fix, indeed.

He only hoped Frank didn't catch on to the state he was in. Andrew counted him as his closest friend, but the thought of Frank's merciless teasing made him shudder. The man could be downright relentless when he caught hold of something that amused him. And the idea of Andrew being smitten with a woman like Bethany Cole would almost certainly strike Frank as a huge joke.

And rightly so, he thought grimly.

Michael Emmanuel had insisted they stay for dinner, so it was nearly nine when they boarded the ferry. The mist-laced wind off the river made the night seem even colder. Bethany secured her scarf more snugly about her neck as they settled themselves for the ride.

"Well," she said, as much to herself as to Andrew, "so much for preconceptions."

Andrew tugged at the collar of his coat. "Preconceptions?"

Bethany nodded. "Michael Emmanuel. And Susanna. I had them pictured altogether different from the way they are."

"What were you expecting?"

Bethany furrowed her brow. What *had* she expected? Certainly not the unaffected ease with which the blind musician had hosted their evening. Nor the surprising quietness and gentleness of the voice that had once thrilled thousands. As for Susanna, Bethany had taken immediately to the young woman's warm demeanor and her quick, friendly smile.

"I would never have guessed Michael Emmanuel would be so . . . comfortable. So easy to be with. He seems so unaffected, so unimpressed with himself. And I really liked Susanna. She's lovely, isn't she?"

Before Andrew could reply, Bethany added, "She's much younger than I thought she'd be, but she has a steadiness about her that makes her seem older, somehow. And I sensed that she might like to be friends."

"No doubt it gets rather lonely for her up here, isolated as they are. Especially since she's relatively new to the area. To the *country.*"

"It's like something from a novel."

"What's like something from a novel?"

"Their story." She turned to look at him. "Really, Andrew — think about it. The sister of a man's deceased wife travels across the ocean to care for a child she's never seen and ends up falling in love with her famous brother-in-law."

Andrew snapped his head around to stare at her. "Why on earth would you think Susanna's in love with Michael?"

Bethany rolled her eyes. Men. You had to hit them over the head with a board sometimes. "Surely you've seen the way she looks at him?"

His eyes grew wider still. "No, I can't say that I have." He paused. "How *does* she look at him?"

Bethany sighed. She didn't consider herself a romantic, not in the least, but there was something about Michael and Susanna that had captured her interest — and her imagination.

"Just take my word for it, Andrew. Susanna Fallon is in love with her brother-in-law. And Michael is in love with her. It's just that neither of them knows it yet."

He laughed. "You seem awfully sure of yourself. Is this some sort of womanly intuition, or are you really as positive as you sound?"

"Both. You'll see."

"I think you might be dangerous," he said, shaking his head. "A physician who also reads minds."

"It has nothing to do with reading minds. It's simply a matter of being aware of those around you. The way they look at each other. Or *don't* look at each other. The way they touch. Or don't touch. A change in the tone of voice."

She went on, intrigued by her own discovery. "I wonder if Michael knows he tends to flush a little every time Susanna opens her mouth. If the man could see, he'd never take his eyes off her. Yes, he's definitely smitten."

The faint amusement that had brimmed

in Andrew's eyes only an instant before now gave way to a look that could only be described as startled. Whatever accounted for the change, he seemed to recover quickly.

"Dangerous," he repeated with a nod. "Definitely dangerous." He nodded firmly, then added, "You did like them, though?"

"Oh, goodness, yes! They're absolutely delightful! I can understand how you and Michael might become fast friends. You think a great deal alike."

Indeed, it struck Bethany that Andrew's friendship with Michael Emmanuel made much more sense than the high regard in which he seemed to hold that awful Frank Donovan.

The thought of the annoying Irish policeman brought a question to mind. "Andrew, what did Frank Donovan mean today, about there being 'talk' when Michael's wife died?"

Andrew didn't answer right away. "It was all gossip, really. You know how people like to speculate on the misfortunes of the famous. Michael's wife was killed in a carriage accident not far from their home. Because of the lateness of the hour and the fact that she was alone, there were some rather wild rumors going round. There was a terrible thunderstorm that night, and no one could quite figure why a woman would have been out alone in such weather." He stopped. "Some of the rumors hinted that there was trouble between her and Michael, that in fact she was having an affair at the time."

Bethany shuddered. "How awful. As if he hasn't had enough tragedy."

"Yes, well, as I said, there was a great deal of gossip, but I have no idea if there was any truth in it."

He seemed eager to change the subject. "I believe Susanna was greatly impressed with you," he said. "Did you notice how many questions she asked about our work — about *your* work?"

Bethany rolled her eyes. "In truth, I don't want Susanna to be *impressed* with me. I'd like it better if we could just be friends." She paused. "Actually, I hope we can be friends with both Susanna *and* Michael. And that little Caterina — what a charmer *she* is! They're a delightful family."

"But they're *not* a family," Andrew reminded her quietly. "Not really."

"True," she said. "But that could change."

EIGHT

A DREAM AND A PRAYER

I prayed for good fortune. . . .
God gave me dreams.
I dreamed of high places. . . .
God gave me wings.

NELL GRACE MACGOVERN

By the looks of him, a body might have thought that the man had either gone daft entirely or else was deep in his cups.

Since Conn MacGovern had never been a man for the drink, Vangie could only conclude that some sort of derangement had suddenly descended upon her husband.

He swept through the door like a mad Viking, an idiotic grin plastered from ear to ear, his face as red as if he had eaten live coals for supper. Now that Vangie knew he was not lying dead in a ditch, the dread that had been building inside her all evening gave way to anger.

"Where have you been, man? I've been out of my mind with worry!"

For a moment he looked puzzled. "I sent a boy —"

"A boy who said you would be away a few hours! In case you haven't noticed, it's suppertime! And a *late* suppertime at that!"

To her amazement, he laughed. A deep, full-throated, booming laugh of a kind Vangie had not heard from him in an age. And then he came charging toward her, lifting her from her feet and swinging her around until the room swam in front her.

"*Conn!* Stop it now! Stop it, you great *amadan!* What's come over you?"

The twins were seated round the table, with Baby Emma in her chair between them. Renny Magee was putting wood on the stove, while Nell Grace ladled soup into the younger ones' bowls. All as one, they stopped to gape, first at their father, then at Vangie. Wee Emma clapped her hands and shrieked, as if she thought the antics of her parents were grand fun.

No more had the words left her mouth

than it occurred to Vangie that only one thing could be responsible for the high spirits of her husband.

"Conn?"

"A job, love! I have me a job!"

Vangie gave a small cry. "You don't!"

"Ah, but I do! And not just any job, my beauty! Oh, no, not at all. A grand job it is, and with a fine place for us to live as well!"

Vangie held her breath, afraid to believe.

He sobered a bit then. " 'Tis the truth, love. I'd not joke about something as big as this."

Vangie knew then that it was so. She knew it from the beam of confidence she had not seen in his eyes for much too long a time, knew it from the scarcely remembered lift of his shoulders, the strong thrust of his chin, and the way he was looking at her as if he had at last brought her a basket of joy instead of yet another bucket of despair.

"Oh, glory be to God," she choked out, barely able to stand without buckling.

"Well, tell us, man! Tell us everything!"

And so tell them he did, and took great delight in the telling. Conn perched himself by the fire and rubbed his hands together in anticipation. He deliberately drew out his tale, gaining great satisfaction as he watched the astonished faces of his wife and children, who were circled about him as if he held court. He stopped to answer their eager questions, sparing no detail, for hadn't it been a long time indeed since he'd had anything worthwhile to relate to them, much less an account that would bring such excitement to their eyes?

"An *estate*, do you say?" This from Vangie.

"Oh, love — wait until you see it! You can't imagine! Why, it's even grander than the Lighton Mansion back home!"

"It *isn't!*"

"I give you my word, the place is a palace!"

"And you are quite sure that we are to come, too, Da?" Nell Grace asked, her eyes enormous and shining. "There's truly room for us all?"

" 'Tis just as I told you. You don't think I'd be going without you, now do you?" Conn reached a hand to his daughter's hair.

"It seems that years ago the estate belonged to a wealthy old man," he went on to explain. "In addition to the big house, there's another lodging on the property, where the caretaker and his wife used to live. It's empty now. The present manager and his wife — the Dempseys, who came across from Ireland just as we did — live in the big house. The caretaker's place is where we will be living. 'Tis a fine, sturdy house, it is, well-built and clean. And doesn't it even have a few pieces of furniture for our use?"

"It's too much to take in, Conn! Can this truly be happening to us?"

"Ah, there's more, love," he assured her. "But first let me tell you about my new employer, Mr. Emmanuel — they call him the Maestro, him being a great musician, you see. He's an Italian man, did I say that? And in spite of his obviously being very well-to-do, he doesn't seem a bit puffed up about himself, not at all. In fact, I'd say he's a real gentleman, exceedingly well-educated and fine-spoken." He stopped. "Poor fellow, though. According to Dempsey, the Maestro lost his wife only last year in a carriage accident."

"How awful!" said Vangie.

"It is that. He has his little girl, though," Conn continued, "a lass of four years. His sister-in-law lives there, too, as well as a cousin — a young Italian fellow who nearly died right in the middle of the harbor from fear of the stallion."

He smiled at the recollection of the boy's pasty face and boggling eyes. "And then there's the older couple I mentioned. Dempsey manages the place, and his wife does the cooking and the cleaning. But the two of them are getting along in years, and Mr. Emmanuel is after making things a bit easier for them. When he discovered that I had a wife and a grown daughter — not to mention two healthy sons — who would be willing to work, he seemed pleased altogether."

He paused to catch his breath. "Did I tell you the man is blind?"

"*Blind?*" Vangie cried. "Oh, the poor man! And him having lost his wife as well. So much sorrow for him to bear, Conn."

Conn nodded. "Aye, but he's not a man who wears his feelings on the outside. He strikes me as the type who keeps his own counsel. He's very soft-spoken and I suspect he's quiet-natured all through. Dempsey says he's a man of great intellect, with the music and all — a famous man at that."

"Oh, Da!" Nell Grace stared at him as if he had risen an extra foot in height even as she watched. "And to think he employed you right then and there as he did! He must place great faith in you."

"And why wouldn't he?" Vangie said. "It's clear this Mr. Emmanuel knows quality when he sees it."

She immediately clapped a hand over her mouth. "But he can't see you at all! Oh,

Conn, what if I say something as foolish as that in front of the man, God forbid?"

Then she smiled at him, her eyes shining. "Well, but whether he can see or not, 'tis obvious he could sense the kind of man you are."

Conn fought down a surge of pleasure at the pride glowing in his wife's eyes. In truth, he couldn't quite forget the way his new employer had made him feel during their discussion. "Well," he said, "the Maestro did consult with his man, Dempsey, and with his cousin as well, in private, before he offered me the position. But only for a short time. Indeed, it seemed to me that he had made up his mind before he conferred with them. And I would have to say" — Conn realized at that instant just how much it pleased him to say it — "that he treated me almost as an equal throughout the entire interview. He treated me with *respect*, Vangie. As one man to another."

Conn's heart threatened to melt at the sight of his wife's damp eyes, her trembling smile. He pulled both her and Nell Grace close, putting an arm around each of them. "It would seem that the good Lord has answered our prayers," he said, feigning a gruff tone to conceal his own unreliable emotions. "I have a job, and we are to have a new home. And not in this wretched city, but in a place where there is land and clean air."

"And *horses!*" put in James. "Don't forget the horses, Da!"

"Well, now, it's not likely I would be forgetting the horses, Son." Conn tousled the lad's hair. "Seeing as how it's a horse I have to thank for getting me this job in the first place!"

Renny had hovered near the stove throughout the entire exchange, her feelings going into a spin as she heard the MacGovern's spirited account of his day.

It was plain that the lot of them had forgotten her presence, not that she would have expected anything else, what with them being so stirred up over the MacGovern's big news.

And it *was* big news indeed, no doubt about it. Vangie was all a-tremble. Nell Grace, the quiet one of the household, had more questions than a judge, while the twins exerted their energy by thumping each other on the head like wee simpletons. Through it all, Baby Emma fought to stay awake so she could emit an occasional squeal.

As for the MacGovern, well, he was about

to rip a seam, so full of himself was he at the moment.

Renny was glad for them all, she truly was. One look at Vangie, her face brilliant with this new joy, was enough to make Renny's own heart swell to bursting. And in truth, it was fine to see the worry lines eased a bit from the MacGovern's rough features, as well. He was a good man, if a hard one, and he did dote on his family, every one of them.

Aye, this was a good thing altogether, and she mustn't mind that they would almost certainly be cutting her loose now. She could hardly expect a place among them in their new situation. More than likely, the MacGovern would not give a thought to the bargain they had struck back in Ireland, but would be relieved to be shut of her, and the sooner the better.

She was assuring herself that she would be grateful to get on with her own life when she noticed himself and Vangie looking in her direction, speaking in low tones to each other. As she watched, the MacGovern gave Vangie's shoulder a bit of a squeeze, then crossed the room toward Renny.

She held her breath, steeling herself for what she was about to hear. She hadn't thought it would come so soon. Couldn't he have waited for a spell, at least until the next day, before giving her the brush? Did he have to be in such an infernal hurry?

MacGovern crossed his sturdy arms over his chest and stood studying her with that keen-eyed look. When he finally spoke, it was with the gruff tone she had become accustomed to. But his words were not what she had expected.

"What with all the excitement, Renny Magee, I might have forgotten to mention that we will expect you to accompany us to our new home."

The cold, hollow place inside Renny suddenly felt the sun. She swiped at the fringe of hair falling over her eyes and stared at him. "You . . . mean to take me with you?"

"Of course, we'll be taking you with us. As I recall, we had an agreement, did we not? That you would stay with us no less than six months in return for Aidan's passage?"

Renny nodded. "Aye, that's so."

"And isn't it only the decent, Christian thing, to keep your word, once a bargain is sealed?"

Renny's gaze locked with his. " 'Tis."

"Then that is that, it seems to me." He uncrossed his arms and hitched his thumbs in his belt. "Unless you can think of a good reason why you should not come along with us, that is."

"No!" Renny blurted out the word like a shot. "A bargain is a bargain. But —"

"But *what?*" he said, his eyes narrowing.

"You're quite certain — there's a place for me? There will be work for me, so that I can earn my keep, I mean? Vangie will still . . . need me?"

"Sure, you've seen how it is with us. There is always work enough." The MacGovern regarded her with a long, thorough look. "You will be assisting me in the stables and on the grounds, as well as helping Vangie. You will not be idle, girl, I promise you that."

Renny pulled her most sober expression, as if to consider his words for another moment. "Then I will go with you," she said, her tone as solemn as a banker's pledge.

"Well, now," said the MacGovern, his expression equally grave. "That is a great relief to us all, I am sure."

NINE

WHEN HOPE AND FEAR COLLIDE

Our feet on the torrent's brink,
Our eyes on the cloud afar,
We fear the things we think,
Instead of the things that are.

JOHN BOYLE O'REILLY

Early December

"Michael?"

Michael straightened, tucking the lap robe more snugly about his legs. It was cold, even inside the carriage, though he had scarcely noticed until now. He'd been too absorbed in his thoughts about this evening's rehearsal, the Christmas concert, Susanna . . .

Most of all, Susanna.

117

He turned slightly to face Paul, who sat across from him.

"Michael, are you all right?"

"Of course. I was just . . . thinking."

"You are still planning to stay in the city tonight, no? Since rehearsal will no doubt go longer than usual."

"No, I've changed my mind. I think we should go back tonight."

"But it will be late. And even colder by then. Snowing, perhaps."

Michael could hear Paul's resistance to the idea of taking the ferry twice on such a night. Paul hated the New York winters.

"Tomorrow the MacGovern family will be arriving. I should be there. But you can stay at the hotel tonight, if you like."

After a long silence, Paul made a valiant reply. "No, I will go back with you."

"We have had this conversation before, Pauli. I can manage the ferry alone."

Paul muttered something, then started in on a different subject. "You're very serious today, *cugino*. What occupies you so? Not the program, surely. It is going well. We will be ready in good time."

"No, I'm very satisfied. There was much improvement at last night's rehearsal."

"Then what is it?"

Michael delayed his reply just long

enough that Paul answered for him. "Ah. Susanna. You are thinking of Susanna."

It was not a question. And there was no mistaking the note of smugness in Paul's voice.

Michael made no attempt to confirm or deny, but Paul was clearly not going to be put off by his silence. "So, I was right. It *is* Susanna."

Michael gave an exaggerated sigh, but he already knew it would take more than a show of impatience to stifle the other's curiosity.

Then, strictly on impulse, he surprised himself by shooting a question at Paul. "What does she look like?"

When Paul hesitated, Michael prompted him. "Susanna — what does she look like?"

"You have asked me this before."

"Then I am asking again."

"Hmm. But to describe Susanna is not such an easy thing."

Paul was obviously enjoying this.

"You may spare me the dramatics, *cugino*."

"*Sì*. Well . . . Susanna is like . . . *una principéssa!*"

"A princess? High praise," Michael said dryly. "And exactly *how* is Susanna like a princess?"

"She has a . . . stillness about her. The way she walks, holds her head, her every movement. She has . . . much grace. Even a kind of elegance."

Michael had actually sensed the grace, the "stillness" Paul referred to. For the first time in years, there was peace in his home. The kind of peace he had longed for — for himself, for Caterina, for his entire household.

And Susanna had brought this peace.

"As I have told you before," Paul rambled on, "Susanna is very attractive. But hers is more a . . . *quiet* loveliness. There is no pretension about her."

"But she doesn't know she's attractive," Michael said, more to himself than to Paul. "She thinks she is plain."

"Ah, but she is mistaken! Susanna is not plain. Not by any means."

Michael knew he was pressing, but couldn't seem to stop himself. "So, then — Susanna is both pretty and poised," he said, trying for a casual note. "It's fortunate, I think, that you are a musician, *cugino,* for you are certainly no poet."

He leaned back against the seat. "What color is her hair?"

"Ah, yes. Susanna's hair. It is . . . the color of honey. Like honey, with streaks of the sun. And she has, what do you call them? The *freckles*. Freckles on her nose. Only a few. Perhaps four or five."

Something in this whimsical reply set Michael on edge. Paul had actually *counted* the freckles on Susanna's nose? It seemed an unwarranted intimacy. Intrusive — presumptuous, even — for Paul to have studied Susanna so closely.

When he could not . . .

And then he recognized the scalding bilge that came crashing over him. He was jealous. Jealous of Paul.

This wasn't the first time he had wondered if his cousin might not have feelings for Susanna — or she for him. Nor was this the first time he had felt this same resentment at the thought. Paul could *see* Susanna, could look into her eyes, observe her movements, her reactions. Paul didn't have to depend on some questionable sixth sense to interpret Susanna's feelings. Paul was —

Michael stopped himself. How could he be so childish as to resent *Paul,* whom he loved like a brother? He was being unreasonable, and he knew it. A jealous, petulant schoolboy spoiling for a fight.

Overcome with self-disgust, Michael dragged one hand through his hair. He had thought himself finished with the ugly business of jealousy once and for all. He had battled it throughout most of his marriage. He would not — *could* not — allow it to shred his spirit again. And certainly not because of Paul. The bitter taste of self-reproach remained on his tongue.

Paul was still reciting Susanna's virtues. "What more can I say? She is lovely. Very lovely. But I think you are right, that she does not realize this. Always she makes less of herself. She . . . diminishes herself, even her music. I wonder why."

Before Michael could venture a reply, Paul offered his own. "Perhaps . . . because Deirdre seemed to cast such a bright light, Susanna became accustomed to walking in her sister's shadow."

Michael swallowed against the knot in his throat.

"I wonder, Michael — why do you always ask me about Susanna's appearance? Why have you not looked at her for yourself by now?"

The question, typical of Paul's directness, caught Michael completely off guard. "With my hands?"

"*Sì.* As you do with others."

"I suppose," he said, searching for an answer, "because I've never felt quite free to do so. I'm not at all sure Susanna would be . . . comfortable with the idea. So I have not presumed."

But, oh, how he had wanted to! Wanted to take her face between his hands, to trace the line of her temples, her chin, touch her hair, to look at her and see her in the only way left to him — with his touch, and with his heart. Yet something had always stopped him.

"I don't believe you would be presuming, *cugino.* I believe you are mistaken about what Susanna wants."

Michael frowned. "Meaning, I suppose, that you *do* know what she wants."

"I know what I see."

And Michael could not see.

Abruptly, he lifted a hand to put an end to the exchange. "I need to concentrate now on the music," he said, turning toward the carriage door.

But he couldn't concentrate on the music. He could think only of Susanna, of his adolescent jealousy, of the revulsion engendered by his own pettiness.

His life was spiraling out of control. And all because of Susanna.

How had his feelings for her managed to engulf him so subtly, yet so completely? When, exactly, had he first begun to listen for the sound of that low, modulated voice, so thoroughly Irish despite the British over-tones of her uncommon education? When had he come to recognize the moment she entered a room simply by the soft rustling of her skirts and her faint but unforgettable fragrance, like a dusting of rose petals?

How had she slipped so quietly into his life, become such an essential part of him, stirring in him the beginnings of a desire — a *need* — to love again . . . and the incredible hope that he actually could?

And what was he going to do about it, now that it had happened?

If Paul was right about Susanna's feelings, the impossible had suddenly become pos-sible, and for an instant Michael was para-lyzed by a need to protect himself. The memory of Deirdre's betrayal came roaring in on him in all its stark, tearing ugliness, its soul-destroying anguish.

How would he ever find the courage to open himself up to another person again, to risk another failure, another loss? His mar-riage to Deirdre had for years stripped him of his self-respect, his pride, his very man-hood. Did he seriously believe that he was ready to try again, that he was even *capable* of trying again to love, to trust, to build a life together . . . with Deirdre's sister?

TEN

NIGHT MUSIC

The high that proved too high,
   the heroic for earth too hard,
The passion that left the ground
   to lose itself in the sky,
Are music sent up to God.

ROBERT BROWNING

Susanna had been restless all evening. Since dusk, an uncommon stillness had engulfed the house and the grounds. The air itself seemed hushed with expectation, as if waiting for something to happen.

It was well after eleven when she felt the change settle over the night. She had let her hair down and sat brushing it in front of the vanity when the wind suddenly blew up with a wail like a wounded beast rising from the river. Almost immediately a volley of sleet followed, pounding against the house with a vengeance.

She hurried to close the shutters, then went to secure the ones in Caterina's bedroom as well. Gus, the wolfhound, lying at the foot of the bed, lifted his great head and looked at her. Susanna took a moment to rub his ears, then made certain that Caterina was well covered and sleeping soundly before returning to her own room.

Moira Dempsey had warned her about the fierce winter storms that often whipped through the valley, but the ferocity of the wind never failed to put Susanna on edge. Tonight, the awareness that both Michael and Paul were gone made her feel even more anxious and isolated than usual.

Not so long ago, she would have felt *relieved* knowing Michael was away.

How quickly things could change . . .

She was as fidgety as if she'd consumed an entire pot of tea and knew she might just as well give up all thought of sleep, at least until the storm passed. With a rueful glance at her nightclothes laid out on the bed, she put down her hairbrush, got up, and went to the window.

There was nothing to be seen, of course — nothing but darkness and bits of icy filigree on the windowpane. She stood listening as the sleet went on beating against the house. The gutters babbled with melting ice — a sound she'd found soothing in her childhood. But tonight, that musical murmur was accompanied by the sharp percussion of tree limbs cracking in the wind, and the ferocity of the storm unnerved her.

She went into the hallway. The gas lamps cast the length of the long narrow corridor in shadows. The door to Caterina's bedroom was ajar, and the wolfhound stuck his head out just enough to satisfy himself that it was only Susanna before turning and going back inside.

Somewhere something banged, and Susanna jumped. But when the noise continued, she recognized it as the loose shutter at the drawing room window and hurried downstairs to close it. Dempsey had been grumbling about the annoyance a few nights past but hadn't gotten around to fixing it yet.

After closing the shutter, she left the room and stood for a moment in the vestibule, unable to decide what to do. She wasn't accustomed to wandering about at so late an hour, when the rest of the household was abed. The storm battering the house and the night creaks of the large old mansion all around her made her feel peculiarly small. Vulnerable. Even *alien,* as if she didn't actually belong here.

Foolishness. It was just a house, just a storm. Still, she would be glad when tomorrow came and the MacGovern family would arrive. There was a husband and wife — and children. Perhaps Bantry Hill would no longer seem so austere, with more children about.

And the MacGoverns were Irish. Ever since Michael had told her about them, she had found herself entertaining hopes that she and Mrs. MacGovern might become friends. The longer she was here, the more she missed the companionship of other women. Rosa Navaro visited as often as she could and made every attempt to be kind, but most of the time she was almost as busy as Michael. She traveled a great deal, and even when she was at home, she was most often involved with her private students or some civic event.

Moira Dempsey had been decent enough to her, but the housekeeper was aging right before Susanna's eyes and seemed either unwilling or unable to expend the effort a real friendship would require. Not to mention Susanna's bewildering suspicion that the woman harbored some sort of resentment toward her. Occasionally she would make a sour remark about "too much education" or "those who get above their raising." "Uppity" was the word she used to describe these unidentified pretenders to a higher plane. And more confusing still was the baleful look the woman would occasionally fix on Susanna when she and Michael were together — a look that seemed to border on distrust.

Susanna knew the Dempseys held great affection for Michael; indeed, their behavior toward him was almost like that of doting parents with a favorite son. But why their fondness for Michael should translate to resentment of her was a puzzle.

She finally willed herself to move, starting down the hall. In spite of the gas lights, the rooms all the way down were dark and unwelcoming, and the house was cold. Moira Dempsey didn't hold with the "extravagance" of leaving a fire in an unoccupied space, so before leaving her room, Susanna had grabbed a shawl to throw over her gingham shirtwaist. Now she gathered it more snugly around her shoulders against the chill.

On impulse, she headed for the music

room. She would build a fire, she decided, and she would play. When nothing else could still the unrest in her, music would. Neither the smell of wood smoke nor the sound of the piano was likely to rouse the Dempseys, who slept at the opposite end of the house, and if Caterina happened to wake, she would merely turn over and go back to sleep.

Michael had told her to use the room whenever she liked, after all.

First she laid a fire, knowing the large, drafty room with its high ceilings and tall windows would take some time to heat.

As she sat down at the piano, she felt oddly shy, almost like an intruder. It wasn't as if the keyboard were foreign to her; she accompanied Caterina and Michael when they sometimes sang together in the evenings and played for Caterina's lessons. On occasion she even helped Michael with his composing.

But it was different coming to the magnificent instrument alone, with no purpose except to please herself, and with the luxury of knowing she could play whatever she liked with no one to listen.

At first, she touched the cool ivory keys tentatively, as if they might crack under too much pressure. She roamed over the bass, its rich timbre calling forth a sigh of satisfaction from her. After a few arpeggios, she ran the scales, grimacing at the stiffness of her fingers from lack of practice. Finally, she slipped into a Bach invention. After that, there was nothing else in the room for her except the piano and the music.

At the conclusion of the Bach, she moved to Chopin, as she always did when seeking an emotional — or even a physical — release. The delicate, fragile composer, whose sentimentality often belied the storm in his soul, never failed to absorb her with his elegant and brilliant artistry, flawless even in the most intense, anguishing passages.

At first she sought the grace and peace of the nocturnes, but it took only a few moments to realize that she wanted more than the simple tranquillity of the night songs. Like the storm roaring down over the river valley, a tempest seemed to be gathering in her spirit. She needed to empty herself of the turbulence — or else tame it.

She turned away from the nocturnes and tried the G-minor *Ballade* — a mistake, she knew almost at once, because she was clumsy and out of form. She could not maintain the intensity and passion of the piece, nor could she endure its tragic undertones.

At any other time she might have stopped then and there, frustrated by her own lack of discipline, but by now she was beyond quitting. Her agitation had built a fire in her that even the music seemed powerless to contain. She dived headlong into the tempestuous C-minor etude — the *Revolutionary*. It was more an *attack* than an interpretation, but Susanna didn't care. This was not intended for the ears of an audience, after all — indeed, not even for her own ears, but more for her heart and her spirit.

Encouraged that she had not entirely decimated the great Pole's creation with her rusty technique, she next went to the *Military Polonaise*. In her present fever, she was ready to do battle, but she was also growing tired, and the demands of the polonaise worked to still the storm.

Fatigue set in as she began the *Fantaisie-Impromptu*, a work personally disliked by Chopin himself, but for some reason a favorite of Susanna's — perhaps for the very extravagance of emotion the music's composer had disdained.

Her fingers caressed the keys now, her pulse slowing as the chaos in her spirit dissipated. As inept and out of practice as she knew herself to be, the aching melody of the *Fantaisie* nevertheless adhered itself to her soul, sweeping her up and carrying her along, making her a part of the music.

She completed the piece and rested for a moment. The effort demanded by the music had drained much of the day's tension from her. And even through the fatigue, an unexpected sense of elation infused her. She felt revived and strengthened.

Her glance came to rest on the manuscript on top of the piano — Michael's *American Anthem* — and she reached for it, flipping through the first few pages. Paul's musical notation was neat and precise, and, knowing him, Susanna felt certain he took great pains to transcribe every note and dynamic exactly as Michael communicated it.

After a slight hesitation, she chose a portion of the manuscript she hadn't yet played through and propped it on the music rack in front of her. She remembered the afternoon she'd first played a portion of the music at Michael's direction, how enthralled she had been at the genius that blazed from each page. What a thrill it must be, to perform a magnificent work such as this — an unparalleled experience, surely.

She began to play; forgetting about her inadequacies, she gave herself up to the music. From childhood, she had possessed a keen ability to "hear" sounds in her inner ear, even to re-create complicated musical structures in her mind. But when she tried to imagine the ultimate performance of this work, she could never capture more than a faint echo of its greatness. For now, she could only content herself with what she was able to reproduce at the keyboard, and even that was enough to move her to tears.

No matter how confusing her emotions toward Michael might be, when it came to his incredible musicianship, she could only stand in awe. It was more than artistry, more than skill, or even genius. Something far less tangible, something indescribable, marked Michael's music. Rosa Navaro and Miss Fanny Crosby would call it *anointing,* the touch of the Divine.

When she had first come to Bantry Hill, Susanna might well have scorned the thought, but no longer. Dwelling under Michael's roof, observing the way he lived his life, seeing the father he was to Caterina — and being a recipient of the kindness and grace he extended so freely — had finally compelled her to turn from the suspicion and distrust that had molded her earlier opinion of him.

Eventually, as she was drawn more and more into his life — and especially into his music, which was almost like being drawn into his soul — she'd had to concede that this man, whom her own sister had despised and even tormented, was a *good* man. A man of integrity and faith and a generous spirit. A man to respect.

And a man she feared she was growing to love.

Michael brushed the icy rain from his hair as he stood outside the closed doors to the music room. He had waited a long time to hear Susanna play like this — unobserved, free, abandoned.

Although the Chopin was rough in places and her technique not entirely under control, he warmed to the fire with which she imbued the latter part of the C-minor etude, the *Revolutionary*. Chopin was not one of Michael's favorites. He admired his unwavering perfectionism and artistry, but much of the composer's music was too fussy for his personal taste. As for the *Revolutionary*, the only time the tempestuous piece failed to annoy him was when he was in excessively high spirits.

But that was before tonight. He found himself captivated by Susanna's interpretation of the piece. A kind of angry defiance drove her. More than that, she seemed to sense what most pianists — even Michael himself — tended to forget or ignore about the puzzling combinations of emotion that characterized Chopin's work and made him unique. Critics often pointed to Michael's own mix of Italian and Irish in an attempt to analyze the varied palette his heritage inevitably brought to his music. In the same way, Chopin, while most passionate about his native Poland, had inherited from both his French father and his Polish mother the traits that contributed to his genius. Strict form and passion, lyricism and bravura, whimsy and melancholy — an entire spectrum of attributes worked together to shape the composer's music and no doubt accounted for the brilliance others might imitate but could never emulate.

Susanna managed to unearth this diversity in her playing, and yet she considered herself, in her own words, merely "competent." What could possibly account for her skewed self-perception, her conviction that her musicianship was somehow lacking? Had she never performed for anyone but herself? Had no one ever recognized her gift and affirmed it?

Surely, if no one else had realized, Deirdre would have. And yet once, when he'd questioned Deirdre about her younger sister, she had carelessly discredited Susanna's musical skills as "pedestrian, at best."

But of course, she would have. In Deirdre's estimation, the abilities of all others paled in the light of her own.

Scarcely aware of what he was doing, Michael followed her through the music, instinctively directing her now and then, nodding his head with pleasure and approval. He thought he could hear her begin to tire a little by the time she ended the *Polonaise* and turned to the dreamier *Fantaisie*. There was a long silence, then the rustling of paper and, thinking she had finished, he reached for the doorknob. But he stopped when she suddenly launched into a portion of his own *Anthem* — the *cantare* section, in which he had developed a blend of brief works from various nations, a multicultural set of hymns as well as selections incorporating the newer gospel music form.

Michael's pulse began to race with excitement.

Somehow, she heard what *he* had heard as it poured from his spirit. In her playing were the same subtleties of emotion, the same reaching and receiving, a soaring past the limits, then a subsiding. The separateness and the coming together, the divisions and the harmony . . .

She *understood*. She had found a link to his

heart, his spirit, and was now pouring out her perceptions into the music and, in so doing, giving him a glimpse into his own soul.

And hers.

A thrill of elation seized him as the music with which he had so long struggled and experimented echoed behind the closed doors. Hearing her grasp and deliver what he had created only made him burn even more to move forward, to continue the work, to go on discovering and creating and refining.

Moreover, the realization of Susanna's understanding, her *partnership* in this, his most important venture, brought her closer to him. Hearing her play helped him to know her . . . and made him wish to know her even better, to know everything that made her . . . *Susanna.*

And with that realization came an urgency to make her grasp and accept her own ability — her *exceptional* ability. Her gift. Always, when he tried to convince her, she would dismiss him with either an awkward protest or a pretense of amusement, as if he were merely being foolish. And always he retreated, fearful of exerting unwanted pressure.

Perhaps Susanna suffered from her own

sort of blindness: an inability to see herself as she really was. He wanted to find a way to make her believe him, to help her comprehend what he had sensed the first time he had ever heard her at the keyboard.

Perhaps there *was* a way. A way that might benefit them both, even bring them closer together.

At last, silence fell behind the doors, and, taking a deep breath, Michael slipped the dark glasses from his pocket, put them on, and walked quickly into the room.

"*Brava,* Susanna! Well done."

Susanna turned to see Michael standing in the doorway. He was still dressed as he had been earlier in the day, in soft gray tweeds and a black sweater.

Humiliation flooded through her. How much had he heard? "Michael — I thought you were staying in the city."

"I decided I should come back." He walked the rest of the way into the room, not stopping until he reached the piano. "The MacGoverns are moving in tomorrow. I didn't want to be away when they arrived."

"Oh — yes. Yes, I . . . should have reminded you . . . I'm glad you remembered." She closed the keyboard and twisted her hands in her lap. "I . . . perhaps I shouldn't have come down so late. I couldn't sleep . . . I didn't think there was any danger of waking anyone."

He dismissed her concerns with a wave of his hand. "Don't apologize. As I told you, Susanna, the piano is for your use anytime you wish. I enjoyed your music." He paused. "I must tell you, Susanna — the more I hear you play, the more I believe you are just the person I am looking for."

When she didn't answer, he went on. "For some time now," he said, "I have been in need of a dependable pianist and organist for the orchestra. Someone who would be willing to work with us full-time. I believe you would be perfect."

Susanna sat dumbstruck, staring at him in disbelief. "Well," she finally managed, "I'm relieved to see that you couldn't have been listening very long."

"I expected you to say something like that," he said, smiling. "Actually, I have been listening for quite some time, and I am entirely serious. I continue to use guests on a temporary basis because I have yet to find the right person for a permanent position. I would like it very much if you would consider my offer."

"You can't be serious! You *know* I'm not capable."

"I know nothing of the kind," he said evenly. "I believe you are exactly what I am looking for. In fact, I *know* you are. But we have discussed your abilities before, no? My challenge is to convince *you* of what I already know."

He *was* serious. Or else somewhat mad.

"You really don't understand," she said, trying to steady her voice. He had triggered a disturbing mix of panic — and something akin to hunger — in her.

"Even if I *were* capable — which I know very well I'm not, no matter what you say — I could never carry it off. I literally freeze when I have to perform. I've always been that way — I *hate* being in front of an audience! I'd humiliate myself. I couldn't possibly do what you're suggesting."

Susanna hadn't meant to be *quite* so truthful and was mortified by her outburst. But perhaps it was for the best. His suggestion was unthinkable.

"I would never pressure you to do something you truly do not want to do, Susanna. And I understand about the stage fright. I was once acquainted with that particular demon myself."

When Susanna attempted to voice a protest, he ignored her. "It's true," he said. "You'd be surprised. But I learned that stage fright can be managed, even turned to your benefit. You can master the fear by confronting it — and relying on God to complete the work he's begun in you. I know you trust God's faithfulness, and if you trust my musical instincts at all, then believe me when I tell you that you have the ability to do this."

"Michael — I've told you before —"

"*Siete dotati!* Do you not hear me? You are *gifted.* Truly gifted! Why can you not accept what I tell you? Susanna, listen to me, please. We are friends now, are we not?"

"Friends? Yes. Yes, of course."

"And so then, do you trust me — as your friend?"

Confused, Susanna watched him closely, even as she searched her heart for the answer. "Yes, Michael," she said softly. "I trust you."

"And you trust my ability as a musician, no?"

"Oh, Michael, you *know* I do! You're an *incredible* musician —"

He waved off anything else she might have said. "Then I ask you to trust my *judgment.* As a musician. As your friend. And as someone who . . . cares for you and wants only your best. Can you do that, just for this moment?"

He was leaning over her, his damp hair falling over his forehead, the dark glasses securely in place. Then, without waiting for her to reply, he extended his hands toward her.

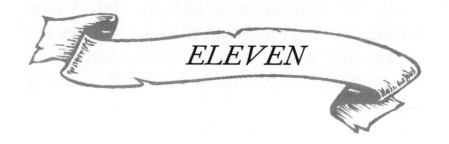

A RISK TOO PRECIOUS

Is this my dream, or the truth?

W. B. YEATS

"I can help you. We will work together," Michael said, clasping her hands in his.

Susanna had no idea what he meant, and she was far too aware of the warmth and strength of his hands to think clearly. Something had shifted between them. A boundary had blurred. The moment she admitted that she trusted him, the reins of restraint — which had provided not only a pattern for behavior but, at least for Susanna, a kind of self-protection — seemed to have slackened.

144

She wondered if Michael felt it, too, but if he did he gave no sign. He seemed more intent on keeping her immobile, as if he feared she might bolt from the room.

If he only knew . . .

Susanna had no desire to be anyplace but where she stood. Close to him, so close she could count every line in his face, except for those concealed by the dark glasses. Close enough to see the silver in his hair. Close enough . . . to be overwhelmed by the closeness.

And then she realized what he was saying, and the feeling quickly dissipated.

". . . The orchestra will perform the *Anthem* in sections — in movements — until it's completed. I have need of someone for the piano. Or organ perhaps. You play both. And I would not rush you. I promise to work with you until you feel ready. We can —"

"No."

Above the glasses, his dark brows knitted together. "Susanna, I can help you. I can help you gain confidence, lose the stage fright —"

"*No,* Michael." She forced the words through gritted teeth as she freed her hands from his.

"But you could be — you have so much to offer —"

145

Something in Susanna seemed to wilt, to shrink and die, like a blossom too frail to survive. She should have known. Why had she ever imagined she could be enough for a man like Michael?

What she heard him saying was that he wanted to change her, make her into something more than what she was. But why had she expected anything else? He lived in a different world from anything she had ever known.

And he was accustomed to a different kind of woman, a kind of woman she couldn't even pretend to be. He had fallen for Deirdre, hadn't he? Deirdre, who had glittered like the brightest jewel, with a zest for life and a sense of the dramatic that bedazzled every man she met. Deirdre, who had always been so *alive*. Whatever else she might have been, Deirdre was never dull, never timid. Audiences hadn't intimidated her — they energized her. Nothing was ever too large, too grand for Deirdre. She rode through life like a princess royal, driving her own chariot, trampling beneath her wheels anything — or anyone — that got in her way.

A man like Michael would hardly be interested in a country mouse who turned to pudding at the very thought of mingling in a crowd, much less walking onto a stage.

"I can't do what you want, Michael. I'm sorry."

"But how can you know this unless you try? I don't understand."

He seemed genuinely puzzled, and for an instant Susanna found herself torn between self-doubt and the desire to please him. But there was a gaping chasm between where she wished she could go and the conviction that she could actually make the leap.

No more had the inner struggle begun than she felt a surge of anger at herself. Was she really so hungry for his approval, his affection, that she would actually wish to become someone else? Someone like Deirdre?

She had never entertained the least desire for greatness. Her entire life had been unexceptional. Indeed, she knew herself to be just an ordinary person, had no thought of ever being anything else.

But she couldn't expect Michael to understand that. Everything he *did* was extraordinary. He basked in the spotlight of success and glamour and celebrity. Even after the loss of his eyesight and the demise of his operatic career, he still enjoyed the life of a hugely popular, successful musician. Renowned, respected, and revered, how could he possibly understand why she wanted no part of that world?

In truth, Susanna wasn't at all sure she understood it herself.

"Susanna?"

He was waiting for some sort of an explanation. But how did she go about explaining her very *nature?*

Frustrated and confused, she fumbled for the right words. "Michael, this isn't something I can explain. Please, can't you just accept the fact that what you're asking goes against everything I am? I'm simply not made that way."

"And you think I want to change you."

Susanna bit back a reply. That was *exactly* what she thought.

"This is not about *changing* you, Susanna. I meant only to help you overcome an unwarranted lack of confidence. Possibly I can be more objective about your abilities than you. You are much more gifted than you realize." He paused. "But perhaps for me it is a selfish thing as well, because I would like very much for you to be a part of what I do."

His voice dropped even more, and she strained to hear him over the moaning wind and the rattle of sleet on the windows. "Susanna, believe me, I have no desire to change you. You are . . ." He hesitated. "I would not change you for anything."

Susanna searched his face for any sign of

insincerity. But without eye contact, it was impossible to read his intent. What she *did* know was that Michael was not an impulsive man. Yet she had the distinct feeling that he had just spoken on impulse.

She saw that he was clenching and un-clenching his fists. Watching him, sensing his discomfort, Susanna felt her resistance waver. Her pique with him, and with herself, began to drain away.

"It's not that I don't value your opinion, Michael. To the contrary, I'm flattered that you would even consider me, and I'm sorry —"

He shook his head and lifted a hand to stop her. "You need not apologize. It's not my intention to make you uncomfortable or try to coax you into doing something you don't want to do. I respect your wishes. But if the time should ever come . . . if you should ever change your mind, you will tell me?"

"Of course," Susanna said, unable to imagine such a time.

"Susanna," he said, moving a little closer, "would you allow me to . . . look at you?" He lifted his hands, palms outward.

Completely unprepared for this, Susanna felt her throat constrict. Tom Donoghue, her mother's cousin, had been blind. And the Widow Blaine. What Michael was asking was a fairly common practice for the unsighted, the only way they could "see" another's features. But with Michael, it seemed more significant. More intimate.

Her hesitation was just enough to make him step back. "If you would prefer that I not —"

"No, I . . . don't mind."

When he still delayed, she tried for a lighter, more casual tone. "It's fine, Michael. Really." Then a brash thought seized her. "One thing —"

"*Sì?*"

"I wonder . . . would you please do something for *me?*"

He tilted his head and waited.

"Would you *please* take off those glasses?" The words spilled out all at once. "You never wear them with anyone except me, though I can't think why! In truth — it hurts my feelings."

For a moment he seemed to freeze, and Susanna cringed, ashamed of her crassness. She had made him angry, and she wouldn't have blamed him if he had bludgeoned her with a scathing retort. But even as she braced herself, he slowly lifted a hand, removed the dark glasses, and slipped them into his pocket.

His eyes remained closed. "Just so you'll know, Susanna," he said, his voice exceedingly quiet as he stood facing her, "I never intended to hurt your feelings. I wear the glasses in order that I *not* . . . offend you."

Susanna held her breath, her nails digging into her hands. After the accident Deirdre had written that his eyes were scarred. Ugly, even *frightening*.

And then he opened his eyes.

They were beautiful. Blue crystals, deeply set and thickly lashed. They lacked focus, of course, but this merely gave him a contemplative, intense expression that conveyed a depth of feeling she would not have thought possible.

There were no scars, no disfigurement of any kind.

It was inconceivable that Deirdre would have lied about this, too. And yet the evidence of her sister's pitiless deceit stood before her.

Oh, Deirdre . . . Deirdre . . . how could you?

"I am not offended by your blindness, Michael," she managed to say. "How could you have thought I would be?"

He shrugged, but Susanna already knew the answer. "What did Deirdre tell you?" she said.

He stilled, lifted a hand to one temple,

then passed it over his face. "My eyes —"

"Your eyes are perfect. But that's not what Deirdre said, is it?"

He paled, silence his only reply.

"Surely Paul told you the truth? Rosa? Someone . . ."

"*Sì*. Of course. But even after they convinced me, Deirdre insisted I wear the glasses. She hated the blindness." He paused. "But, Susanna, I wear them on other occasions, not only with you. I almost always wear them in a crowd — especially in an unfamiliar setting. I am a large man. I could easily hurt someone if we should collide. The glasses, at least, call attention to the fact that I cannot see where I'm going. You understand?"

Always, it seemed, he thought of others before himself. And this was the man Deirdre had repeatedly called "selfish." "Inconsiderate."

When she spoke again, her voice trembled. "I didn't realize . . ."

"You prefer I not wear the glasses when we are together?"

Susanna's gaze went to his eyes, and in that instant she was struck by the irrational sensation that he was looking directly at her. She swallowed, then shook her head as if to expel the feeling. "I think . . . yes, I think I'd rather you didn't."

"So, then — I won't."

Inordinately pleased by his quick response, Susanna moved to close the distance between them, lifted her face, and waited. "Yes . . . well, then . . ."

He dipped his head, resting his hands lightly on her shoulders.

"Michael?"

He hesitated.

"I'm nothing like Deirdre," she blurted out.

His countenance went solemn. "I know," he said softly.

"People never took us for sisters, unless they knew us. I don't resemble her in the least." She stopped. "I'm quite plain."

Why had she felt the need to tell him that? He would find out for himself soon enough, after all.

His mouth quirked. "That is not what I have been told."

"But it's true —"

"Susanna?"

"Yes?"

"Hush now."

Susanna drew in a sharp breath and closed her eyes, holding her breath as he began to trace the oval of her face with his fingertips.

It was an unsettling experience — but not

unpleasant. As Michael himself had stated, he was quite a big man, and when he conducted the orchestra or embellished his speech with dramatic gestures, Susanna invariably caught a sense of great power in his hands. She hadn't expected such gentleness. But as he molded her face with his fingers and began to skim every feature, his touch was light and deft — and in no way overly familiar.

"You need not hold your breath, Susanna."

At the note of amusement in his voice, she opened her eyes and found him smiling as he continued his exploration. Once he nodded, as if his touch had confirmed what he already knew. His expression intent now, he continued to trace her features.

His fingertips were calloused — from the mandolin, she supposed. And from gardening — Michael loved to work in the gardens. He brushed over her forehead, lightly winging out from her eyes, even seeming to take note of her eyelashes before moving down over her cheekbones and the hollows beneath them. Susanna tensed, but he allowed his thumbs to graze the corners of her mouth only for a second before briefly skimming his fingertips along her jaw line.

He fanned his hands outward, noting the

length of her hair, and only then did Susanna remember that she hadn't bothered to put it up again. Heat rose to her face, but of course he couldn't see her disarray. Somehow, the thought didn't help.

Finally, he gave a slight nod — Susanna thought he might have sighed as well, though she couldn't imagine why. She was keenly aware of his hands clasping her shoulders, just as keenly aware that she didn't really want him to release her.

"Thank you, Susanna."

There was a huskiness, a tenderness in his voice she had never heard, a softness to his features she had never seen, but she tried not to attach too much importance to either.

"You are wrong, you know," he said, his voice even lower now.

Susanna looked at him. "What?"

He was still smiling. "You are not in the least *plain.*"

And it occurred to Susanna that, for the first time in her life, she didn't *feel* plain.

And then he bent to touch his lips to her forehead. In that moment, her last slender thread of caution pulled free and dropped away. The kiss, in its gentleness and poignancy . . . and *carefulness* . . . seemed more like a benediction. She did not so much feel herself kissed . . . as *blessed.*

Michael had been almost overcome by her closeness. Both elated and unnerved, he stood stunned by the force of his own feelings. The cool softness of her skin under his fingertips and the subtle fragrance of roses he had come to identify with her very nearly distracted him from "seeing her," being able to form his own image of her appearance rather than depending on Paul to convey that image to him.

And now he knew why he had refrained for so long.

Her features were delicate but distinct, her face thin, but not gaunt. Her youthful skin was cool and silken. He grew almost dizzy when he realized her hair fell free, when he tested the weight of it. *Honey,* Paul had said. Her hair was the color of honey.

Feelings he had suppressed for years blazed up in him: a deep, humming pleasure in her loveliness, a loveliness of which she was completely unaware. The unfettered lightness of simply being close to her, being in her presence. The wrench of pain at the very thought of parting from her.

Still holding her, he struggled to clear his head. He couldn't bring himself just yet to let her go. Whatever boundary had stood between them seemed to be gone. It was a moment that signaled either a crossing or a retreat. They were poised at the edge of what was safe and familiar, facing each other across an unknown terrain. They could back away and maintain the amicable, comfortable relationship they had forged — a relationship without risk, for the most part. Or they could cross over into a new province where nothing was charted, nothing was absolute.

Only a few years ago, he would have pursued her, courted her, with all the confidence and arrogance of a youthful buccaneer. But the disaster of his marriage, the tragedy of Deirdre's death — and, yes, the loss of his sight — all stood between the man he had once been and the man he was now.

He could not afford the luxury of daydreams or assumptions where Susanna was concerned. God had healed him, restored him to wholeness, that was true. But there were parts of him, deep and hidden, that were still bruised from the years of rejection and humiliation — and from the soul-shattering realization that he had allowed himself to be used by a woman who had never loved him, who had simply seen him as a means to an end.

But Susanna was, as she herself had said, "nothing like Deirdre." She was totally without guile. And perhaps it wasn't only her directness and lack of pretension that inspired his trust. Perhaps the fact that in the beginning *she* had so obviously mistrusted *him* made it easier for him to sweep his own doubts and suspicions aside.

Still, he was afraid. Afraid to risk, unwilling to chance losing her friendship, her acceptance of him. He would rather have *something* than nothing.

And as much as he wanted to be completely free with Susanna — free to love her, to hope that she might come to love him — in his spirit he knew this wasn't the time. What they had right now, at this moment, was too precious to risk. She brightened his world and lighted his life and brought grace and joy and peace to his existence. For now, that must be enough.

Even so, he could not stop himself from bending to touch his lips to her forehead in a light, decidedly chaste kiss.

And she did not pull away.

TWELVE

AN UNLIKELY
GUARDIAN ANGEL

Some have entertained angels without
knowing it.

HEBREWS 13:2,
The Holy Bible (NASB)

Andrew Carmichael was alone in the dispensary, measuring medicines and filling bottles when the office bell rang. He glanced up, wiped a hand over the front of his laboratory coat, and went out into the waiting room.

It was going on five, a miserable evening with a punishing wind and a mixture of ice and snow. A blast blew into the waiting room as soon as he opened the door.

The woman who stood before him was

quite different from the usual run of patients who showed up on his doorstep. She wore a tastefully designed hooded cloak that had probably cost more than the sum total of his accounts due. Although her face was partially concealed by the fur trim of the hood, he could see that she was a woman of refined features.

"Are you Dr. Carmichael?" she asked in a breathless voice.

Andrew nodded, quickly standing aside to let her enter.

She stepped inside at once, glancing about the waiting room. She was a small woman, scarcely reaching Andrew's shoulder, but something in her bearing gave the impression of greater stature.

"How can I help you?"

She withdrew a piece of paper from her handbag and gave it to Andrew. "I wondered if you would be good enough to call at this . . . residence. I believe you will find a need for your services there."

Andrew looked at her, then at the paper. It was an address on Mulberry Street, a particularly wretched area of shanties and log hovels.

He glanced up to find the woman watching him closely.

"You'll be paid whatever you require, of

course," she said. "I'll send my driver around tomorrow to take care of your fee, and if further visits are necessary, you've only to give him your bill."

"May I ask who the patient is?" Andrew said, puzzled by the lack of information being offered.

"Patients," she corrected. "You'll find a woman . . . and young children."

"The entire family needs treatment?"

The hood had fallen away from her face, and Andrew saw that she was probably in her forties, an attractive woman in an unpretentious sort of way.

"I . . . I'm not sure," she replied. "The mother, for certain, and the youngest child. Perhaps all of them." She lowered her eyes.

"This situation — is it urgent?"

She still didn't look at him. "I believe it may be, yes. Could you possibly go today, Doctor?"

Andrew studied her. Despite the quiet elegance of her features, she appeared drawn, as if she hadn't slept well for some time.

"I — yes," he said. "I expect I can arrange to go yet this evening."

The tautness of her features gave way to a look of unmistakable relief. "Thank you so much."

"May I have the mother's name, please?"

She hesitated, swallowing with some difficulty. "Lambert. Mary Lambert."

"Is she a relative?"

Something flickered in her eyes. "No," she said, her tone unexpectedly sharp.

Abruptly, she turned to go, but Andrew stopped her with another question. "And may I have *your* name, Mrs. —"

"I don't believe that's necessary."

Andrew was tempted to press, but decided against it. He had a sense that her self-control was exceedingly fragile.

"Very well, then," he said. "I'll look in on the family later this evening and see how I can help."

She only half turned, inclining her head and murmuring a word of gratitude before hurrying out the door.

Andrew stepped outside just long enough to watch a driver clad in black carefully hand the woman into a handsome — but not ostentatious — carriage. The sting of the wind and the ice-laced snow drove him back inside before he could see which way they went.

As he finished up his work in the dispensary, he decided to wait for Bethany's return from the children's home before making his call on the Lamberts. As usual, she'd insisted on walking, though he had urged her to take the buggy. Of course, it hadn't been this cold and wet when she set out, and Bethany seldom chose to ride when she could walk. She could be stubborn at times.

He smiled a little at the thought. After locking the medicine cabinet, he went to wash his hands. The hot pain in his swollen wrists and fingers warned him that an outing in this weather would do the arthritis no good, but there had been no mistaking the importance of his mysterious visitor's request. Quite simply, he hadn't the heart to refuse.

His gaze went to the medicine cabinet, lingering there for a moment until a shudder seized him and he turned away. With an angry toss of the towel, he wheeled toward the door.

Perhaps he should take the buggy and pick up Bethany on his way to Mulberry Street. But it was after five, and the streets would be crowded. He was almost sure to miss her in passing. Besides, he was fairly certain she'd want to make the call with him once she returned.

He decided to wait, hoping she would turn up soon.

Bethany was thankful with every treacherous step that she had had the foresight to wear her boots. The streets were slippery, darkness was drawing in fast, and impatient pedestrians weren't inclined to give one another much room.

She should have listened to Andrew. Hadn't he warned her the weather was going to turn nasty before dark?

She was about to turn the corner onto Mott Street when a wiry little man wearing a fisherman's cap and a baggy overcoat jostled by her, nearly shoving her into the street. She had no more righted herself and started off again when a gaggle of shopgirls came sloshing toward her, laughing and poking at each other, seemingly oblivious to her approach. In an effort to avoid them, Bethany darted sideways into the street and only barely escaped being struck by a coal wagon. The driver cursed at her, splashing her with dirty water as he rumbled on.

Incensed by now, she stood glaring at the back of the rickety wagon. Someone behind her gave a shout, and almost too late she turned to see one of the police department's Black Marias hurtling toward her. She sidestepped it just in time, though she turned her ankle in the process.

The vehicle clanged to a stop, and Bethany hobbled backward, skidding and nearly falling on a patch of ice.

"Dr. Cole!"

Bethany gritted her teeth as she recognized the policeman hanging onto the side of the Black Maria. She was wet and shivering, and she wanted nothing so much as to get back to the office. The last person she wanted to see right now was Sergeant Frank Donovan.

The big policeman jumped down and raked her over with a quick scowl. "You all right?" he said, not waiting for a reply before adding, "You're drenched."

"No, I'm not all right," she snapped. "And, yes, I'm drenched."

He grinned at her. "Well, unless you're out for an evening stroll, I think you'd best let me give you a ride." He jabbed a thumb over his shoulder in the direction of the police wagon. Before Bethany could reply, he took her arm and began propelling her toward the wagon. "It might be a bit rank inside, but it's dry for all that. And you look as if you could use some drying out."

She yanked her arm free. "Thank you, Sergeant, I can manage. I haven't that much farther to go."

He ignored her, encircling her waist and sweeping her up to the inside of the wagon, then jumping in behind her. "Doc would have my hide if he knew I'd left you on your own in this weather. What was he thinking, anyway, sending you out in this?"

Bethany glared at him. "Andrew — Dr. Carmichael — didn't *send* me out, Sergeant. It was entirely my decision."

"Ah. But not a very smart one, if you don't mind my saying so." He gave a whistle, then shouted at the driver of the wagon.

"You can sit on the floor if you want," Donovan said as they hauled off down the street.

Bethany looked around at the foul interior of the Black Maria. "I'll stand, thank you," she replied with forced civility.

"As you like. So, then — what brings you out on such a wretched day?"

Bethany had the feeling he was deliberately trying to annoy her. The last place she wanted to be was inside this disgusting wagon with Frank Donovan, but she refused to give him the satisfaction of amusing himself at her expense.

"We have a patient at the orphanage," she said, keeping her voice cool and steady. "The weather hadn't turned this bad when I left the office, so I decided to walk."

"I see." He regarded her with a detached, clinical expression. "Well, how do you like your work by now, Dr. Cole? Not quite what you're used to, I expect."

"And just what exactly do you think I'm used to, Sergeant?"

His dark eyes snapped with insolence. "Whatever it was, I doubt it was anything much like the Bowery."

"As a matter of fact, I find our practice very rewarding. We're obviously needed here."

Frank Donovan rolled his tongue along the inside of his cheek. "I'll not argue that you're needed. All the same, I can't help wondering what possesses a woman like you to become a sawbones in the first place. And to set up practice in a neighborhood like this —" He broke off, shaking his head.

"A woman like me?" Bethany countered. "And exactly what kind of woman might that be?"

An impudent smile played at his lips beneath the dark red mustache. "Well, now, it strikes me that an attractive young woman of good family — as you obviously are — would find it more . . . suitable . . . being a doctor's *wife* rather than being the *doctor*." He paused. "You wouldn't be one of those women's rights females, would you? Sure, and you don't look much like the rest of 'em."

Bethany held her temper only by an iron

act of will. "Are you goading me on purpose, Sergeant, or are you really as boorish as you seem to want me to believe?"

He gave a harsh laugh. "I've offended you. I apologize, Dr. Cole — that wasn't my intention. Not at all."

His apology was a farce, and they both knew it. "You needn't apologize, Sergeant. I didn't make it through medical college by being thin-skinned. Unfortunately, my chosen profession has more than its share of buffoons."

Again he laughed, even harder this time. "I do admire your spirit, Dr. Cole. No wonder Doc is so smitten with you. I doubt he's ever met up with your kind before."

"My *kind?*"

"Ah, now, don't get yourself in a twist," he said, doffing his hat and affecting an unconvincing look of remorse. "I didn't mean any harm. But it's true about Doc, you know. The poor fella is as love-struck as any man I've ever seen."

Bethany groped for a last remnant of self-control. "You know, Sergeant, Andrew — Dr. Carmichael — considers you a friend. To save me, I can't imagine why."

Without warning, the policeman's mouth went hard. "Oh, I'm Doc's friend, right enough. Don't you be doubting it. That's why I'm more than a little concerned about him."

Bethany frowned at him. "What are you talking about?"

"I think you know exactly what I'm talking about." He leaned against the wall of the wagon and crossed his arms over his chest. "Doc is a very trusting sort, as you may have noticed. Indeed, if there is such a thing in this infernal town, the man's an innocent entirely."

In a flash of insight, Bethany realized that despite his crudeness, his rough demeanor, and his cutting cynicism, Frank Donovan *was* a friend to Andrew. Not only a friend, but his self-appointed protector as well.

And just as clearly, she understood something else: Donovan was protecting Andrew from her. He considered *her* a threat to his friend.

Her anger boiled to the surface, and she turned on Donovan. "Just what is it about me that you don't approve of, Sergeant? What exactly do you think I'm going to do to Andrew? Stab him in the back with my scalpel? Run off with all the exorbitant fees we're bringing in?"

His mouth twisted into a humorless smile. "Now, Dr. Cole, I think you know exactly how it is with Doc where you're concerned. The poor man is so besotted with you he can't find his own tongue when you're close-by. Why, he'd open a vein for you if you so much as crooked your little finger at him."

Bethany stared at him in astonishment. "That's the most ridiculous —"

"I think not," he said, his tone sharp as he uncrossed his arms and slipped his hands into his pockets. "Mind, now, Lady Doc — I'm no fool. And neither," he added with a calculating look, "are you."

Bethany had just opened her mouth to reply when a sudden, unwelcome realization siphoned the strength of her outrage.

Donovan was right.

The occasional moments of attraction that had passed between her and Andrew early in their relationship had deepened almost daily. At least she sensed that to be the case with Andrew.

But what about her own feelings?

"That's what I thought."

She stiffened at the sound of Frank Donovan's mocking voice, the look of utter contempt in his eyes.

"You know full well you're going to hurt him. Oh, not on purpose, perhaps. But you'll hurt him all the same."

"What I know is that you're badly out of line, Sergeant."

"If you have any feelings for the man — and I'm not saying you don't — you'd be doing him a kindness by letting him know just where you stand. Somehow, you don't quite strike me as a woman with a yen to settle down and tend to the hearth fire while Doc goes about his work of healing. You'd rather be toting your own medical bag around town alongside of him. You don't want to be *any* man's wife, do you?"

His tone turned even more caustic as he went on. "Even if you don't admit it, I think you know that one of these days — and maybe not too far off — Doc's going to need a wife more than he needs a *business partner.* He's going to need someone to take care of *him* instead of taking care of everybody *else.*"

When she did not respond, his lip turned up in a sneer. "Come on, you know how it is with him! Faith, woman, you *work* with him every day. You've seen his hands, the stiffness in his legs — the way he can barely make it up a flight of stairs on a bad day! He's getting worse all the time; even I can see it! The man is more likely than not to end up an invalid eventually. *Isn't* he?"

Stricken, Bethany could only stare at him. He'd seen more than she would have thought. And yet . . . it was becoming difficult *not* to see. Andrew was getting worse. Some days he could scarcely manage to stitch a wound.

Bethany forced herself to stand there, trying to breathe evenly, to show no reaction. Not for the world would she give this . . . rube . . . the satisfaction of knowing he had triggered an unexpected, unsettling rush of bewilderment.

She had her life in order. Her education was complete. Her career was underway. She had a practice, an office, and a growing list of patients. And, thanks to Andrew, she had finally obtained hospital privileges.

Indeed, she had everything she had ever wanted, everything she had dreamed of and hoped for since she was a schoolgirl. Her life was satisfyingly full; she had no need for more. There was no *room* for anything more.

But thanks to Andrew's so-called *friend,* she could feel her complacency beginning to slip away. In its place rose a boiling cloud of confusion, conflicting emotions, and questions she wasn't yet ready to answer. Not even to herself.

Why had she ever gotten into this disgusting, squalid wagon with Frank Donovan anyway? And why couldn't he have simply kept his unsolicited opinions to him-self?

"Here we are, then. I'll just stop in and say hello."

He jumped easily from the wagon and reached to help Bethany down, flashing a smile that didn't quite mask the flinty edge in his expression.

As he set her to the ground, he held her a moment longer than necessary, his gaze raking her face. "I meant no offense, Dr. Cole," he said, his tone oddly impersonal and detached. "Just looking out for a friend."

Bethany tugged free of him. "And is Andrew aware, Sergeant, that you've appointed yourself his guardian angel?"

He burst out laughing. "I hardly think so. It's not likely that anyone — even a saint like Doc — would ever mistake me for an angel!"

THIRTEEN

WHO SEES THE HEART

Give me, O God,
    the understanding heart.

GEORGIA HARKNESS

Too late, Andrew recognized the searing flash of resentment that shot through him.

Any jealousy on his part was wholly irrational. Frank had made it clear upon entering that their meeting had been merely a chance encounter, and Bethany followed up by explaining in greater detail.

And yet the sight of them together had unsettled him. He despised himself for such an adolescent reaction, especially since it had to do with a friend. This was *Frank,* after all.

174

Andrew had never seen any indication that Frank might harbor an attraction for Bethany. The man hardly lacked for feminine companionship — the ladies seemed to fall at his feet anytime he passed by.

Well, a certain *kind* of lady, at any rate.

Bethany's appeal was, on the other hand, of a *quieter,* more subtle nature than that which Frank typically seemed to favor.

Still, what a striking pair they made! Bethany with her fair, patrician loveliness in contrast to Frank's dashing, flamboyant good looks.

With relief he noted that Bethany distanced herself from Frank as soon as they entered the waiting room. He greeted both of them with as much enthusiasm as he could muster, and was just about to speak to Bethany about his mysterious visitor and her urgent request that he visit this Mary Lambert and her children. But the door opened again, this time to admit the petite blind hymn writer, Miss Fanny Crosby.

Ordinarily, Andrew would be glad to see Miss Fanny. But he had the call pending on Mulberry Street, and he was anxious to get away. Stifling his impatience, he went to her. "Miss Fanny! What in the world are you doing out in this weather?"

"Why, I'm paying you a visit, of course,

Andrew." She smiled at his fussing and brushed the light coating of snow from her shoulders. "Aren't you glad to see me?"

She stood in the middle of the waiting room, her head slightly lifted as if she were listening to something in the distance. "Who else is here, I wonder?"

Frank made his presence known, as did Bethany, while Andrew helped Miss Fanny remove her coat. "I'm always glad to see you," he assured her, leading her to a chair beside the iron stove that warmed the room. "But you ought to be scolded for venturing out on such a day. Please tell me you're not on foot!"

"Oh, listen to you! As if I'm not used to being out in worse weather than this. But, no, I'm not walking. Or at least I didn't walk *here*. Ben Drummond gave me a ride from the Women's Mission House. I decided I could use a brief respite to warm up a bit, so I decided to stop and visit with you for a spell."

"Well, we're very glad you did." Andrew forced a smile at Bethany over the top of their visitor's head.

Miss Fanny gave him a motherly pat on the hand, then turned in the direction of Frank Donovan. "Sergeant, I stopped at the precinct house earlier today to check on the boys, and I heard all about patrolman McNally's lovely bride and their wedding, bless them both."

"Aye," Frank said, drawing a little closer. "Patrick went and tied the knot at last."

"Yes, well, I keep praying for a good Christian woman to bring you to your senses as well. A man your age needs to be thinking of settling down."

Frank grinned and winked at Andrew. "Now, Miss Fanny, what would you know about my age?"

She waved a hand as if to dismiss his prattle. "I know a good deal more about you than you might expect, Frank Donovan. I know, for example, that you fancy yourself quite the rascal. But I also know that even a rascal can be saved from his own foolishness by the good Lord — and a good woman."

Before Frank could make a comeback, Miss Fanny turned toward Bethany. "Dr. Cole, I was at the children's home this morning, and dear little Maylee told me about your frequent visits to her. And yours, too, Andrew. Bless you both for taking an interest in the child."

Her expression grew more solemn. "But I wonder how she is, really. She never complains, you know. Not a word."

Bethany glanced at Andrew before replying. "Maylee is fairly stable for now, Miss Fanny. But . . . you understand she'll never be well. Her condition is degenerative."

"I know," said Miss Fanny with a sigh. "And I pray for the poor child daily. She simply breaks my heart. But do you know, the sweet girl would much rather sing me a song about Jesus than talk about herself. How our dear Lord must cherish her!"

They made light conversation for a few minutes. Then Miss Fanny got to her feet, saying, "Well, Sergeant. Dr. Cole seems to have survived her jaunt in your foul-smelling old wagon well enough, so perhaps I could impose on you to deliver me to my apartment?"

Frank replaced his hat, tipping it to the back of his head with one finger. "It would be my pleasure, Miss Fanny, but I have to say, I don't understand why your husband didn't keep you at home in the first place. Days like this aren't fit for you to be out."

Andrew watched the two of them as the diminutive Miss Fanny took Frank's arm. "Van is my husband, Sergeant, not my guardian. Besides, he has his work to do, and I have mine. The Lord takes very good care of us."

She smiled up at him. "But thank you all

the same for your concern. You're a good man."

Frank looked at Andrew and lifted an eyebrow. "We both know better than that, Miss Fanny."

"Oh, would you listen to yourself! The trouble with you, Frank Donovan, is that you really don't know *what* kind of a man you are. One of these days, when you stop running long enough, the Lord is going to get hold of you, and then you'll realize what I've been trying to tell you all along."

"Now don't you start on me, Miss Fanny," Frank grumbled. "You know I won't argue with you."

Still holding on to his arm as they started for the door, Miss Fanny gave a wave to Andrew and Bethany. "And I expect I must be the only person in New York who can claim that distinction. Well, come along now. It's time I was getting home."

As soon as the door shut behind them, Andrew turned to Bethany. "I have a call to make. I thought you might want to go with me, although I feel I should tell you that I have no idea what it's all about."

Andrew went on to explain then about his strange visitor. "I don't know what to expect," he finished, "so if you're tired and would rather not go —"

"No, I'm going with you. It sounds intriguing." She was already collecting her coat and her medical bag. "You said the entire family might need treatment?"

Andrew nodded, shrugging into his own coat. "It's possible, although she didn't seem to know for certain."

"And she didn't tell you anything else? Not even her name?"

"Nothing more." He stood thinking a moment, then opened the door and looked out. "I think we'll take a hack. I don't know about you, but an open buggy ride in this weather doesn't hold much appeal for me this evening."

"So long as you pay the fare." She grinned at him.

"Yes, well I'm feeling extravagant."

"Imagine that," she said, whirling about and starting for the door. "And you a Scot."

FOURTEEN

RESCUE THE PERISHING

Down in the human heart,
Crushed by the tempter,
Feelings lie buried
    that grace can restore:
Touched by a loving heart,
Wakened by kindness,
Chords that were broken
    will vibrate once more.

FANNY CROSBY
(from "Rescue the Perishing")

Bethany had been mired in a slough of despondency ever since her visit to Maylee.

The encounter with Frank Donovan had only intensified her gloomy feelings. For the most part, she thought she'd managed to conceal her dark mood from Andrew, but the sight that greeted them when they walked into the hovel on Mulberry Street depressed her low spirits even further.

A boy of twelve or thirteen opened the door and stood staring at them with bleak eyes. After hearing Andrew's explanation as to their call, he stepped aside for them to enter, then went to stand in a dim corner of the room, arms crossed over his thin chest.

Bethany tried to be discreet as she scanned their surroundings. Two small girls huddled close together under a pile of rags on a rude, unpainted bedstead with nothing but straw ticking for a mattress. Directly across the room from the bed, a small, fragile woman lay uncovered and shivering on a sagging divan, muttering and ranting to herself.

Next to a narrow basin, a dilapidated cupboard leaned against one wall and appeared to hold two or three tin cups, some unmatched plates, and a piece of stone crockery. The only other furniture in the room was a scarred wooden chair. The lone window was merely a hole without glass, stuffed with rags. There was no fire, and the room was cold and damp. Permeating the dreary surroundings was a strong stench of sickness and neglect.

Bethany looked at Andrew and saw that his mouth was white rimmed, his features drawn tight. He was angry. As angry as she had ever seen him.

He made a gesture that he would see to the woman on the divan, so Bethany went to the little girls in the corner.

And all the while, the boy with the sharp features and inscrutable expression stood watching them in silence.

It took Andrew only seconds to recognize an opium addict in the throes of early withdrawal. The woman's eyes shot open at his approach, but in spite of the sly, almost calculating furtiveness, he could see that she was disoriented.

Clad only in a tattered nightdress, she was emaciated, her hair wet with perspiration and matted about her face. The stench that engulfed her person and the entire corner of the room was nearly overwhelming. She was trembling so hard the divan shook beneath her.

The minute Andrew reached her, she kicked out with both legs and began to flail her arms in front of her. He turned his face away for a moment, drew in a long breath, and willed himself not to condemn her.

But the woman sprawled before him was a

bad dream with which he was all too familiar.

"Mrs. Lambert?"

She continued to thrash about and moan.

Andrew waited, but she showed no sign of quieting. "Mary? Can you hear me?"

She squeezed her eyes shut and threw her hands over her face.

Andrew bent over her. "Mary, I'm a doctor. I've come to help you."

He reached to brush the tangled hair away from her face, but with an unexpected show of strength, she struck out at him, knocking his hand away.

Andrew persevered, even though the very sight of her made him want to retch. Not with nausea; he'd overcome that hazard of his profession years ago. But Mary Lambert dredged up something much deeper, much darker. Something he would have preferred to keep buried forever.

Suddenly impatient with himself, he straightened and turned to Bethany. "I'm going to need help with her.

"See if you can calm her down," he said as Bethany approached. "Otherwise, we'll have to restrain her long enough for an examination."

Bethany hesitated only a moment before seating herself on the edge of the divan. She grasped one flailing hand and brought it to rest on her lap. At the same time, she began to murmur words of reassurance to the woman.

Almost instantly, Mary Lambert stopped her thrashing about, obviously distracted by Bethany's soft voice and firm touch.

"Now, Mary, we need you to be very quiet so Dr. Carmichael can examine you. We're here to help you."

The woman squirmed but continued to watch Bethany with wary eyes.

"You're very ill, Mary. And so are your children. We're here to help. But we need you to help us as well."

"What about the girls?" Andrew asked as he adjusted his stethoscope.

"They're both severely malnourished," Bethany told him. "I suspect the younger of the two may have pneumonia. They're dehydrated, of course, and feverish. They need to be hospitalized right away."

With her free hand, Mary Lambert reached as if to knock Andrew's stethoscope away, but Bethany intercepted her move, and she dropped her hand without protest.

As Bethany continued to soothe the woman, Andrew made a brief but thorough assessment of her condition. He found exactly what he had expected. She was badly jaundiced. Her pulse was racing, her heart-beat fast and erratic. Twice she wrenched herself into a fetal position, gripping her abdomen with one hand as if to squeeze off the cramps he knew she was having. By now she was thoroughly drenched with sweat, and she'd taken to muttering again — something about spiders and rats. She was delusional.

No surprise there, either.

He checked both her arms and saw the needle tracks that indicated she was injecting the narcotic instead of smoking it. Like her little girls, she was malnourished and close to dehydration. Her stomach was undoubtedly empty by now, so he went ahead and gave her a minimum dose of strychnine for her heart, then prepared a bromide of soda to help quiet her, although at the moment there was no combativeness about her, no attempt to block his treatment.

Andrew was keenly aware of the boy watching from the corner of the room. "Fetch me a blanket, son. And a cold cloth."

The boy didn't move. "We don't have no blankets."

Andrew and Bethany exchanged glances. "Some rags then," he said. "Your mother needs to be kept warm."

Finally the boy pushed himself away from

the wall and disappeared behind the curtain separating one room from the other. When he returned, he held a thin coat and a wet gray rag.

"This is all I could find," he said, handing Andrew the coat without looking at him.

Anger shot through Andrew. *Money for opium, but not for blankets . . .*

He covered Mary Lambert as best he could with the coat, then left Bethany to bathe the woman's face and hands with the dirty cloth.

Andrew motioned the boy to one side. "What about you, lad?" he said quietly. "Have you been ill, too?"

The youth shook his head. "I'm okay."

"How long has it been since you've eaten, son?"

The youth shrugged but made no reply.

Andrew sighed at the lack of response. "Does your mother drink liquor, too? With the opium?"

The boy darted a glance across the room at his mother, then turned back to Andrew. He blinked once, and Andrew recognized his attempt to keep his feelings well under wraps.

"Sometimes. Not always."

"How long has she been like this?" said Andrew.

"Like she is now?" The youth shrugged. "Three or four days, I guess. Before that she was sick a lot." He paused. "But she weren't never — out of her head, not until lately."

"Has she been using opium for very long?"

The boy hesitated. "A year or so. Maybe more."

"What about your father?"

In an instant, the impassive expression disappeared, replaced by a look of such raw hatred Andrew felt as if he'd been struck.

"We don't have a father," the boy bit out.

Andrew regarded him curiously. "What's your name, son?"

"Robert."

"Why do you say you have no father, Robert? Are your parents separated? Divorced?"

A look of loathing swept over the boy's face. "They weren't never married. He just comes down here every now and then. When he gets tired of his *real* missus."

Andrew's chest tightened at the shame and anger in young Robert Lambert's eyes. "He doesn't provide for you at all?"

The boy gave a contemptuous laugh. "There's what he *provides.*" He gestured toward his mother. "Not that he ever gave us that much to begin with. She had to work and all, when she still could. But at least she used to spend the money he gave her for food and rent. Lately, though, she's spent it all on the opium and the drink." He glanced away. "Landlord is threatening to throw us out now."

"Does he still come here — your father?"

The boy shook his head, a look of contempt darkening his features. "He ain't been around for months now."

Andrew tried to think. He knew what had to be done, but he wondered how the boy would react. "I need to confer with Dr. Cole a moment," he said, leaving the boy and returning to Bethany and Mary Lambert.

Bethany looked up at him. "I've never seen anything like this before. What's wrong with her, Andrew?"

"A lot of things. Liver disease for one, I expect. Anemia. Withdrawal. She's in a bad way."

"Withdrawal?"

"Opium," Andrew said shortly. "And alcohol."

He caught a glimpse of disgust, but Bethany was too professional to give sway to her feelings for long.

Andrew turned and gestured to Robert Lambert. "Your mother and your sisters will have to go to the hospital, son. I'm going to make arrangements to have them moved to Bellevue."

As the boy approached, his previous stoicism seemed to fall away. A look of panic flickered in his eyes. "All of them?"

Andrew nodded.

"But we don't have money for any hospital!"

Instinctively, Andrew put a hand on his arm. "Don't worry about the money. They'll be taken care of; I'll see to it. There's really no choice, Robert."

He hesitated. "You need a place to stay as well, and I know of one. Whittaker House. It's run by a pastor named Ted Whittaker and his family, and —"

"I'll not stay in any preacher's house!"

Andrew glanced at Bethany, then at the youth. "What do you have against preachers, Robert?"

"*He's* a preacher!"

The boy's words didn't register right away. "Who's a preacher?"

"*Him!*" Robert's face was splotched, his eyes blazing. "Our *father!*"

The room seemed to grow very still. "Your . . . father is a pastor?" Andrew said softly, struggling to take in the lad's meaning. "Who — what's his name?"

"Warburton. *Robert* Warburton." The boy

spit the words from his mouth as if they were laced with poison. "She named me for him!"

Andrew stared at him in numb astonishment. It must be coincidence. Another Robert Warburton.

"You're quite certain — he's a pastor?"

"He talked about it often enough. Bragging on his big church and all the traveling he has to do and the speeches he's asked to make and the books he writes. Oh, he's a preacher all right!"

A big church. Speeches. Books. It couldn't be — but it *had* to be. Robert Warburton. Pastor of one of the largest, most influential congregations in the city — in the *state*. A man looked up to by hundreds, perhaps even thousands, as if he were a saint.

Robert Warburton . . .

Bethany touched Andrew's arm and he saw the recognition in her eyes. Most likely, just about everyone knew who Robert Warburton was.

A thought struck him, and he turned to the boy. "Robert, do you have family in the city? A grandmother, perhaps?"

The boy frowned. "Mama's not from here. Her folks are back in Ohio." He paused. "She told us she wanted to be an actress. That's why she moved here. Only she couldn't get a job and was down on her luck. I guess that's when she took up with *him*."

Andrew's mind groped for answers. With no family in the city, who was the woman who had sent him here? And *why* had she sent him, if she and the Lambert family weren't even related?

"I'll be all right just stayin' here," the boy said.

"You can't possibly stay here," Bethany said firmly before Andrew could make a reply. "You've no food. No heat. And you said yourself the landlord was threatening eviction. No, Robert, Dr. Carmichael is right. Besides, I promise you, you'll like Whittaker House. Ted Whittaker is a young man himself, with a wonderful family. All the boys who live there seem to like it. It's a good place." She paused. "That's where you need to go, Robert. At least for now."

Andrew looked at Robert and saw him gazing at Bethany with something akin to awe. What sort of effect might Bethany have on a youth like Robert Lambert — a boy trapped in the midst of squalor and despair, with a mother who had become something less than human to him? Bethany, with her impeccable dress, her exquisite, delicate features, her loveliness — not to mention the almost maternal tone she was taking with him.

And where had that maternal tone come from? He hadn't heard it before, not even with Maylee.

"You'll need to stay with your mother and your sisters," Bethany went on, "until we can arrange for an ambulance. I'll wait here with you while Dr. Carmichael takes care of all the arrangements. Then he and I will take you to Whittaker House."

Robert looked from one to the other. "You'll both go with me?"

"Of course we will."

Robert studied her as if he were searching for some additional reassurance. Finally, he thrust his hands into his pockets and nodded. "All right, then."

"Good." Bethany smiled at him, and Andrew — not for the first time — counted himself blessed to have her at his side. Bethany could usually persuade just about any patient of *anything*.

He thought that might be particularly true if the patient happened to be male.

To Step Aside Is Human

Then gently scan your brother man,
Still gentler sister woman;
Tho' they may gang a kennin wrang
To step aside is human. . . .
One point must still be greatly dark,
The moving why they do it;
And just as lamely can ye mark
How far perhaps they rue it.

ROBERT BURNS

The hack was nearing Bethany's apartment, and she had yet to utter more than a few words since leaving Whittaker House. The experience with Mary Lambert and her children had proven difficult for both of them,

Andrew sensed, but even more of an ordeal for Bethany than for himself. He was having serious doubts about whether he should have asked her to accompany him, and he voiced those regrets.

"Don't be ridiculous," she said with a frown. "I have no intention of avoiding the difficult calls because I'm a woman. I thought you knew me better than that by now."

Andrew took her hand. "It has nothing to do with your being a woman. But I couldn't help seeing how it distressed you, and I could have handled the call on my own. Asking you to come was pure selfishness on my part. I simply wanted you with me."

She glanced down at their clasped hands but made no attempt to pull away. "You said you'd read my grandfather's papers on narcotic addiction?"

Andrew nodded.

"Well, so did I. But since much of his research concentrated on the War years and the soldiers who became addicted to painkillers after being injured, I suppose I've assumed that addiction was mostly confined to men. Seeing Mary Lambert and what the opium has done to her disturbed me. It seemed worse, somehow, to encounter a woman — a mother with obviously neglected children — in that awful condition."

Something dark and troubling squeezed Andrew's chest, but he couldn't quite bring himself to reply, not just yet.

"No doubt you think I'm naive," she went on, "and perhaps I am."

"No," Andrew said. "Not at all. We don't hear very much about women becoming addicted to liquor or narcotics," he said. "Nevertheless, it's all too common. Especially in the slum districts. I've seen it time and time again. Women or men — it's a vicious, devastating evil."

He should tell her. He should tell her now. This was as good a time as any, and eventually she would have to know. She had confided in him, after all. She'd been open and candid with him about many things in her life. The longer they were together, the more she seemed to open her thoughts, her memories, her feelings to him. But how did he begin? And how could he face what he would surely see in her eyes once she knew the truth?

He pulled in a deep breath. On impulse, he squeezed her hand, saying, "It's late, and neither of us has eaten since noon. Why don't we stop at Upton's and have a late supper?"

"Oh, you read my mind! A decent meal

and a cup of tea will go far to lift my spirits; I'm sure of it."

Andrew forced a smile to mask the sick awareness that what he planned to tell her over supper would almost certainly do anything *but* lift her spirits.

"Andrew, you've scarcely eaten at all. I thought you were hungry."

They were midway through a late dinner at Upton's, and Andrew still hadn't initiated the conversation he'd been dreading. He pushed his food around on his plate, not answering her.

Bethany gave a long sigh and put her own fork down. "I can't get them out of my mind either," she said. "And do you know what I find myself thinking, Andrew?"

He looked up.

"I can't help but wonder about the church."

"What do you mean?"

"When I see a case like Mary Lambert — and when I realize that there must be tragedies like this all throughout the city — I have to question how it happened, how it came to this. There are also *churches* throughout the city, filled with people who claim to abhor poverty and neglected children and godless parents. How does an entire family come to utter ruin without the church *doing* something about it?"

She clenched one hand into a fist. "Worse still, if the Lambert boy was right, it was Robert Warburton — a *clergyman* — who led Mary Lambert into this appalling state! How could a man — a pastor — do such a thing and live with himself? With his *wife?*"

"Don't you think *we* are the church?"

She frowned and leaned forward a little. "What?"

"You and I. And anyone else who's willing to take Christ's mercy to the world." Andrew pushed his plate away. "*People* make up the church, Bethany, and *people* are inclined to forget about the Mary Lamberts of this world. The problems seem so overwhelming that even people who *do* care feel as if they can't do anything to change the situation. They forget that one person *can* make a difference. That's where it has to begin: with one person."

He stopped, raking a hand over the back of his neck. A fiery shaft of pain shot up his arm, and he caught his breath before going on. "For the most part, we assume that one person can't make a difference, and so we leave it up to 'other people' — those who are 'in charge' of that sort of thing: the clergy, the benevolent societies, the physicians. But the truth is, there aren't nearly enough 'other people' to do the job. And for those of us who *do* try to help, there's never enough time or energy to do as much as we'd like."

Again he paused and leaned back with a sigh. "Sooner or later, fatigue and discouragement set in. At least that's how it is for me. At times, when I think about all the poverty and illness and hopelessness in this city, I can't help but become frustrated with my limitations. And my own self-centeredness."

Bethany leaned forward. "If there's anything you're *not*, Andrew Carmichael, it's self-centered. You're the most selfless person I've ever known."

Andrew cringed inwardly at the compliment, especially since he had vowed to set the record straight tonight. He braced himself to change the subject.

As it happened, she did it for him.

"I need you to teach me all you know about addiction, Andrew," she said. "I want to learn as much as I can."

Andrew knotted his hands together. "Surely, with your grandfather's studies and expertise in that area —"

She interrupted with a shake of her head. "I'm not talking about what I've learned from books and papers. Yes, I've read as much as I could about various addictions, but I've had no real experience in treating them. Obviously, you have. After tonight, I can see that I need to know more."

Andrew swallowed against the dryness in his mouth. She had opened the door to the very subject he'd intended to raise — and now he wanted nothing so much as a way to avoid it.

But before he could utter a single word, he looked up to see a young patrolman named Liam MacGrath bearing down on their table.

"Evenin', Dr. Cole," the policeman said, doffing his hat to Bethany. "Dr. Carmichael. Sergeant Donovan said if you weren't at your office or at home I might find you here or over to Axel's. You're needed down at Paradise Square."

Andrew scraped his chair back and retrieved his medical case. "What's happened?"

"Big explosion at the powder factory. We got several with real bad burns."

"We'll need transportation," Bethany said matter-of-factly as she got to her feet, her case in hand. "We took a hack here."

The young patrolman looked at her. "Well, now, I don't mind tellin' you, Dr. Cole, Paradise Square is no place for a lady."

Bethany fixed a look on him and smiled. "I appreciate your concern, Officer, but I've been there before. Will you drive us?"

The policeman darted a glance at Andrew.

One look at Bethany's face and Andrew knew better than to try to dissuade her. Paradise Square was as foul a place as any city ever harbored, but by now most of the rogues and rabble who peopled the area had come to recognize Bethany and himself — indeed, seemed to hold a grudging respect for them. Besides, it sounded as if they would both be needed.

"She's right," he conceded. "We should be on our way."

Not until they had left the restaurant and were nearing the infamous Five Points district did it strike Andrew that only the most craven of cowards would welcome the squalor of Paradise Square as a means of withholding the truth from the woman he loved.

SIXTEEN

A Sorrow Shared

Too long a sacrifice
Can make a stone of the heart.

W. B. YEATS

In the snug little caretaker's house at Bantry Hill, Vangie MacGovern lay beside her husband, watching him as he slept. He was peaceful as a boy, smiling in his dreams.

Here it was, three weeks before Christmas, and Vangie was still hiding his rightful gift from him.

It was becoming harder and harder not to tell him. Soon he would guess. She had been in the family way too many times for him to be entirely ignorant of the signs.

202

And why *hadn't* she told him? With each of the other children, she had been eager to make the announcement. She would have thought she would be even more impatient with this one. This would be their *American* child after all. Their first child born out from under the English boot of persecution. Their first child born to freedom.

The enormity of her deceit gnawed at her. By not sharing the news with Conn, she was depriving him of the elation he experienced each time he learned that a new babe was on the way. He had every right to share this joy, and she had no right to withhold it.

Yet she continued to keep silent. God forgive her, for some inexplicable and no doubt sinful reason, she did not *want* to see her husband's joy, that familiar light of happiness and pride that always accompanied such news.

What kind of wicked, ungrateful woman had she become?

It wasn't that she resented the babe. To the contrary, she had already begun to experience that familiar rush of love and fierce protectiveness for a new life growing inside her. No matter how many times she might give birth, each time was a wonder, an incomparable gift.

No, she could never resent her own child.

It was *Conn* she resented . . .

The truth had been lurking at the edges of her mind for days, but she had kept it at bay. Now she was confronted with the full force of its shame and fury. How could she possibly resent her husband for loving her and for giving her yet another expression of that love? Hadn't she been blessed more than any woman had a right to be? To be married to a man who still loved her with all the passion of his manhood and the fullness of his heart after more than twenty years — surely she should be overcome with happiness and gratitude, not filled with resentment and bitterness.

The crux of her mutinous feelings toward her husband was Aidan, of course. She still resented Conn for the way he had set his head — and his heart — against their oldest son. She had begged him to write to the boy and initiate a reconciliation. Surely if Aidan knew of their unexpected good fortune, and if he could be convinced that Conn wanted him here, *needed* him here, then he would join them. But Conn met her every plea with the same hardheaded refusal. He simply would not take the first step.

And so day after day, week after week, the stone in Vangie's heart — the stone that stood between her love for her husband and her forgiveness of him — seemed to grow harder and more resistant.

She had written her own letters to Aidan, a number of them. But no reply had come, not so much as a note. And Vangie knew with a sick certainty that a reply would *never* come unless Conn himself made the first move to break down the wall between himself and their son. And how likely was that, himself the stubborn fool?

Vangie feared she might never see her oldest son again. And for that, she could not bring herself to forgive her husband.

Both the pain and the unforgiveness burned in her day and night. Like a pool of acid eating away at her insides, little by little, joy by joy, dream by dream. She could find little more than drudgery in the very act of living. The anticipation of a new baby couldn't fill the void of her firstborn's absence any more than her love for her husband could bridge the widening gap between them.

Conn stirred in his sleep and moved to draw her closer to him. But Vangie resisted, lying still until at last, overcome by the soul sickness dredging up in her with a vengeance, she rose and left their bed.

Renny Magee lay awake on her cot in the

narrow loft, listening to the night sounds of the river and the rising wind. She could tell by the draft coming through the window that the air had turned sharply colder.

At first she thought the strange noise below was merely the wind keening through the pine trees at the side of the house. She burrowed deeper under the bed covers. But after a moment more, she heard the sound again and sat up, listening.

It wasn't the wind. Someone was in the kitchen, directly below her.

Someone weeping.

She hesitated only a minute before flinging the covers aside and, shivering in the cold, tiptoed down the wooden steps from the loft in her stocking feet.

At the doorway to the kitchen, she stopped short. There was no light in the room, save for a candle flickering weakly on the shelf of the cupboard near the window. Still, she could see Vangie, sitting alone at the table, her head resting on her arms, her slender shoulders rising and falling as she wept.

Dread immobilized Renny as she stood watching. What terrible thing had happened? But then it struck her that Vangie would hardly be weeping alone at the kitchen table had some awful event occurred. In times of difficulty, members of the MacGovern family didn't keep to themselves, but drew together.

The sight of the strong, kindhearted Vangie sorrowing in the lonely silence of the night pierced Renny's heart like a darning needle. Yet she resisted the fierce desire to cross the room and offer comfort. Vangie would most likely not welcome an intrusion upon her solitude.

And so she backed away, hovering just outside the door where she wouldn't be seen, half in fear of what had brought Vangie to such a state of despair, half in despondency at the awareness that it was not her place to approach this woman she loved as she might have loved her own mother . . . had she ever known what it was to *have* a mother.

Conn woke from a restless sleep to find Vangie gone from their bed.

After another moment he heard her in the kitchen, weeping. He rose to go to her, then stopped, sinking back onto the mattress. This wasn't the first time she had left their bed in the middle of the night.

And he knew why. She meant to conceal her pain from him.

Apparently, she believed he didn't hear

her sobbing alone in the kitchen, didn't see the evidence of her sadness in her swollen eyes at the breakfast table. She continued to pretend that all was well, that she was happy and content in their new home. But to his own grief, Conn knew better. For a long time now, Vangie had kept a part of herself closed, shut away from him, even when they made love.

There was a place in her reserved for someone else, he knew. An empty place that not even the depth of his love, the needs of the children, and the richness of their life here on this sprawling, wondrous piece of land could ever fill. It was Aidan's place, and it was growing inside her, growing to such proportions that Conn feared before long it might shut out all else, including him.

At last he turned and, even though the urge to go to her was almost more than he could bear, he fought against it. He couldn't bring himself to face her resentment yet again, to see the accusation in her eyes. He knew what she wanted from him, and although he would have moved mountains for her, sure, there would be no moving Aidan. He had seen it in his son's face that day on the docks, when he'd turned and walked away from them, from all of them, even his mother. The boy had made his choice, and he had chosen Ireland over his own family.

What could be done about such a son?

Besides, did Vangie really think this was easy for *him?* Didn't she realize that the knife in her heart sliced as deeply into his own? Aidan was *his* son, too. Didn't she understand that the loss of their son was as much his loss as hers?

There was nothing more he could say to her that he hadn't already said, nothing to ease her pain or purge her resentment toward him. Surely in time, she would come to see that there was nothing either of them could do. Aidan would come to America only if and when *he* wanted to come, and until then they might just as well let go of the boy.

He considered himself a man, after all, so let him be a man. They had their other children to care for. The good Lord knew that in itself was a full-time job.

Conn sighed. Morning would come soon, and he'd have to be up and ready to work. And so he buried his head in the pillows, trying to drown out the heartbreaking sound of his wife's unhappiness, even as he attempted to ignore his own.

SEVENTEEN

SURPRISES IN THE MORNING

A little love, a little trust,
A soft impulse, a sudden dream . . .

STOPFORD A. BROOKE

Christmas was less than three weeks away, and the orchestra would perform its annual holiday concert — the final concert of the year — in just ten days.

Susanna had been seeing evidence of Michael's usual pre-performance tension for days now. This morning, however, he seemed more energized than edgy, consuming his breakfast in a rush and replying to Caterina's questions in a vague and disjointed fashion. None of this was like him at

210

all; Michael was a man who typically savored not only his food, but mealtime itself, taking advantage of the time at the table to enjoy Caterina's chatter.

Come to think of it, Caterina was also acting peculiar. Instead of Susanna having to call her at least twice before she stirred, she had appeared in the hallway a little before seven, still in her nightgown and wrapper, but wide awake and fairly dancing with high spirits.

By the time they were finished with breakfast, Susanna was convinced that both Michael and Caterina were indeed behaving oddly, as if they were conspiring together. Caterina kept darting glances at Susanna with a puckish smile, and several times she left her chair to whisper in her father's ear, despite Susanna's pointed remarks about rudeness.

Normally Michael would have reprimanded his daughter for such conduct, but this morning he appeared to be enjoying her mischief. And Caterina, the little minx, was clearly intent on taking full advantage of her father's indulgence.

They had taken to eating their morning meal in the small breakfast room off the kitchen instead of in the dining room. Susanna herself had suggested the change;

both Michael and Caterina seemed less restrained in the small, cheerful setting that looked out onto the gardens. Besides, the vast dining hall was too stuffy a setting for breakfast. Since Paul was almost always up and about before the rest of the household and rarely sat down for the morning meal, it was normally just the three of them at the table.

As Michael's time with his daughter was limited, Susanna had offered more than once to take her meal alone, but in truth she had been pleased when Michael wouldn't hear of it. She looked forward to these early-morning times with him and Caterina. Michael also seemed to enjoy beginning the day in this fashion. He was more relaxed and animated at breakfast than at any other time.

Susanna admired the way he so diligently reserved a part of his mornings and as many evenings as possible for his daughter. His travels back and forth to the city and the hours he spent locked up in the music room cut deeply into his time with Caterina, but he was never neglectful. To the contrary, he made every effort to give her his undivided attention — and affection — as often as possible. As for Caterina, she seemed to take her father's busy life in stride, while clearly thriving on the time they *did* spend together.

Michael pushed his chair back from the table and stood. "I trust the two of you have not forgotten this evening?"

His question prompted a muffled giggle from Caterina, which her father quickly silenced with one raised eyebrow.

"No, of course not," Susanna replied. "Is Paul still planning to meet us at the ferry and take us to the hotel?"

"*Sì.* Cati seems bent on dressing in her finest, but if you would prefer not to, Susanna, that's quite all right."

Susanna's "finest" was the black wool dress she had brought with her from home — not quite shabby, but undeniably well-worn. Still, even if she could afford it, which she definitely could not, a new dress would have been an unnecessary extravagance for a simple dinner after rehearsal. Her black dress would do perfectly well.

Still puzzled by his and Caterina's odd behavior this morning, Susanna caught herself — just for a moment — wondering . . .

But, no, neither of them could possibly know about today. Caterina had pried her birth date out of her once, but that had been many weeks ago. The girl was bright, but surely too young to remember a date for so long a time. Besides, even if she *had* remembered, it was foolish entirely to think that Michael might make an effort to acknowledge it.

Unless Caterina had coaxed . . .

Really, she was being *too* foolish. Still, it was rather nice, even *pretending* that someone might remember her birthday.

She watched as Michael bent to press a good-bye kiss on the top of Caterina's head. Immediately the child leaped from her chair and whipped around to him. "I wish it were tonight right *now*, Papa!" she burst out, flinging her arms about his waist.

"Someday soon, *mia figlia*," he said dryly, "I hope for you to make the acquaintance of a virtue called 'patience.' "

"But I know about patience, Papa," she said, still clinging to him. "Mrs. Dempsey says it means not to rush the cook or we'll eat the potatoes raw."

He chuckled. "Mrs. Dempsey is a wise woman, no?"

"She also taught me a poem about patience."

"Ah! And I expect you are about to recite it."

Caterina tilted her head, curls bouncing, and looked up at him: *"Patience is a virtue. Have it if you can. It's rarely seen in woman — and never in a man."*

Michael's dark brows shot up in surprise. Then he threw back his head and laughed.

Beaming, the child turned to look at Susanna.

"I think it's time for our morning devotions, miss," she said sternly, then lost the struggle to keep a solemn expression.

Michael tugged at a lock of his daughter's dark hair. "I must get ready to leave," he said. "I will see you this evening."

Caterina was watching Susanna closely, the fingers of one hand pressed against her lips as if to contain another giggle. Yes, there was definitely some sort of collusion between the child and her father. She rose from her chair and started to follow Caterina out of the room.

Michael, however, stopped them. "Caterina, I need to speak with your Aunt Susanna for a moment. You go along to your room and wait for her."

The little girl frowned, glancing from her father to Susanna, but finally went bouncing out of the room, looking back only once.

"I wanted to talk with you about this before I raise the subject with Caterina," Michael said, gesturing that Susanna should again sit down.

His lighthearted demeanor had sobered.

"Is something wrong?" Susanna asked.

He shook his head, taking a chair across the table from her. "No, but there is something I want to discuss with you, something that will involve you just as much as it will Caterina or myself. I want to know how you feel about it before I initiate anything or bring it up to Caterina."

Exceedingly curious, Susanna listened carefully, her astonishment growing as he told her what he wanted to do, indeed what he felt God was *calling* him to do.

When he had finished, he paused for only a second or two. "What do you think? Would you be willing that I should do this? And to help out if needed?"

Susanna wiped the dampness from her eyes. "I think it's a wonderful idea," she said quietly. "And of course, I'll help however I can."

"And do you think Caterina will agree?"

"Oh, Michael, you know she will! Caterina has a generous heart entirely. And I have no doubt but what she'll be more help than you can imagine."

Slowly, he nodded and smiled. "I think you are right. We will tell her together, no?"

He sought her hand across the table. "Thank you for understanding, Susanna."

Susanna looked at their clasped hands.

After so long a time, they had moved from suspicion to acceptance, from acceptance to trust, from trust to friendship. And now they had come together as allies in a common cause.

He squeezed her hand as if he had read her thoughts. How could such a simple touch, Susanna wondered, make her heart feel as if it were overflowing with warm oil?

EIGHTEEN

TO GO AGAINST THE GIANT

Use well the moment;
   what the hour
Brings for thy use is in thy power;
And what thou best canst
   understand
Is just the thing lies nearest
   to thy hand.

JOHANN W. VON GOETHE

During the first few minutes of rehearsal, Susanna found it difficult to concentrate. Her thoughts kept drifting to Michael and the surprise he'd revealed after breakfast. If she had had any remaining doubts about the kind of man he was, what he had divulged to her this morning would have erased them all.

She could never say this to Michael — he had a way of deflecting any praise that came to him — but Susanna was deeply moved by the thought of what he meant to do. It was a good thing, even a *noble* thing. She found herself genuinely enthusiastic about the experience ahead — and inordinately pleased that Michael had placed so much confidence in her cooperation.

But for now, she really needed to pay attention to what was happening on stage. In addition to the orchestra, Michael had assembled three choirs: two large choirs from local churches and a smaller but highly talented children's choir from several of the city's shelter houses. They could not have been more diverse.

Watching Michael work was a fascinating experience. Most of the time he seemed relaxed, even casual with his people, and their high regard for him was obvious. Even so, in spite of his informal bearing, he insisted not only on perfection, but on total involvement in the music. Under Michael's baton, no musician dared to daydream or indulge in idle chatter with a neighbor.

He had built a magnificent orchestra, one that rarely received anything but the highest of praise from the critics. There were exceptions, of course. One or two columnists seemed incapable of anything but the most scathing reviews — not only of the orchestra, but of Michael himself. He routinely discarded those reviews that were transparently personal, petty, or spiteful, but seemed to pay close heed to the comments of the few critics he respected, even if their judgments were less than glowing. Clearly, he was not a man to grow complacent with his own abilities or accomplishments.

Susanna's gaze roamed over the orchestra and the choirs. It was an awesome array of talent, yet with every number rehearsed, she became more keenly aware of the absence of an organist. Up until now, the rehearsal had consisted mostly of varied renderings of seasonal carols — some from other countries — and a number of traditional selections, such as Schubert's "Mille Cherubini in Coro" and "Jesu Joy of Man's Desiring." Michael typically developed his own arrangements, even for the simplest Christmas carol, so perhaps he had purposely omitted the organ. But when he instructed just before the break that they would end the rehearsal with "For unto Us a Child Is Born" and the "Hallelujah Chorus" from the *Messiah*, she fully expected an organist to arrive on the scene, albeit late.

During the break, Caterina went running up to the stage, where Paul and Michael still lingered, engaged in some private discussion. Michael smiled when his daughter tugged on his coattails, then lifted her into his arms as the few orchestra members remaining on stage came over to them.

Susanna watched with wry amusement as Caterina proceeded to charm them all with her dimples and laughter. After another moment, Michael set her to her feet, and she led him down the stage steps to the front row, where Susanna was seated.

"So — how are we doing?" he said, sitting down beside her. "Do you have any suggestions?"

"Papa, may I go play the harp?" Caterina begged.

"Don't interrupt, Cati," said Michael. Then he nodded. "Only for a moment. We will be starting again soon."

He smiled at Susanna. "One time it is the harp, next the cello," he said as Caterina scampered off. "I think she means to play all the instruments in the orchestra."

"Like her papa," Susanna said. It was true: Michael seemed capable of playing whatever instrument he chose, although at home he clearly favored the simple mandolin.

He gave a turn of the wrist, saying, "But we will hope that Caterina plays them *well*. Her papa is a virtuoso with none." He paused, his expression growing more serious. "Speaking of virtuosos, I need to ask . . . if you would be willing to help us a little before we finish today."

Instantly, Susanna's guard shot up.

"Now, before you say no, let me explain. I would have asked you at the beginning of the rehearsal, but I knew you would think I arranged it on purpose — and I promise you, Susanna, I did no such thing."

"Arranged *what?*"

He hesitated, as if reluctant to explain.

"Arranged what, Michael?" she repeated sternly.

As if he could feel her scrutiny, he turned his face away. "It seems that Christopher Redding, our organist . . . ah, what has happened is . . . that he fell on the ice yesterday afternoon and broke not only his ankle, but a wrist as well. I thought perhaps . . . you might consider helping us. For this evening, at least."

Susanna stared at him, speechless. An unexpected twinge of excitement was immediately swallowed up by a surge of annoyance and disappointment as she remembered his and Caterina's behavior of the morning: the sly smiles and furtive whispers between the two. To think she had actually allowed herself to believe, even for a moment, that they might have been plotting something . . . special.

"Do you really expect me to believe you didn't plan this?"

He turned back to her with an infuriating ghost of a smile. "You see," he said, "I knew what you would think."

"Then you also knew what I would say."

He shrugged, a gesture that merely heated Susanna's irritation.

"You can't possibly think I would humiliate myself in front of all these people."

Paul and Caterina had left the stage and now stood watching them, Caterina with eyes wide and curious, Paul with his gaze averted, as if trying to pretend he wasn't listening.

But Susanna was beyond the point of caring.

"Michael, I haven't been near an organ for nearly a year! And I've never played an organ like *that!*" Forgetting Michael's blindness for the moment, Susanna stabbed her index finger toward the immense grand organ at the far right of the stage — a massive instrument with five manuals in addition to the pedals. An organ like this would surely intimidate all but the most outstanding of musicians.

And she had been longing to get her hands on it all evening . . .

She shook her head as if to banish the treacherous thought.

"But you once played for the worship at your church," Michael pointed out.

"That was ages ago! And a poor excuse of an instrument it was at that. Certainly nothing like that behemoth on stage."

His jaw clenched in a stubborn look, and he murmured something about it being "just an organ."

"It is most assuredly not '*just* an organ,' " Susanna shot back.

"But only for this evening," he said, his tone deceptively mild. "You need not play — how do you call it? — full organ. If you would merely accompany us as best you can. Otherwise the rehearsal will not be what it should."

Was there no end to his attempt to manipulate? "And I suppose your Mr. Redding will be fully recovered in time for the concert? He must have quite an impressive capacity for healing."

Michael's expression turned sheepish, but he made no reply.

Susanna shook her head. "I simply cannot believe you did this. And to bring Caterina into it as well! So *this* was what all the whispering and scheming at breakfast was about."

"But, Aunt Susanna — that's not what we were whispering about —"

"Caterina —" Michael's tone was unusually sharp.

"Well, we weren't," the child repeated with uncharacteristic sullenness. "I didn't know anything about Mr. Redding."

Susanna looked from one to the other. Michael's expression was impassive, closed, but Caterina's lower lip could not have protruded any farther, and tears glistened in her eyes. Could Susanna possibly be mistaken about Michael's having deliberately contrived this scenario?

"I'm sorry you think I would try to deceive you in such a way," Michael said quietly. "The truth is that I only learned of Redding's accident when I arrived this afternoon. As I told you, I was hesitant to approach you about the organ. I was fairly certain that you would react . . . just as you have."

Paul, obviously bent on redeeming the situation, gave Susanna a look of appeal. "It is true, Susanna. Redding's son brought the word of his accident only moments before rehearsal began." He paused. "As a member of the orchestra, I wish, of course, that you would reconsider. We do feel the lack of the organ. It would be a great help if you would play for us. And it's not as if you would be a soloist. Why, with the instruments and all the voices you would scarcely be noticed!"

Susanna lifted an eyebrow at this; they both knew the likelihood of the organ not being noticed.

"But if you really feel incapable, I understand," Paul added with a cherubic expression.

"I don't know that I'm *incapable*." Susanna was growing nearly as exasperated with Paul as she was with Michael. "I expect with some warning I could have managed. But even the most accomplished of organists, which I would never pretend to be, needs to practice."

"But of course," Paul quickly agreed. "It would take a long time — perhaps weeks? — before you would feel competent, no?"

"Not *weeks*," Susanna said. "But certainly a few *days*. It hardly matters in any event. You need someone sooner than I could be prepared."

Michael broke in then. "*Sì*, as you said, there is no possibility that Redding would be back with us in only a few days. I admit that I probably *was* hoping that if I could convince you to assist us today — and if you managed well enough — then you might consider playing for the concert itself."

"Michael, we've talked about this before —"

He nodded. "I know, I know. And I do understand your fear —"

"I'm not — it's not *fear*. Not exactly." Susanna bit her lower lip. Several times. "All right. It *is* fear. But you can't possibly understand what it's like for me."

"As I have told you before, I *do* understand."

"I know what you told me, but —"

"But aren't you brave, Aunt Susanna?"

Susanna turned to look at her niece.

"When we read the story about David and Goliath, you said that being brave doesn't mean we're not afraid. It means doing what we're supposed to do even if we *are* afraid."

Susanna stared at her niece. Caterina was gazing up at her with the uncompromising, guileless look of a child who has found a truth, made it her own, and now decided to test it.

She saw the look on Paul's face — not smug, exactly, but definitely keen to hear her reply. Michael, too, was obviously curious as to how she would answer Caterina.

But Caterina had not finished. "You said David was probably *very* afraid of Goliath, because he was just a boy and Goliath was a *giant*. But David went to meet Goliath anyway, and God helped him. And if the organ is like a big, scary giant . . ."

If Michael had not been blind, his gaze would have easily burned a hole through Susanna. And in Paul's eyes, she encountered a distinct glint of challenge.

To her surprise, Michael moved to ease the tension, lifting his hand as if to put a halt to any further discussion. "I understand, Susanna. You simply do not feel . . . ready . . . to do this. So, then, we will stop trying to coerce you and get back to rehearsal."

"But, Papa —"

Michael shook his head. "It is enough, Caterina. Your Aunt Susanna has said no. We will speak no more about it."

"Thank you, Michael."

Throughout the remainder of rehearsal, Susanna could feel Caterina watching her. The little girl's disappointment pierced her heart. And she knew that, because of her stubbornness, Handel's crowning achievement would suffer for the lack of an organ's depth and richness.

But Michael had it coming. He had attempted to trick her into doing something he knew she wouldn't want to do. All her earlier warm thoughts toward him went flying from her mind, replaced by a cold, wrenching disappointment of her own.

Still, no matter how she tried to justify her resistance to his maneuvering, her excuses seemed to bounce off the wall of her conscience. They all added up to nothing more than fear. The fear of calling attention to herself. The fear of failing — failing not only the expectations of those who were counting on her, but failing the music itself. The fear of not being . . . *adequate.*

It was a fear that even she could not explain, so how could she expect anyone else to understand it? Least of all a man who almost certainly had never felt inadequate in his life.

NINETEEN

LIGHT AND SHADOW

My heart is like a trembling leaf
carried by the wind.

ANONYMOUS

For the past hour, Bethany Cole's mood had
seesawed from exasperation to anticipation
so many times she was getting a headache.

The exasperation stemmed from the time
and effort spent on decking herself out in an
exceptionally uncomfortable dinner dress
and a new hair style, which she immediately
decided made her look somewhat like a
ferret.

By the time she'd removed some of the
froufrou from the dress and secured her hair

to its usual nape-of-the-neck twist, her hands were trembling. She felt three kinds of fool for working herself into a state over what should have been nothing more than a pleasant evening among friends.

As for her earlier anticipation, it had been all but swept away by her impatience with herself. This was not some sort of a . . . a rendezvous, after all, but simply a social gathering to which Andrew had offered to escort her.

And wasn't Andrew the reason she was so jumpy in the first place? He seemed bent on making more of the occasion than it really was. He had even sent her flowers, for goodness' sake! Not to mention the fact that, with all the time she'd wasted fussing over her appearance, she could have seen a few more patients or even made hospital rounds. Certainly, she could have accomplished something more worthwhile than giving herself a roaring case of hives.

Not that she actually had hives just yet, but if she didn't calm down and stop fussing over her appearance, it could still happen.

And wouldn't that be just fine and dandy? No doubt poor Andrew would be positively elated at the thought of escorting a red, bumpy-faced partner into Gaulerio's elegant dining room.

She took one more quick glance in the mirror, decided not for the first time that her hair was too pale — was it just the light, or was she starting to go gray around her temples? And one side of her neckline was draped lower than the other. Well, it was too late to do anything about that. Leaning closer to the mirror, she jabbed another hairpin into the back of her hair — and discovered a spot on the tip of her nose, a blemish that she was quite certain had not been there a minute before.

She groaned, slapped some more talc over her face, and resigned herself to the dismaying fact that she was going to be a huge disappointment, if not an all-out embarrassment, to poor Andrew.

But why did she keep thinking of him as "poor Andrew," when this entire debacle was all his doing anyway?

Andrew Carmichael fumbled with his neckcloth, finally giving up in utter frustration.

He should have left the office earlier. He had insisted that Bethany take some extra time, sending her off a good hour and a half before they usually closed up. Now he wished he had left when she did. But the three patients remaining in the waiting room had all seemed serious enough to warrant attention, so he had stayed.

So much for allowing some extra time for himself tonight. As it was, he'd barely managed to shave and change clothes.

Bethany, of course, would be absolutely lovely. As always.

Which raised the question he'd been asking himself all day: given the fact that Bethany Cole would steal the breath from any man at twenty paces, why on earth had she agreed to accompany him tonight?

What a picture they must make to anyone else: the Princess and the Peasant.

Beauty and the Beast.

He actually groaned in self-disgust. What had ever possessed him to think that Bethany might *want* to spend an entire evening with him? She spent most of her days with him as it was.

Had she consented only because they were associates? Did she view tonight as just another event to be endured because they were partners?

Or had she simply not been able to think of an excuse quickly enough to beg off?

Anxiety tore at him even more as he recalled the conversation he'd had only last week with Frank Donovan. Frank's cynicism often rankled him, but on this particular occasion, he had found his friend's sarcasm particularly annoying. In truth, Frank's remarks had hurt, and hurt deeply. And yet his barbs had held such a ring of truth that Andrew had actually found himself fighting off a kind of bleak despondency for days after.

Frank had come to the office just as patient hours were over, and Bethany was on her way out. Andrew had watched her leave, not realizing that Frank was watching *him*.

When he turned back, Frank's face was creased with a smirk. "Ah, Doc, you're in a bad way, it seems to me."

Andrew had known exactly what Frank was getting at, but he'd managed to feign a questioning look.

Frank shook his head. "I don't reckon there is a sorrier sight than a man in love."

"Frank . . ."

"Have you given this sufficient thought, Doc?"

Frank's abrupt change in tone, from his usual wry banter to this unexpected gravity, caught Andrew off guard. "Have I given *what* sufficient thought?"

"Have you considered the consequences if things don't work out?"

"Am I supposed to know what you mean?"

"Oh, come on, Doc! You know what I'm

talking about. You're in love with the woman, and that's the truth."

Andrew felt mortified. Had he been that transparent? And if he had, what business was it of Frank's?

"Even if you were right — and I'm not saying you are — shouldn't you let me worry about it?" He forced a short laugh. "I'm not exactly wet behind the ears anymore, you know."

Frank had a most irritating way of eyeing a man as if he were nothing shy of a fool. "Well, that's true enough, Doc. But you wouldn't be the first man to go diggin' yourself a grave with the wrong shovel. If you take my meaning."

Andrew frowned but said nothing.

"I'd hate to see you make a bad mistake, is all."

Andrew clenched his fists at his sides.

"The thing is, Doc, if it's settlin' down to home and hearth fire you're wanting, I confess I don't quite see that happening with your Dr. Cole. She may be a fine doctor — by all accounts, she is exactly that — but can you honestly see the woman with a passel of young'uns hangin' on to her skirts while she stirs the soup?"

For the first time in their friendship, Andrew found himself angry with Frank Donovan. No, more than angry — furious. Frank's intentions might be the best; he might sincerely believe he was doing nothing more than looking out for a friend, but that did nothing to cool Andrew's anger. This time Frank had gone too far.

Andrew gave a shrug, intending to put an end to the conversation before he said something he might later regret.

As it turned out, it was Frank who brought the exchange to a halt. With an idle wave of his hand and in a tone thick with exaggerated Irish, he said, "Ah, well, 'tis none of my business after all, is it now? I'm naught but a thickheaded mick who needs to mind his own affairs."

They parted with an unresolved — and unfamiliar — tension between them. They hadn't encountered each other since, but Andrew knew how it would be when they did. They would make an attempt at small talk, pretending nothing had happened, but the tension would still hang between them until either time or circumstance managed to expel it.

He quit fiddling with his tie and picked up his hairbrush. His hands were so swollen he could scarcely manage the brush, but he made one more hasty attempt to coax his hair into place. He had never thought much about his hair one way or the other. Lately, however, he bemoaned the color, an odd shade, neither brown nor black, rather like the bark of a tree. And that dreadful fore-lock that simply would not be constrained; had he been a woman, he could have an-chored it in place with a hairpin, but as it was, he went about most of the time looking like a one-eyed sailor.

He passed a hand down his nose. The hawkish, too prominent beak of the Carmichael men was definitely not one of the familial traits he might have coveted.

By now he was thoroughly disgusted with himself. This was a simple evening out with friends, not some sort of a . . . a tryst. And yet he'd made a royal botch of things when he asked Bethany if he could escort her, and then gone on to compound his humiliation by behaving like a lovesick poet most of the week. Sending her flowers this afternoon, for goodness' sake, and insisting she take time away from the office when he would have really preferred to have her there — had needed her there, in fact.

He'd rather just call the whole thing off. But of course that was impossible. Then he really *would* make himself out a total fool.

He swiped the stubborn lock of hair away from his forehead and grabbed his coat and gloves from the back of the chair. He looked for his scarf, found it at his feet, then struggled to pull his gloves on over his swollen knuckles. Finally, stomach churning, he left the room, uttering a hasty prayer as he went that he wouldn't knock anything over at dinner to embarrass himself or Bethany.

At least one piece of news he had saved for tonight was almost guaranteed to please her. And he hoped she'd also like the surprise he'd planned for after dinner.

All in all, it would be a lovely evening, except . . . except for what he planned to tell her later — something he *must* tell her. Tonight.

SUSANNA'S SURPRISE

He that is down needs fear no fall,
He that is low, no pride.

JOHN BUNYAN

Susanna was still smarting from the scene back at the concert hall when they walked into Gaulerio's restaurant. The setting that greeted her, however, caused her to forget everything else — for the moment, at least.

This was Michael's favorite eating place, and Paul's as well. Gaulerio's was known to be a favorite meeting and dining establishment for many among the music community. Even so, Susanna was surprised at the lack of gilt and glitter. Instead, the restaurant had a quiet elegance, warmed by a great deal of wood and rich tones of burgundy and deep blue. The room was illuminated with candles and low-hanging chandeliers. Although every table seemed to be occupied, the sounds of conversation and the clink of silver and china were unobtrusive, muffled by the thick floor coverings and heavy draperies.

A small, trim man with a neat mustache rushed up to them. "Ah, *Maestro! Benvenuto, benvenuto!* We were beginning to think you had abandoned us!"

Michael laughed. "Surely you know better than that, Enrico."

Enrico greeted Paul just as effusively, then bowed low to Caterina. "Ah, the *principéssa!* See how quickly you are growing up!"

The three men exchanged a few words in rapid Italian before Michael took Susanna's arm and introduced her as "*Signorina* Fallon — Caterina's Aunt Susanna."

With a huge smile and a sweeping bow, Enrico kissed Susanna's hand, then said something in Italian too quickly for her to catch. Straightening, he turned to Michael and took his arm. "Everything is ready, *Maestro.* We will go upstairs now."

Michael and Paul, obviously well-known

here, had to stop several times before reaching the stairway to acknowledge greetings from the various diners. A number of men stood to shake hands, while the women, Susanna noticed, watched Michael closely with unconcealed interest.

At the top of the stairs, Enrico led them down a narrow hallway and flung open the paneled double doors at the end. "Here we are! Come, please!"

Caterina scampered ahead of her, and Paul, too, moved quickly forward. Susanna started into the room, then stopped. At the same time, Paul's good-natured face split into a wide smile as he stood watching Susanna.

Directly ahead of her, a small group was gathered around a large oval table, lavishly decorated with winter greenery, candles, and sparkling china. Nearby, on a smaller table, several brightly colored, beribboned packages were heaped.

Susanna stared in astonishment. Rosa Navaro was there, along with Dr. Cole and Dr. Carmichael. Pastor Holt. Even Miss Fanny Crosby had come. The moment they caught sight of her, they all stood, laughing and applauding. "Happy Birthday, Susanna!"

Caterina danced circles around her. "Did

we surprise you, Aunt Susanna?" she piped. "*Did* we?"

Susanna smiled down at Caterina and took her hand. "How clever you are, *alannah*. And how well you kept your secret — you and your papa!"

"Papa did all the work," Caterina said with the utmost seriousness. "He and Cousin Paul."

"Well . . . I'm very grateful. This is . . . a wonderful surprise."

Susanna didn't trust herself to so much as glance at Michael. This, then, was what he and Caterina had been whispering about this morning. Not a scheme to replace the missing organist, not a ploy to "advance" her to a place where she had no desire to be. A party.

A surprise party. For her.

Michael had been telling the truth, after all. Just as Caterina insisted. And fool that she was, she had made a scene, humiliated herself, disappointed Caterina — and embarrassed Michael.

Susanna wished she could fall through the floor, so great was her self-reproach. Two things struck her in that instant: she was dismayed at how quickly the old mistrust of Michael could reappear, confounding her other feelings for him; and at the same time she was shaken by a surge of relief, in spite of her shame, to realize that she'd midjudged him so badly.

"Michael," she said, her voice low as she turned to him, "I didn't know . . . this morning, when you and Caterina —"

"*Sì.* I know," he said, his tone quiet and unmistakably sad.

She had mistrusted him, misunderstood him, hurt him. He was *still* hurting — she could hear it in his voice, see it in the slump of his shoulders, the white lines that bracketed his eyes.

"I don't know what to say. I'm sorry . . . so sorry . . . for thinking —"

"It's all right, Susanna. Come — we should go in now." He waved off her apology, but his demeanor was restrained, his expression inscrutable.

"I must talk with you later."

He offered his arm as if he hadn't heard her. "Your friends are waiting."

Somehow Susanna managed to ignore her raw feelings as the evening progressed. The heaviness in her heart seemed to recede in the laughter and the warmth around the table, and at one point she realized she was actually enjoying herself.

If Michael bore her any grudge, no one

would have guessed. He was his usual affable, congenial self, greeting all their guests and drawing Andrew Carmichael aside for a private word. No one else seemed to notice that he seldom spoke directly to her, that he avoided even the most casual touch of the hand or brush of the sleeve when passing a dish or a condiment her way.

The only bad moment came after all the gifts had been opened. There was a soft indigo shawl from Rosa, a delicate, lace-edged handkerchief from Miss Fanny, and a pair of fawn-colored gloves and matching neck scarf from Dr. Cole and Dr. Carmichael. From Paul she received copies of Miss Alcott's *Little Women* and *Little Men*, and Caterina presented her with a portrait she had painted — a remarkably realistic likeness of Gus, the wolfhound.

Only after all the other gifts had been opened and an elegantly decorated cake had been served did Michael surprise her by quietly pushing a gift wrapped in shimmering paper and satin ribbons in front of her.

Susanna looked at the package, then at Michael. Her fingers trembled as she loosened the ribbons and pulled the paper from an exquisite ivory jewelry box. The lid was adorned with an intricately carved minstrel's harp, also in ivory.

She caught a sharp breath. "Oh . . . how *beautiful!*"

Bethany Cole and Rosa echoed her sentiment, while Paul described the gift in detail to Miss Fanny.

Caterina tugged at her sleeve. "It plays *music,* Aunt Susanna!"

Susanna wound the spring, and "Dear Harp of My Country" by Ireland's own poet, Thomas Moore, began to chime its plaintive melody in bell-like tones.

Susanna's eyes filled, as did her heart. Her gaze went to Michael, who sat quietly, his lips curved in a faint smile.

"It's . . . *exquisite,* Michael."

"It was my mother's," he said softly. "My papa gave it to her when I was born."

She stared at him, shaken by the value his words attached to the gift, a gift she would have counted as highly precious even without its personal significance to Michael.

"It's . . . the most wonderful gift ever. I don't know what to say."

"I hoped you would like it," he said simply.

Like it? Susanna felt like weeping. She was thrilled that he had chosen to give her something that obviously meant a great deal to him. And yet the personal nature of the gift only served to sharpen her feelings of guilt.

She looked around the table and saw the well-meaning but curious smiles. Somehow she managed a smile of her own.

"Thank you . . . so much, every one of you. This has to be the most special birthday party I've ever had."

In truth, it was the *only* birthday party she'd ever had. At home, there had never been enough money for such extravagance. The enormity of what Michael had done for her, the trouble he'd gone to for her, overwhelmed her anew.

She should probably say more, especially to Michael, but she couldn't think of a thing that wouldn't have sounded gauche or mawkish. "I'm truly grateful for your kindness," was all she could manage.

The buzz of conversation and laughter rose again as they shared the birthday cake. When the evening ended, Susanna felt almost relieved. She had enjoyed herself, certainly, and she appreciated the kindness of these friends whom she had known for only a brief time. But the collision of her emotions was taking its toll on her, physically and emotionally. She felt depleted by the time they left the restaurant. All she wanted was to get away and be by herself.

Because of the snow, Michael had arranged in advance for rooms at a nearby hotel; they would be staying in the city the rest of the night. This thwarted any chance for a conversation with him, but Susanna thought it might be just as well. She didn't think she could possibly muster the energy for a coherent exchange with anyone tonight, especially Michael.

Yet she couldn't bear the thought of leaving things so . . . *bruised* and strained. So in the lobby of the hotel, she drew him aside with the intention of thanking him once more for the party and, of course, for the gift.

She struggled for the right words, but they came out awkward and disjointed. "Michael . . . I don't know how to thank you. For tonight. I've never . . . nobody has ever done anything like this for me. And the music box . . . I'll cherish it. Always. Truly, I will. It means — it's very special."

"That's why I wanted you to have it, Susanna," he said quietly. "Because you, too, are very . . . special."

Without giving her time to reply, he brought her hand to his lips, then released her. "*Buona notte,* Susanna. I hope you rest well. Would you take me to Paul now, please?"

It was impossible to gauge Michael's emotions when his feelings were shuttered as they were now. Susanna did hear the note of weariness in his voice when he said good night, however, and sensed that he, also, was ready to end the evening.

Later, after Caterina and Rosa had retired, Susanna walked into the sitting room of their suite and stood at the window, looking out. The snow, still falling, muffled the usual night sounds, wrapping everything in an otherworldly stillness, the kind of quiet that seems to slow the passing of hours and calm even the most restless of hearts.

But Susanna's heart would not be quieted tonight. Only an hour ago, she had been craving solitude. Now that she had it, a sense of abandonment and isolation crept over her. She stood at the window, weighing every word that had passed between her and Michael earlier in the evening.

Why, she wondered, had she been so quick to judge Michael's motives, so resistant to his encouragement? What was the source of her self-doubts, her sense of inadequacy? She treasured the gift of music more than almost anything else in life. But until now, she had never allowed herself to confront her fear of failure for what it really was.

Earlier, Caterina's childish but incisive words had ambushed her, opening up something in Susanna that, at the time, she had known she must examine more closely when she could. Those words came back to her now, unsettling her just as much as they had before:

". . . *but aren't you* brave, *Aunt Susanna? You said that being brave doesn't mean we're not afraid. It means doing what we're supposed to do even if we are afraid.*"

As she allowed her thoughts to slip back across the years, Susanna knew it would be all too easy to blame Deirdre for the fear and insecurities that had plagued her for as long as she could remember. Her sister had never let her forget that *she* was the *artiste,* Susanna the *plebeian.* Contemptuous of Susanna's timidity, Deirdre had dubbed her "Mouse" and disparaged her every attempt at accomplishment.

Susanna had tried to rationalize Deirdre's behavior as typical of the older sibling lording it over the younger. But she knew better. Even as a child, Deirdre had been spiteful toward Susanna, as if any recognition of her sister diminished her own share of the limelight.

And yet despite her vindictiveness, Deirdre was not to blame for Susanna's weaknesses. In truth, Susanna knew that what she had become was what she had made of herself.

In admitting her fear of failure, recognizing her own inadequacies, she had contented herself with the shadows, avoiding even the slightest pursuit of prominence or status. She had made excuses to avoid taking a risk. The place she had claimed for herself, the place where she was most comfortable, was in the background.

She had long thought of it as humility. Now she saw it was false humility.

For years she had convinced herself that the "Christian way" was to avoid any form of self-aggrandizement, when in fact she had simply been avoiding any possibility of failure. Rather than pursuing and developing the gifts God had bestowed upon her, like the unfaithful steward she had *buried* them. She had been not only ungrateful, but *unfaithful.*

And yet how did one distinguish genuine humility — a virtue God not only approved but even commanded — from a desire to be "safe," a deliberate attempt to stay backstage out of fear of failure?

Susanna already knew the answer. What

she had claimed as humility was utter self-ishness. Self-deception on a grand scale. Even when she *knew* herself capable, she refused to try, refused to risk. She hadn't been exhibiting Christian virtue at all. She had merely wrapped herself in a cocoon, protected herself from the possible humiliation of not being perfect.

All her life, from girlhood to womanhood, she had chosen safety over adventure, security over opportunity, contentment over change. Deirdre might have fed her self-doubts, might have even chipped away at her confidence, but Susanna knew that she, and she alone, was ultimately responsible for this stifling of the spirit. She had placed restraints upon herself. She had let herself become the "Mouse" her sister despised.

And in one blistering moment of insight, she realized that she was also the only one who could free herself from that confinement.

But even if she *wanted* that freedom, was she willing to pay the price for it? *Could* she pay it? It would mean changing the way she saw herself, what she believed about herself. It might even mean changing her life.

"No, Caterina —" she whispered the answer to her niece's question — "I'm not brave. I don't even know if I *want* to be brave. Or if I can . . ."

TWENTY-ONE

A RIDE IN THE PARK

What if the dream came true?

PADRAIC PEARSE

Frank Donovan holstered his gun, donned his coat and hat, and took the steps two at a time as he left his second-floor rooms.

He still had to pick up his mount at the stables and see to Tommy Brennaman. He had plenty of time, but he planned to have himself a bite of supper before going on duty.

No doubt Brennaman would show up late as usual. If the rookie patrolman were not such a good hand with the horses, Frank would have done his best to get him booted off the force long before now. He always had an excuse, did Tommy, and a lame one at that.

Well, Frank intended to tell him the way of things tonight once and for all. There were other men who could handle a horse. He'd had just about enough of Brennaman's slouching.

It was still snowing, coming down even heavier now, and snow made the job just that much harder. The only good thing about it was that it covered up some of the garbage heaped in the streets and made the pigs run slower than usual.

In all likelihood the park would be busy. Everyone and his brother would be out on an evening like this, to test the skating or have themselves a sleigh ride. For himself, he wouldn't like to be on the ice just yet, in case it wasn't quite safe. But that wouldn't stop a host of eejits from giving it a try.

His mood blackened still more as he tramped across the street at the Orphan Asylum. Ordinarily he wouldn't have volunteered for park duty, especially on a night such as this — it was well off his beat. But most of the precincts were short on men due to a particularly beastly wave of grippe, and since he had nothing better to do, Frank had opted to take an extra shift or two.

After all, there was something to be said for trotting a fine horse around the park in the snow while watching a gaggle of pretty young girls on their skates. One never knew when he might be called upon to rescue some lovely young thing from a fall on the ice or a runaway sleigh.

There was nothing like a hero to a lassie in distress. Even an Irishman would do.

If she were desperate enough, that is.

Andrew had hinted that he might have a surprise for her after the party. When they pulled up to the park and got out of the buggy, the first thing Bethany saw was a sleek, dark green sleigh, the body trimmed with red and gold stripes. Two midnight black horses, their harness bells jingling in the light wind, stood pawing at the snow.

Bethany whipped around and found Andrew smiling at her.

"Oh! Andrew! This is the surprise?"

"You're pleased?"

"*Pleased?* This is incredible." The snow crunched under her feet as she went over to the sleigh and peeked inside for a closer look at the figured carpet, the crimson velvet seats and braided trim. She ran her hand over one of the ornamental plumes and then turned back to him. "How did you ever think of such a thing?"

He shrugged. "I just thought you might enjoy it."

"But where did you get it?"

"I rented it. It's ours for the rest of the evening."

Bethany looked back to the sleigh, then lifted her face to catch the snowflakes drifting down. She caught Andrew's arm. "Well, what are we waiting for?"

Laughing, he helped her into the sleigh and settled her snugly under an enormous bearskin blanket before going around to the other side. Bethany had never been in the park before tonight, had only passed by it on occasion. To her delight, she found it was lovely: elegantly landscaped and well-maintained, its hills and meadows blanketed in white, and trees that looked to be sprinkled with diamonds of ice.

She was surprised to see crowds almost everywhere they passed. "I had no idea so many people would be out on a night like this."

"Winter is one of the favorite times for park goers," he said. "The big thing in the winter is ice skating on the lakes and ponds — and sleigh riding, of course. Central Park has become one of the city's most popular recreational spots."

Sleighs were everywhere, filling the night with the sound of harness and bells and laughter. Men tipped their hats and women smiled and nodded as they passed by each other on the track. Dozens of people thronged one of the lakes, skating in singles or couples or entire family groups.

"Do you skate, Andrew?"

He smiled a little as if reminiscing, but shook his head. "Not for years. There was a pond near my home, in Scotland. When I was a boy, my sister and I used to skate there. I doubt I'd be able to stay on my feet now, after so long a time."

"You have a sister? You've never said."

His expression sobered. "Jean was several years older than I. She married after I left home, but died in childbirth not long after I came across."

"I'm sorry." Bethany studied his profile. "It occurs to me that you really haven't told me very much about your childhood or your family, even though I've told you all about mine."

"There's not that much to tell. I grew up in Glasgow, as you know, had a perfectly ordinary childhood. My father still lives there. He's a clergyman. My mother passed on when I was still a boy. Jean took over and ran the household after that. And mothered me."

Still watching him, Bethany felt a twinge of sympathy. She knew what it was like to grow up as the only child among adults. While it had certain benefits, it could also be lonely.

As if he'd read her thoughts, he said, "How was it for you, Bethany, growing up without brothers or sisters?"

"I didn't mind. Not usually. Oh, there were times when I would have liked a brother or sister, but for the most part I was content." She ducked her head sheepishly. "It's not all bad, really — being the center of everyone's attention."

Andrew raised an eyebrow. "Somehow you don't strike me as the kind who enjoys attention all that much."

He paused for a moment, and his next remark caught Bethany off guard. "I've heard that one who grows up as an only child often wants a large family after marriage."

"Is that a question?"

"Well . . . no, not necessarily," he replied, not looking at her.

An unpleasant thought filtered through Bethany's mind: the memory of Frank Donovan's accusations about the unlikeliness of her domestic — and maternal — aspirations. "I suppose I haven't thought much about the future. I always seem to be so focused on the present."

He nodded. "I think perhaps you and I are a lot alike in that respect. There's always so much to do —"

"And never enough time in which to do it," she finished. "Unless you have the energy and the initiative of Miss Fanny Crosby, who I find to be absolutely amazing! Honestly, Andrew, however does she manage to do everything she does?"

"She is a wonder."

"Of course, she has no family depending on her," Bethany mused. "That would allow her more time for her work." She reached to tuck a strand of hair back under her hat. "I understand she and her husband tend to go their separate ways."

"Where their work is concerned, that's true. But they're devoted to each other."

"Her husband is blind, too, isn't he?"

"He is. In fact, I believe they met when they were both at the Institute for the Blind. Mr. Van Alstyne teaches, but not at the Institute. He's a music teacher and a church organist as well. A very gifted man, so I've heard."

"Van Alstyne? But I thought Miss Fanny's name was Crosby?"

"That's her maiden name. I believe they agreed that she would continue using it.

Perhaps because of her music — that's how everyone knows her."

She shook her head. "Well, I'm absolutely in awe of both of them. Accomplishing so much, in spite of the fact that they can't see."

"It seems to me you needn't take a backseat to anyone when it comes to accomplishment. I'd say you've managed rather well yourself."

Bethany waved off the compliment. "Some days I feel as though I'm not accomplishing *anything*," she said with a sigh. "Especially when it comes to the patients I can't help."

"You're thinking of Maylee."

"Yes, I *hate* not being able to do anything for her, Andrew! She's such a wonderful child. She's smart, she's curious about everything, and she has the sweetest spirit. And yet just look at what she's forced to endure — and who knows what still lies ahead for her!"

"But you *have* helped her, Bethany. More than you realize. She absolutely delights in your visits, you know. She tells me all about them every time I stop by. You've given her something she's never had before."

Bethany frowned at him.

"Don't you see? You've become her

friend. I think any little girl could count herself blessed to have someone like you in her life. I'm not so sure but what you haven't become a kind of . . . mother figure to her as well."

"Goodness, I hope not! I don't consider myself a model for motherhood, not by any stretch of the imagination!"

"You're always so hard on yourself, Bethany. I happen to think you'd make a wonderful mother!"

Clearly, he'd spoken on impulse. He went crimson the moment the words left his lips.

"Well . . . be that as it may," said Bethany, feeling awkward, "I have no particular ambitions in that direction."

Andrew suddenly seemed intent on the horses pulling the sleigh. "Never?"

"I wouldn't say 'never.' I haven't actually thought that far ahead. What about you, Andrew?"

"Me?"

"You'd obviously be a good family man. Why haven't *you* ever married?"

He kept his eyes fixed straight ahead. "I don't necessarily prefer things this way," he said evenly. "But with the practice . . . and my health . . ."

Their eyes met, and Bethany recalled Frank Donovan's words about Andrew's condition, how it would eventually grow worse. And in that wistful, uncertain gaze she saw that Andrew also feared that, in time, he might become a burden.

She wanted to say something to reassure him, encourage him. But she knew too much about the possible progression of his disease to try to put a good face on it.

Thankfully, his unfailing sense of humor came to the rescue. "Besides," he said, a ghost of a smile touching his lips, "why would any woman willingly marry a doctor?"

"Why would any *man* marry a doctor, for that matter?" she tossed back recklessly.

"Perhaps doctors should only marry doctors?" he said, not quite meeting her gaze.

He let the question hang. Bethany decided not to touch it.

Frank Donovan saw them from the hillside. Doc and Lady Doc, as he'd come to think of them.

Still mounted, he saw them drive by in their fancy sleigh as they came round the near side of the lake. Doc had himself a fine-looking hat on, and Dr. Cole was decked out like one of the swell-looking matrons from the carriage trade.

Except that Dr. Bethany Cole looked

nothing at all like a matron.

He cracked a grim smile. Maybe he would ride down and catch up with them, say hello.

But then he remembered that things weren't quite as they had been between him and Doc. And Dr. Cole, of course, froze up at the very sight of him.

So he stayed where he was, watching, as their sleigh began to slow down, not far from one of the snow-covered arbors near the lake.

Neither of them spoke for two or three minutes more. Finally, Andrew cleared his throat. "About Maylee — I have something to tell you."

Bethany sat up straighter, immediately interested. "You've learned something new about her condition?"

He shook his head. "I only wish that were the case. But I think this will please you, all the same. Do you remember the night we were at Bantry Hill, the night we told Michael and Susanna about Maylee?"

"Of course. I remember how sympathetic they were."

"Yes, well, last week Michael asked me to take him to visit her."

"What a nice gesture. But then, Michael

is a very kind man."

"As it happens, it was more than a gesture. Michael has suggested that Maylee come and live at Bantry Hill."

"Andrew! He can't be serious?"

"Oh, he's very serious. Michael isn't a man to make idle propositions, I assure you. He was quite taken with Maylee — you should have seen how well they hit it off right from the start. When he pulled me aside at the party tonight, he said he'd spent considerable time in prayer and discussed it with Susanna. They haven't told Caterina yet, but Michael is sure she'll be delighted."

"But why would he do such a thing?" Bethany frowned in disbelief. "Does Michael really understand Maylee's condition, that she's going to require more and more care eventually, and that she won't ever be well?"

"I assure you, Michael understands. I made certain of that. As to why he's willing to do this, why he *wants* to do it" — he smiled a little — "all he would say was that God had put it on his heart. He's quite resolved."

"How amazing!"

Andrew slowed the horses and turned in toward the lake. "Let's watch the skaters for a bit, shall we? Or are you too cold?"

"No, I'm fine," Bethany said, distracted. "Does Maylee know about this?"

"Not yet. I thought you'd want to be with me when I tell her. Perhaps we can go and see her tomorrow."

He paused. "This will be a good thing for her, Bethany. There's certainly room for her at Bantry Hill, and Michael says she'll have plenty of attention and care. In addition to Susanna and the Dempseys, he's employed a new man and his family from Ireland. They're already living there, on the premises. There's a wife and a grown daughter, and they've agreed to help with Maylee."

"He's thought this through, then? You're quite certain?"

Andrew leaned back against the seat of the sleigh. "He seems to have considered everything very carefully," he said. "He's already broached the subject with the MacGoverns — that's the family he recently hired on. And as I said, he's discussed it with Susanna and by now, I'm sure, with Caterina, too. Actually, he makes it sound as if the lot of them are looking forward to having Maylee there." He paused. "This means she'll have a real home, Bethany. She won't have to spend what's left of her life in an institution."

According to Andrew, Maylee's parents

had abandoned her when she was still a toddler. Once they realized they had a desperately ill child on their hands, they had deposited her at a church door and fled. The cruelty of that abandonment never ceased to anger Bethany.

She suspected that Andrew had been praying about Maylee's situation for some time now. As a matter of fact, so had she, although God hardly needed her prayers when he had Andrew's.

She scanned their surroundings for a moment. The park looked like one of those lithographs by Mr. Currier and Mr. Ives: the skaters on the lake, the trees, some of which had grown quite tall, the rustic, snow-covered arbors, and in the distance the graceful Bow Bridge. Were it not for the crowds of people everywhere, they could have been in the country instead of a city park.

Bethany knew that Andrew came here sometimes, when he wanted to get away by himself, just to sit and think . . . or perhaps to pray. There had been a time when keeping company with such a godly man, a man given to speaking of God and prayer and spiritual things as easily as others spoke of politics or banking might have intimidated Bethany. But no longer. Andrew might be a man of faith, but he was thoroughly down to earth.

She respected him as she had no other man except for her grandfather, but she was no longer quite so daunted by his faith as she had once been. Actually, Andrew himself was the one who had helped her realize that she needn't be some sort of a spiritual giant to prove herself a Christian, that it was enough to love God, to trust him, and be obedient to his will.

"I'm no more important to God than you are," he continued to impress upon her. "And my prayers carry no more weight with the Almighty than do yours."

Abruptly, Bethany turned to him. "How do you pray for Maylee, Andrew? If you don't mind my asking, that is."

"Of course, I don't mind," he said quietly. "Well, naturally I continue to pray for her healing. But mostly I've prayed for *comfort* for her — for a place where she'll be truly wanted and loved. I've often wished I could take care of her myself, but I'm so seldom at home —"

Bethany nodded. "Don't think the idea hasn't occurred to me, too. But neither of us is in a position to give her full-time care."

Her mind was racing. "Monitoring her care will be an ongoing need. That will mean frequent trips upriver."

"We can manage that, don't you think?"

"Traveling to Bantry Hill would hardly be a burden. You know I love going there. I still can't comprehend Michael doing this," Bethany went on. "And for a child he's only just met."

"I don't know that we can ever understand someone like Michael." Andrew flexed the fingers of one gloved hand, then the other, as if to ease the stiffness. "I *do* know he's a man of genuine compassion — a kind of compassion so rare that surely it can't be anything but a gift. A *God* gift. I must say I admire him tremendously."

They were sitting very close together now. Bethany looked into his face — the strong features, the boyish shock of hair falling over his forehead, the faint web of lines at the corners of his eyes. Something tugged at her heart. When had he become so much more than a colleague? More than a friend? When had he come to mean more to her than she was comfortable admitting, even to herself?

On impulse, she closed the small distance between them, touching her lips to his lean, clean-shaven cheek. "And *I* admire *you*, Andrew Carmichael."

He turned an endearing shade of pink. "For what?"

"For caring so much about a lonely little

girl. And for being —" She paused. "Just . . . for being yourself."

His gaze fell upon her, intense with unspoken questions. Then without warning this man — her partner in medicine, her closest friend, her only confidant — slowly removed his hat and lowered his face to hers.

He kissed her with uncommon gentleness, one corner of her mouth, then the other. Slowly, she touched his cheek, and he turned into her touch, then took her face between his hands and kissed her again.

In that moment Bethany's complacency with the order of her life, the fullness and satisfaction and independence she'd been so certain her career would bring, seemed to lift away like a mist rising over the frozen lake. She felt herself take a sharp turn and step onto a new pathway. Her present began to fade and recede until the only thing she could see was a future with Andrew.

TWENTY-TWO

No More Secrets

To think, the fullness my yearning heart has long been seeking was here then, and still abides, in your safe-keeping.

ANONYMOUS

Frank had almost changed his mind about approaching them, had actually started to move the horse slowly down the snow-covered hill. But he drew to a sharp halt when he saw what they were about, saw Doc remove his hat, draw her close, and dip his head toward hers.

Something tightened in his chest, and a taste as bitter as salt water burned his mouth as he watched them. He hadn't meant to spy, but for a moment he couldn't look away, even though his pulse was beating in his ears like a drumroll.

He had known jealousy only once before in his life, but it had been nothing like this scalding, squeezing sense of being pushed away, an impotent outsider. The awareness of what was happening to him took him completely off guard, and, shaken, he struggled to rein in his treacherous feelings.

In truth, he was envious of *both* of them: Doc, because he had obviously claimed for himself the heart of a woman Frank could only admire . . . and desire . . . at a distance; and Bethany Cole, because she now wielded even more influence with the only man Frank Donovan had ever called a *friend*.

Slammed by a wall of emotions he couldn't begin to understand — didn't *want* to understand — he hauled his mount around and took off in a fury, throwing snow before and behind him as he charged up the hill.

Andrew drew back. "We need to talk," he said, his voice unsteady. "But not at the risk of your freezing to death. Let's find a coffee shop."

Bethany hesitated, then looked around.

"Over there," she said, pointing to a snow-hooded arbor, ringed by benches beneath its canopy.

"Aren't you cold?"

"No, I'm fine. It's so beautiful here, I'd rather stay outside."

They left the sleigh, stopping to buy a bag of hot roasted chestnuts before claiming one of the benches that faced the bridge. Gas lamps and carriage lanterns cast their soft glow into the night, dappling the riding paths and hillsides with light and shadow.

They were secluded, surrounded by dense vines, trees, and shrubbery frosted with snow. It seemed that everyone else in the park was either on the ice or circling the lake in a sleigh.

Bethany bit into a chestnut, mindful of Andrew's eyes on her.

She felt uncommonly nervous. The chestnut seemed to lodge in her throat. She glanced at Andrew to see that he wasn't eating at all, just watching her. For some reason, she couldn't quite face him yet.

In a matter of moments, everything had changed.

The problem was, she wasn't sure she *wanted* things to change.

Nevertheless, one of them probably

needed to say something.

"Bethany, I've never told you exactly how I feel about you, but I expect by now you know."

Andrew cringed. His voice sounded as if it were coming from someone else. It was too loud, his tone too formal. His words spilled out too quickly, as though he were desperate to say everything at once and get it over with. He knew his face must be crimson, and not from the cold.

"You've . . . probably known for some time," he repeated lamely. "Certainly before tonight."

Bethany turned to look at him, her eyes wide and searching.

"You've become . . . ah, very important to me, Bethany. I care for you. Deeply. You already know that. But I haven't wanted to bring this up until I was . . . until I knew —"

"If *I* care for *you?*" she finished for him.

He nodded, holding his breath. "That, too, but there's more —"

"Andrew, of course, I care for you. Surely, you've realized that." Her lips curved in just the faintest hint of a smile, and she lifted her hand as if she might touch him, but instead dropped it back to her lap.

"I had . . . hoped."

He moved to tuck a stray lock of hair back under her hat, then traced one side of her face with the back of his hand. "You are so incredibly lovely," he said, nearly strangling on the words. "I never get enough of just . . . looking at you."

"*Now* you're embarrassing me," she said, but Andrew thought she looked pleased. And she moved closer to him.

He caught her hand and held it. "Bethany, there are things I need to tell you. Now, before we talk about anything else. I've been meaning to tell you for some time, but I keep putting it off, afraid —"

"Andrew, I'm just not sure —"

He put up a hand to interrupt her. "I think I know what you're going to say, Bethany, and I understand."

Frank Donovan's warning echoed in his mind. *"If it's settlin' down to home and hearth fire you're wanting, I confess I don't quite see that happening with your Dr. Cole . . . Can you honestly see the woman with a passel of young'uns hangin' on to her skirts while she stirs the soup?"*

Before she could say anything more, he hurried to reassure her. "I wouldn't ask you to give up . . . anything, Bethany."

She frowned. "What are you talking about?"

"I wouldn't expect you to give up medicine," he said, the words pouring out in a rush. "Surely you know I would *never* ask that of you! If we were to . . . if we were married . . . I wouldn't for a minute expect you to stop practicing."

"Andrew — are you asking me to marry you?"

"I . . . well, not yet. I mean, yes. Yes, I am, but there's something else I want to tell you before —"

"I should think so."

"What?"

"I believe it's common to at least mention the word 'love' before proposing marriage."

Andrew reared back. "Well, of *course*, I *love* you! I've already admitted that —"

"No, as a matter of fact, you haven't."

Andrew felt his face flame. "I . . . must have *thought* about saying it so often that I just assumed I had."

She shook her head, her lips pressed together.

"Well, now I have."

"So you have." Her eyes glinted with humor.

"I realize I'm no prize, Bethany. Believe me, it's taken every shred of nerve I have simply to get to this point. But I'd be —"

"Andrew —"

He stopped, waiting.

"Let's both admit that I'm not exactly any prize either. At least not for a man who wants a more . . . *traditional* marriage. I couldn't give up medicine, Andrew. I simply couldn't. I've worked too long, too hard —"

"I know you have, and you're an excellent doctor," he interrupted. "You love medicine —"

"Yes, I do —"

"And I love *you* too much to ask you to give up anything that means so much to you —"

"And what if we should have children?"

That set him back. Still, it was a perfectly legitimate question. "I'd like children, of course — eventually — but it *would* mean your taking time off from the practice —"

"But not necessarily giving it up altogether."

"Oh, no. Of course not. We'd . . . work it out."

She said nothing for a moment, but he could tell she was thinking. As much as he hated to give her anything else to think about, he knew he must.

"Bethany, there's the matter of my health —"

She tried to preserve a calm front, but inside she was churning. She should have known he would raise the issue himself, wouldn't leave it to her. And ever since Frank Donovan had drilled her with his cynical diatribe that day in the police wagon, she had played this very question over and over in her mind. But now that she knew that he loved her — and that *she* loved him — she could no more give him up because of his poor health than she could have struck him and left him to die.

"Your health isn't an issue with me, Andrew."

"Perhaps it should be. It will most likely get worse, Bethany. We both know that."

She nodded. "I won't lie to you, Andrew. Of course your health worries me. But it worries me because I care for you, and because I *hate* the idea of your being in pain. But this illness is a *part* of you. And if I'm to be a part of your life, then we'll face everything together. Including the arthritis."

It struck her then that she wasn't simply reassuring him or trying to convince herself. What she was saying was true — as true as her love for Andrew. Frank Donovan had been wrong.

Very wrong.

"Think about this, Andrew: if it were turned around, if *I* were to be afflicted with an ongoing illness, would you want me any less? Would you reject me?"

"Of course not!"

"Well, then?"

He nodded, his gaze never leaving hers. "Point taken. And I won't deny it's a huge relief to me. But there's something else, Bethany. Something I should have told you long ago, and certainly before I asked you to marry me."

Bethany laughed. "My goodness, Andrew, you certainly are taking a long time getting around to proposing to me."

But he didn't share her laughter. He looked pale, the shadow of his beard darker than before. His eyes smoldered with pain. For a moment Bethany wondered if the arthritis had flared, but she sensed that this was a different kind of pain — and that whatever he was about to say might be of a far more devastating nature than the issue of his health.

When he began to speak, he looked . . . and sounded . . . weak. Weak and miserable. In spite of the cold, perspiration lined his forehead and upper lip, and his hands were trembling visibly.

"You can't imagine how I hate telling you this. I'd give anything if I didn't have to, but then I wouldn't be able to live with myself."

He stared out across the park in the direction of the bridge. "I need you to know that when I've finished, I will completely understand if you want nothing more to do with me. Perhaps you won't even want to practice with me. No matter what else has happened between us, no matter what's been said tonight, you owe me nothing. No commitment."

"Andrew, nothing could be so bad that I'd walk away from you." Bethany spoke the words, but his bleak stare sent a chill coursing through her. He hadn't replaced his hat, and he began to run it around and around between his fingers.

"Do you remember the day we talked about your grandfather? I told you I'd read some of his papers on narcotics addiction?"

Bethany nodded.

"In truth, I'd read everything I could get my hands on about the subject, not just your grandfather's research. But medical curiosity wasn't my reason for studying your grandfather's publications."

Bethany watched him, a cold knot forming deep inside her as he went on.

"I was an addict, Bethany. I was addicted to opium."

His tone was as wooden as before, but his eyes were heavy with shame. They sat staring at each other for one long, terrible moment as Bethany fought to hold on to her composure.

"How?"

"Are you quite sure you want to hear this?" Andrew's voice was still flat, but his features were sculpted in anguish.

"Whether I *want* to hear it is beside the point. I think I *must* hear it."

His eyes went over her face, and then slowly, he nodded.

"It began when I was still in medical college. One of the faculty physicians — well-intentioned, I'm sure, but careless, now that I look back on it — started me on small doses of opium, to help me manage the pain. This was at the outset of the arthritis, when the symptoms were absolutely brutal, and he'd seen that I was having a bad time of it. But I was determined not to give up my training, and so, meaning to help, he saw to it that I could get however much of the drug I needed, to see me through. As I said, he no doubt meant well, even though he had to know the risk. Before I knew what was happening —"

"You became addicted."

He nodded, and she could almost feel his misery.

"It begins so innocently," he went on.

"For many, it's as simple as purchasing a few compounds from the chemist to ease some sort of physical distress. Or in far too many cases — like mine — a physician who means only to help initiates a deadly cycle. But it almost always ends up the same way: one becomes enslaved by the very thing that was meant to free him of the pain."

"But obviously, you're not still addicted. You've taken a cure —"

His head came up, and he let out a sharp, bitter laugh. "An addict is never *cured*, Bethany. Not completely. You know that." He wiped a hand over his mouth. "I will always be an addict. A *former* addict, God willing, but an addict, all the same."

"I can't . . . it's almost impossible for me to imagine you . . . that way . . ."

"You wouldn't have liked me very much, that's certain. I despised *myself* during that time. Every day I promised myself I'd quit. But when I tried" — he shook his head — "I was scrambling for more of the stuff within hours."

"How . . . did you overcome it?"

"Cold abstinence."

His words came out like bullets, and the turbulence of emotion in his face made Bethany shudder.

He pressed on. "About the same time that

I realized what was happening to me, that I had become dependent, my roommate also became aware. Somehow or other he managed to get permission for both of us to leave the college for several days. He took me to his parents' home in Edinburgh, where he made preparations and then locked both of us inside an attic room."

"I scarcely made it through the first stage. The second stage was pure torture — I'll spare you the details."

"No," Bethany said quietly. "Tell me. I want to know everything you went through."

His features contorted, but he nodded. "Every nerve, every muscle feels as though it's been scraped raw and then left to burn in the sun. Nausea, abdominal cramps, fever, unbearable spasms that set your entire body to shaking —" He stopped, closing his eyes for a moment.

"It's as if everything in you is twisted and crushed and pulled apart. You think you're dying and pray you will. And the entire time this is going on, you know you're not just battling for your health or your sanity — you're battling for your very *soul*."

"Oh, Andrew," Bethany whispered. "How did you ever bear it?"

He made a lame attempt at a smile, but it

quickly fell apart. "Well — let's just say I'll be forever grateful to Charles Gordon. My roommate. For his perception and his prayers and his strong back. He kept me from taking a leap from the attic window more than once. And he stormed heaven on my behalf for days. Not to mention all the abuse he put up with in the meantime." He stopped. "I owe him a debt I could never repay. He literally saved my life."

Bethany's mind felt numb. "I'm sorry you had to go through all that, Andrew."

He turned his face toward hers. "Not half as sorry as I am that I had to *tell* you about it. I saw your shock and revulsion the night we went to see Mary Lambert, and from that time on I lived in terror that I'd see the same thing on your face once you knew about me.

"I'm ashamed for you to know about that time in my life, Bethany. All I can do is promise you that it's over. Completely over. But perhaps . . . that doesn't matter. The very fact that it happened is no doubt enough to shake your faith in me."

Slowly, Bethany took his face between her hands, holding him steady and making him look at her. "Don't insult me, Andrew," she said. "It would be a poor kind of love indeed that would allow the past to destroy the present and the future. I'm sorry for what you endured, and I hate it that you had to go through that, but it doesn't change the way I feel about you."

Please, God, let it be the truth, she thought fiercely. *Let me be strong enough to put this terrible thing behind us and never look back.*

She could. Of course, she could. The man she had kissed only moments before wasn't the same man as that young college student. Awful as the experience must have been for him, it took an incredible measure of courage and strength to go through what he did and survive it. The very fact that he *had* fought it and overcome it only confirmed her measure of the man. In time, she would be able to look at him and never think of the other.

She *would* . . .

"I have to ask you this," he said, his voice almost a whisper. "Now that you know — how *do* you feel about me?"

Their faces were so close they shared a breath. "I believe I've already mentioned the word *love,* Andrew."

Snow was falling again, and the wind blew a spray of it inside the arbor. Andrew freed one hand to brush away a stray snowflake from the corner of her mouth. "You're quite sure?"

"Sure enough that I believe I just might

marry you, Andrew Carmichael."

A slow smile worked its way across his features. "Do you mean that?"

"Oh, I mean it all right. There's just one thing —"

His smile wavered. "What would that be?"

"Are you ever going to get around to *asking* me?"

TWENTY-THREE

WHEN THE
THUNDERBOLT STRIKES

Whiter she than the lily,
Than beauty more fair,
Sweeter voiced than the violin,
More lightsome than the sun;
Yet beyond all that
Her nobleness, her mind —
O God Who art in Heaven,
Relieve my pain!

ANONYMOUS, 19TH CENTURY,
translated by Padraic Pearse

For several mornings now Paul Santi had watched, hoping to catch a glimpse of Conn MacGovern's daughter when she came outside.

Sometimes she appeared at the front of the house, sweeping the porch or picking up stray playthings. Other mornings she would walk out back to toss food to the chickens or to play with one of the cats living in the stables.

So far, Paul had resisted any attempt to engage her in conversation. This morning, however, as he stood on the brow of the upward slope that separated the main house from the caretaker's cottage, she actually started up the hillside, in pursuit of a black-and-white kitten, now bounding toward Paul as fast as its tiny legs would carry it.

The girl stopped halfway up the rise, her gaze going from the kitten to Paul as if she couldn't quite make up her mind what to do. On impulse, Paul reached down and scooped up the small creature before it could dodge past him. After another second or two, the MacGovern girl again started toward him.

With every step of her approach, Paul could see that she was even more lovely than she'd appeared at a distance. Her hair was a cloud of auburn, though not quite so fiery as her mother's. She was slender enough to appear fragile but carried herself with the purposeful, fluid grace of Mrs. MacGovern, a strikingly attractive woman in her own right.

Only a few feet away, she halted again. Paul smiled, hoping to reassure her that he was entirely harmless as he closed the distance between them.

"Yours?" he said, placing the kitten in her arms.

She shook her head without meeting his eyes, snuggling the kitten against her.

For one irrational moment, Paul found himself envying the small creature.

"Well, *he* thinks he's yours," he said. "Or at least he would like to be."

Finally, she smiled, and Paul felt as if a vial of sunshine had been poured out over his head like a blessing.

"His mother is one of the stable cats," she said shyly. "But I've rather . . . adopted him, you see."

Her soft voice, tuned by the lilting Irish accent, was sheer melody to Paul's ear. And those eyes! As shining and as brilliant as the most priceless of emeralds!

He knew he was staring like a great *stupido,* but when he tried to speak, he seemed to have lost his voice.

"You are Mr. Emmanuel's cousin," she said, reminding Paul that in addition to acting like a fool, he was also being rude.

"*Sì,*" he managed. "*Mi scusi.* Forgive me. I am Paul Santi. And you are Mr. MacGovern's daughter." He cringed at the realization that he sounded like a foolish schoolboy.

But she was still smiling at him, so perhaps she was not put off by his awkwardness after all.

"Your father — I speak with him each day. Michael says Mr. MacGovern has already proven himself to be invaluable." He cleared his throat. "We — all of us — are very glad that you and your family are here."

She looked down, and Paul had all he could do not to lay his hand on top of her head to find out if her hair felt as silken as it looked.

At that moment he glanced toward the cottage, only to see Conn MacGovern standing on the front porch, watching them. MacGovern was a big man who typically looked at Paul with an expression of mild contempt. No doubt the Irish trainer had taken note of the fact that Paul, unlike Michael and MacGovern himself, preferred to keep his distance from the horses.

Paul was finding it difficult to concentrate, his attention going from the girl standing only inches away from him to her father, who had stepped off the porch and now stood in the yard, arms crossed over his brawny chest, watching them intently.

"Ah . . . your father," Paul said, inclining his head in MacGovern's direction.

She turned to look, and at the same time MacGovern called to her.

Nell Grace. It suited her, Paul decided. When she turned back to him, she shot him another quick smile. "I'd best be away now."

"Yes . . . of course. I . . . may I say that I'm very pleased to have finally met you, Miss MacGovern," Paul managed to say. She turned and hurried back down the hill, the kitten watching Paul over her shoulder.

He saw her exchange words with her father, then go around toward the barn. MacGovern followed her, taking her by one arm — not a rough gesture but one of protective firmness all the same. MacGovern glanced back at him once, and although they were too far apart to gauge his expression, Paul felt almost certain that the big Irishman's glare would have withered the grapes on a vine.

But he would think about MacGovern later. Nothing must be allowed to spoil this momentous morning, which quite possibly might turn out to be the most important day of his life.

The thunderbolt. He had been struck by the thunderbolt.

At long last, love had come.

Inside the cottage, Conn stood with his back to the sink, finishing his second cup of tea, scalding hot and strong enough to make his ears ring, the way he liked it. No one except Vangie could make tea to please him.

He watched her spoon some stirabout into Baby Emma's mouth, at the same time attempting to quiet the twins, who were far more interested in pestering each other than in finishing their breakfast. Renny Magee was already off to the stables, and Nell Grace had headed for the back of the house the minute she returned from shutting the kitten inside the barn. No doubt to bury herself in her books or her writing pad.

He knew he had embarrassed the lass, but though he dreaded her tears almost as much as those of her mother, he was not about to tolerate her carrying on with that cheeky Italian fellow. He had just come back from saddling the stallion for his employer's early morning ride when he'd spotted the two of them, Nell Grace and that Santi *gorsoon,* standing on the hillside blathering as though they'd known each other most of their days. The thought of that young sneak skulking about after Nell Grace had set his blood to boiling.

To his surprise and annoyance, Vangie had seemed altogether unperturbed when he told her. Determined that she should understand, and growing impatient with the twins' antics, he now ordered them to get their coats and wait outside for the school wagon.

"I don't see why we have to go to school anyway," grumbled Sean, who only the week before had informed his parents that he was an American and now preferred to be called *Johnny*.

"You have to go to school so you'll not be a cabbagehead the rest of your life," said his twin brother, punching him in the ribs.

James was the darker of the two, his hair a deeper red, his skin not quite so pale. When it came to mischief, however, it seemed to Conn that they were perfectly matched.

"That'll do!" he warned. He took a step toward them, and they went scrambling for their coats.

"If you learn nothing else at school," Conn grumbled, "perhaps you'll acquire the means to behave like civilized children instead of troublesome little heathens."

The twins glanced at each other, eyes glinting, but Conn gave them a look that quickly cut short even the thought of a snicker.

"Your lunch, boys," Vangie said before they made it to the door. Sean — *Johnny,* Conn reminded himself — came back to grab their pail off the table, aiming a kiss at his mother's cheek that barely connected before he again dashed out the door. James watched, then he, too, darted across the room to kiss his mother good-bye.

The instant Vangie set Baby Emma to the floor, the child promptly trundled over to Conn. He picked her up and swung her about a couple of times, then off she went behind the stove to play with the wooden blocks her brothers had carved and polished for her.

"Those two," Conn said with a sigh, sitting down beside Vangie at the table. "I don't like to think of the trouble they'll bring when they're older."

"They're good boys. Give thanks they're in good health and have plenty of life in them."

"Oh, I'm thankful enough for that. It's the mischief in them that worries me."

"They're but eight years old, don't forget." She paused. "What happened between you and Nell Grace?"

"She was up the way with that Italian fellow."

"Mr. Emmanuel?"

"No, no, the skinny one. The one with the smart talk and the yellow streak."

"Conn! You don't even know the lad."

"I know what I see. He's all talk, that one is. He won't even go near the horses." Conn scowled. "I say, never trust a man who doesn't take to the horses."

Vangie looked at him, then shook her head. "Conn MacGovern, sometimes I could just box your ears."

"What?" Conn couldn't believe it. She was vexed with *him!* "You can't mean you approve of the girl cavorting with his kind!"

"*Cavorting?* Oh, Conn, would you listen to yourself, you great oaf! I thought you said Nell Grace was merely *talking* with the lad. Sure, there's nothing wrong with that!"

"She ought not to be anywhere near him. Or any other boyo, for that matter! The girl is only seventeen, after all."

Vangie was eyeing him as if he'd grown an extra head. She didn't understand; that was the thing. What did she know about untrustworthy men, after all?

"You can be such a dolt at times," she said matter-of-factly. "Have you forgotten, then, that I was only seventeen when we were *married?*"

"That was different," he said, and of course it was.

"Different, indeed," she muttered. "And your point is, I expect, that the young man at the Big House is Italian instead of Irish."

"Exactly."

"He would also appear to be respectful and well-mannered. A gentleman, from what I've seen of him."

Conn frowned. "I wouldn't be knowing anything about that."

"No, indeed you would not."

Conn couldn't make out her tone, but from the look in her eye it wasn't in his favor.

"He's well-educated as well. You can hear it in his speech." She brushed some crumbs off the edge of the table into her hand.

Conn shrugged. What good was education if a man had no backbone?

"And he's obviously from good people," Vangie went on. "Mr. Emmanuel is a good man, a *Christian* man. You said so yourself. And the boy is his cousin, isn't that so?"

"Be that as it may —"

She arched an eyebrow. "I don't see the harm in Nell Grace making conversation with the lad. She needs friends, especially missing her brother as she does."

They locked gazes a moment more, then she looked away. There seemed to be no understanding Vangie these days. One minute she would dissolve into tears if he disagreed with her even on the least of matters, but then just as quickly she would turn all fire and smoke, taking him to task for a misspoken word.

Still, he'd rather have her vexed with him for his thickheadedness than hollow-eyed with sorrow. Aye, better her fussing than her weeping, and that was the truth.

He leaned forward to plant a quick kiss on her cheek. When she made no response, he got up from the chair and glanced at his pocket watch. "I'd best be getting back to the stables. Himself will be wanting his ride soon."

He stood over her, hesitating, uncertain as to whether he ought to say what was still on his mind. But he was the man of the house, after all. "So, then — you'll keep Nell Grace away from that Santi fellow?"

Her chin went up. "I'll do no such thing. Our girl is not a child any longer, Conn, and it's time you realized it. Nell Grace is at an age where she has the right to speak with anyone she chooses. And she's not a foolish girl. We can trust her judgment, it seems to me."

Confused now, for it was a rare thing entirely for Vangie to openly defy him, Conn went for his coat. He was reluctant to leave things as they were, but couldn't think how to handle her when she was in such a state.

Once at the door, however, he turned back. "Even so," he said, determined to make his point, "no good can come of letting a boyo like that slaver after her. And him a coward at that."

She shook her head, not looking at him as she rose from the table.

"Well, then," he finally said, "I'll be in by noonday."

Conn stepped outside, closing the door behind him. There was no explaining the strangeness in Vangie this morning. For a few moments he had glimpsed the fire he had always admired in her. Indeed, he almost welcomed her impatience with him. But nearly as quickly as the sparks had flared, the heaviness had returned, taking the light from her eyes and the color from her cheeks.

He could not bear the sorrow that seemed to hover over her of late, would have done most anything to restore her spirit. And indeed, though she couldn't know, he *had* tried to do something about it. Still, one thing he would not tolerate, no matter what Vangie had to say: no daughter of his was going have any truck with a useless fellow like that cousin of Mr. Emmanuel's.

Nell Grace deserved better than a great *gorsoon* who was so unmanly as to be afraid of the horses.

TWENTY-FOUR

QUESTIONS OF THE HEART

So simple is the heart of man,
So ready for new hope and joy. . . .

STOPFORD A. BROOKE

The morning was raw and blustery, and the
wind stung Michael's cheeks as he cantered
across the rolling fields surrounding Bantry
Hill, but he didn't mind the cold.

Today he was on Mehab, the Arabian he
had bought from Rosa Navaro after her husband's death. At his side, Conn MacGovern
rode Yasmin, a mare the trainer favored.

Michael had promised himself that by
Christmas he would be riding Amerigo, the
contentious stallion he had imported from

Ireland, but that remained to be seen. MacGovern had worked wonders in gentling the horse and building his trust, but the stallion was still unpredictable, and seemed to enjoy trying to outwit both his trainer and his owner when they least expected it.

Mehab, on the other hand, responded instantly to the slightest pressure of rein or knee, the subtlest shifting of Michael's weight. MacGovern kept to his left, and although Michael sensed his presence, the trainer's comfortable silence allowed Michael the illusion of riding alone, just himself and the magnificent Arabian.

He threw his head back and breathed in the chill morning air, mixed with a faint scent of horseflesh and leather. Downhill and back up again, his body became one with the horse. He leaned in to the reins, urging Mehab into full gallop, his heart beating in time with the drumming cadence of the horse's movement.

A fire blew to life in Michael's veins, a passion much like the rush he felt when he stood onstage and conducted his orchestra. Riding was music — the singing of the wind, the percussion of hoof on turf, the pounding tempo of nature in all its glory. He could feel the Arabian's muscles flowing beneath him like a swiftly running stream, and together they cut a path through the frosty morning as if they were flying.

At last, at the top of a high hill, he reined in and stood waiting for Conn MacGovern to catch up. Mehab snorted and pranced, then quieted as MacGovern cantered the mare up the hill to Michael's side.

Michael had quickly come to respect his new employee, especially MacGovern's love of the land and his willingness to undertake even the meanest of jobs. He sensed in the sturdy Irish immigrant a rock-solid integrity, coupled with a lively bent toward humor. Moreover, the man never seemed the least uncomfortable with Michael's blindness.

Now MacGovern drew his horse to a stop and let out a laugh. "It'd be a great *amadan* indeed who'd wager against you, now wouldn't it, sir? Remind me never to bet my week's wage on any race you'd run."

Michael grinned in MacGovern's direction. "Ah, but if you had been on Amerigo —"

"If I'd been on Amerigo, Mr. Emmanuel, I'd be lying dead in a ditch by now, and that's the truth. But he's coming right along, and you'll be riding him yourself soon."

"Thanks to your training." Michael

reached down to slap Mehab's neck. "I'm very pleased to have you and your family here at Bantry Hill, MacGovern."

"No more pleased than we are, sir."

"And your wife and children are settling in well? The house is suitable?"

"Faith, sir, it's much more than suitable. It's a palace compared to that dismal shack we had in the city."

"Good," Michael said. "If you need anything, be sure and let me know."

They turned and started back, trotting side by side. Silence stretched between them for a time, broken only by the clopping of hooves on the turf and the snorting and blowing of the horses.

Then MacGovern cleared his throat. "If you don't mind my asking, sir, it's . . . well, it's uncommon to see a blind man such as yourself daring to ride. Especially when —"

"Especially when I lost my sight in a riding accident?" Michael turned toward MacGovern and chuckled. "News travels quickly at Bantry Hill, I see."

"Begging your pardon, sir, I didn't mean to —"

Michael dismissed his apology with the wave of a hand. "It's all right. No doubt some think I'm completely mad to keep riding. But my passion for horses came early, when I was a boy in Tuscany. A man doesn't give up a thing like that easily."

" 'Tis true, sir," MacGovern said. "I know for myself, I rarely feel so much a man as when I'm sitting a fine horse."

Michael nodded. "After the accident, a number of well-meaning people tried to convince me not to ride again. Even Paul questioned my judgment. I had a difficult time explaining to him why riding was so important to me."

MacGovern did not reply to this, but Michael heard him take in a deep breath and exhale it heavily. At last he spoke again. "Speaking of that young helper of yours — he's your cousin, is he?"

"Paul? *Sì,* Pauli is my cousin — and my assistant. He is also concertmaster with the orchestra."

"Concertmaster, eh?" Michael heard the lack of understanding in MacGovern's tone. "That sounds like an important job for such a young fellow."

"It is a most important position, yes, and he *is* very young for so much responsibility — only twenty-seven. But Paul is an excellent musician. In many ways, he is invaluable to me. He is — how do you say it — my 'right arm.' "

"Twenty-seven? Is that a fact now? I

wouldn't have thought it." He paused. "He's not a married man?"

"Married? No, Paul is not married."

"I've noticed the lad seems . . . a bit shy of the horses. Unlike yourself, sir."

"That's true. Pauli does not share my love of riding."

MacGovern said nothing, but Michael heard him mutter something under his breath. They urged the horses forward in an easy canter, and did not speak again until they reined to a stop near the stables.

Michael dismounted, gave Mehab an affectionate pat, and handed the reins over to MacGovern.

"It is because of me that Paul has no love of the horses," he offered.

"Sir?"

"Because of the accident," Michael said. "Pauli never had any real interest in riding, even before then. But the accident only made things worse. Since then, he cannot bring himself to trust a horse. Any horse."

"I see."

Michael thought he detected a kind of grudging understanding in MacGovern's voice, and perhaps a trace of awkwardness as well, for having raised the subject of the accident at all. The exchange seemed peculiar, to say the least, and he wondered where it was leading.

Apparently, he wasn't to know. "Well, then, here comes the lad now, sir," MacGovern said abruptly. "I'd best be on my way and tend to the horses."

Michael frowned. Why had MacGovern taken off in such a rush, as if he was deliberately avoiding Paul?

Perhaps Paul had done something to provoke the man, although given Paul's diligent avoidance of the stables, he couldn't think how.

Michael didn't raise the subject of MacGovern right away. Paul was getting ready to leave for the ferry, but first had some questions about the evening's rehearsal. He was standing in as conductor tonight, as he did on occasion, to give Michael a break.

Only after they'd gone to Michael's office and discussed the selections that still needed the most work did Michael make an attempt to satisfy his curiosity.

"Is there a problem between you and MacGovern that I should know about?"

There was a distinct delay in his cousin's reply. "MacGovern? No, not at all. Why — should there be a problem between MacGovern and me?"

The hesitation only made Michael more curious. "He was asking about you this morning, that's all."

"MacGovern was asking about *me?* Why?"

Michael shrugged. "I have no idea. He seemed . . . very interested in you for some reason."

There was a long silence. "He . . . he *did* see me talking with his daughter this morning. Perhaps he . . . does not approve?"

"Ah. His daughter." So that was it. Michael smiled to himself. "And is she pretty, *Signorina* MacGovern? Hmm?"

"*Em bella!* She is — beyond description!"

Michael's interest sharpened. "And how old is this young lady?"

"How old? I have no idea. What — does that matter?"

Michael shrugged. "I was just wondering why MacGovern asked *your* age."

"My age? What did you tell him?"

"I told him the *truth,* of course. You are twenty-seven, are you not?"

"*Sì.* But did he mind that I am so old?"

"*Old?*" Michael laughed. "I should be so old, *cugino!*"

"His daughter is . . . very young, I think," Paul said, a touch of uncertainty in his voice. "Perhaps MacGovern thinks I am too old for her."

"Very possibly," Michael said, poker-faced. He enjoyed needling his cousin almost as much as Paul enjoyed teasing *him*. "But it seemed to me that he was more concerned about your lack of affection for the horses."

"The *horses?*" Paul sighed. "Of course. MacGovern has seen that I do not like the horses. No doubt he holds that against me."

"Mm. Perhaps you should spend more time in the stables, Pauli."

"I will do whatever it takes," the younger man said solemnly. "Anything at all."

Michael leaned forward across the desk. "Paul? You're serious?"

Again Paul sighed. "It is the thunderbolt, Michael," he said, his voice grave and heavy with significance.

Relief coiled through Michael. If Paul's affections ever *had* been directed toward Susanna, that was clearly no longer the case.

"Paul, how well do you know this girl?"

"We met only this morning," his cousin said, his voice dreamy. "But I know, Michael. I *know!*" He stopped. "It is the thunderbolt, I tell you. You will pray for me, yes?"

"To be sure," Michael said dryly.

He heard Paul rise from his chair. "Thank

you, Michael!" he burst out, grasping Michael's hand across the desk. "You understand that this is difficult for me. I know nothing about women! I have never been in love. Not until now."

"Paul," Michael cautioned, "you only spoke to the girl this morning —"

"That is true, but as I told you —"

"*Sì*. The *thunderbolt*. It would seem that I must begin to pray at once."

"I knew you would understand, *cugino!*" Paul paused, and when he resumed, his voice held an edge of sly humor. "But of course, you *would* understand. It is the same for you and Susanna, no?"

Michael frowned. "*Che cosa?*"

"Oh . . . nothing. I meant nothing." He sounded even more cagey.

"I think you meant *something.*"

Paul remained silent, but Michael could feel his scrutiny. "Out with it, Pauli."

"With you, Michael, one is never certain. But with Susanna, one can tell . . ."

Michael lifted an eyebrow. "*Must* you speak in riddles always, Pauli? One can tell *what?*"

"You know. That she cares for you."

Michael swallowed. "Clearly, the *thunderbolt* has struck your brain as well as your heart."

There was a long silence. When Paul spoke again, the teasing note had left his voice. "You cannot see the way Susanna looks at you, Michael. But *I* have seen."

An unbidden rush of hope swept over Michael, so strong he very nearly gave himself away. He quickly reminded himself that Paul was caught up in the throes of a romantic seizure and might well be seeing his own infatuation in everyone else.

Paul came around the desk and put a hand to Michael's arm. "Michael — forgive me if I speak out of turn. I know I often do. But I also know what I see. With Susanna, there is much feeling for you. And I think it is the same with you, but for some reason the two of you are determined to fight against it."

"Susanna still doesn't trust me," Michael ventured quietly. "Have you forgotten the incident at rehearsal, how quickly she suspected the worst when she thought I had . . . *conspired* against her?"

"No, I have not forgotten. But I think perhaps you make too much of what was nothing more than a bad coincidence."

Michael started to interrupt, but Paul stopped him. "Listen to me, Michael. Susanna may have jumped to conclusions, but you told me yourself that she apologized. Or at least attempted to, once she realized that she had misunderstood. She admitted her mistake. Why can you not simply accept the incident for what it was? It was not that important, Michael, except in your mind. You are so . . . thin-skinned . . . where Susanna is concerned."

Michael weighed Paul's words, and something in him resonated to his cousin's defense of Susanna. No doubt he *had* made too much of what had merely been a misunderstanding. But it had been such a *painful* misunderstanding . . .

He heard Paul mutter a sound of frustration, though when he spoke his words were conciliatory. "I apologize if I have made you angry, Michael."

Distracted by the confusion simmering in him, Michael waved off his cousin's apology. "I'm not angry."

And he wasn't. At least, not with Paul.

If he was angry with anyone, it was with himself, for the morass of his emotions, the uncertainty of his judgment. And he was also angry with Deirdre. It was a futile, misdirected, and wholly irrational anger, he knew, but at times he felt as if his dead wife would always be a barrier between him and any possible chance to love again. Because of Deirdre, Susanna would never fully trust him. And because of Deirdre, his *own* capacity for trust had been so badly fractured he wasn't sure that even love would ever be enough to heal the breach.

He clenched his hands at his side, then reached for the back of the chair, swaying a little on his feet. Since the accident, he was occasionally plagued by vertigo, and now it swept over him.

"Michael —"

He heard the alarm in Paul's voice and lifted a hand. "It's nothing. I'm all right." He sank down onto the chair, waiting for his head to clear. "You should go now or you'll miss the ferry."

"But —"

"I'm fine, Pauli. A little dizzy, that's all. It will pass in a moment. Go on now."

After Paul left, Michael sat, not moving, with his head in his hands. In spite of his best intentions, his mind wandered back to Paul's words about Susanna: ". . . *you have not seen the way Susanna looks at you . . . but I have seen . . . she cares for you . . .*"

And what if Paul was right? What then?

He sighed. He, too, had been struck by the thunderbolt.

But in his case, the lightning had brought not only the revelation of love, but the recognition of its futility as well.

TWENTY-FIVE

A PUNISHING SILENCE

I was mute with silence,
I held my peace even from good;
And my sorrow was stirred up. . . .

PSALM 39:2 (NKJV)

When Conn returned to the house for the midday meal, he found only Nell Grace and Baby Emma in the kitchen. Nell Grace was stirring something on the stove — cabbage soup, from the smell of it — while the tyke played near her feet. There was no sign of Vangie.

"Where's your mother?"

Even before he asked, he knew something was amiss. At this time of day, he never walked into the kitchen but what Vangie wasn't either at the stove or the sink, putting the finishing touches to their meal.

Nell Grace's expression was troubled as she inclined her head toward the rear of the house. "Out back," she said. "I think she's sick, Da."

Conn immediately started for the outhouse, only to find Vangie a few feet from the back door, crouched on her haunches, head down, her hair hanging in her face.

"Vangie!" He hurried to her, dropped down at her side, and put his arms around her. In spite of the cold, she wore only a shawl, and he could feel her trembling.

"What is it, love? What's wrong?"

She shook her head as if too weak to reply.

"Let me get you inside. It's too cold for you to be out here like this."

He drew her up, alarmed when her hair fell away from her face and he saw how pale she was. She looked as if she might faint at any instant. Suddenly a spasm shook her, and she wrenched herself from his arms to go to her knees again. She gagged, but nothing came up. She moaned, but it was more a sob.

As Conn stood there, watching her and feeling helpless entirely, it struck him that this was familiar. He had seen Vangie like this before — many times, in fact. His mind registered the memory, and a thrill of excitement shot through him, only to give way to a pang of hurt pride. If he was right, then why wouldn't she have told him by now?

But this wasn't the time for questions. He bent to steady her. "Better now, love?"

She nodded and let him raise her to her feet and help her inside. In the kitchen, Nell Grace followed their movement with worried eyes, while little Emma whimpered for her mama.

"Your mother will be all right," Conn told them. "She just needs to lie down for a bit. She's feeling poorly."

In the bedroom, he lifted her onto the bed, covered her, and then sat down beside her. She was still shaking, but when Conn reached to pull an extra quilt up from the foot of the bed and tuck it around her shoulders, she turned her face away, saying nothing.

He watched her for a long time, wanting to touch her but sensing her withdrawal from him. "Why haven't you told me, Vangie?" he said quietly.

She turned a dull look on him, then shrugged and quickly glanced away. "I was waiting . . . to be sure."

Conn studied her. "As I recall, with the

others you knew quite some time before ever the sickness set in."

She didn't answer, didn't even look at him. He took the hand clutching the bed linens and found it limp and cold.

"Vangie?"

At last she turned and met his eyes. Conn was taken aback at the hard look to her, as if she was angry with him.

"Is it that you don't want the babe?" He could barely get the words out. A heaviness had lodged in his chest, and he was beginning to feel sick himself as his mind scrambled to make sense of Vangie's behavior.

" 'Tis not that I don't want it."

"What then?" He pressed her fingers, trying to ignore the alarm welling up in him.

The look she turned on him made the hair at the back of his neck stand on end. Her gaze seemed to burn right through him with something he had never seen in Vangie's eyes before, not even in the heat of their worst arguments. He felt himself indicted, censured for some unknown crime.

But just when he thought she was about to lash out at him for whatever dire offense he had committed, she again turned away. Conn thought she looked to be caught up in the effort of making a particularly difficult, even a grudging, decision.

"I . . . wasn't certain how you'd feel about it," she said. "With Emma scarcely out of didies herself."

She was lying. Vangie knew exactly how he'd feel about a new babe, how he had *always* felt. That was what hurt the most. By not telling him, she was keeping from him something she *knew* would give him pleasure. It was as if she had deliberately chosen to withhold a blessing.

He moistened his lips against the dry sourness in his mouth. "I would feel the way I have always felt, Vangie. Proud and happy. Has there ever been a time when I *didn't* feel so, once I learned a new babe was on the way?"

She dragged her gaze back to him. "I thought it might be . . . different now. We're not young anymore, after all."

Conn stared at her. Was she serious? "Not *young?*" he said, trying to make light. "And were we so much younger, then, when Baby Emma was conceived?"

His words brought not even the trace of a smile to her lips. "That was different."

"Oh, I see. And *how* was it different?" Conn felt his temper begin to heat, even though he sensed that the worst thing he could do at this moment would be to allow himself to get angry. "I confess you're confusing me, love. I don't understand what it is you're trying to tell me."

She regarded him with a look that made Conn feel as if she had already judged him guilty of some terrible crime. "You wouldn't understand even if I explained it to you."

Her words were laced with a mixture of weariness and resignation. She didn't look well, not at all. Possibly, any discussion of whatever wrong she thought he had committed ought to wait until she had rested.

Yet he couldn't bring himself to simply let this go. He would have been relieved to learn that her condition accounted for the recent mood changes and erratic behavior. But the way she was looking at him! She had nearly admitted that there *was* something wrong, and that, whatever it was, she considered it beyond his understanding. Was it merely the pregnancy affecting her emotions, or was she actually turning against him because of some imagined sin on his part?

"*Help* me understand, then, Vangie. Sure, and you know by now that I can't bear it when you shut me out."

Conn thought he saw a faint trace of regret in her face. But when he moved closer to her, she flinched and pulled her hand away.

She was still as stone as she looked at him. "I suppose I meant to punish you," she said in a chillingly impassive voice.

Conn reared back, gaping at her. "*Punish* me? For what?"

"For Aidan." Her eyes were so fierce upon him that Conn felt as if his soul had been seared. "It's because of you I've lost my son."

TWENTY-SIX

ACTS OF FORGIVENESS

For a man to be himself,
he must know himself.

IRISH SAYING

Vangie could see the battle taking place in Conn. She watched every stage of it: the flaring of his temper, his struggle to control it, his inclination to deny everything she said.

An angry red stain splotched his cheeks, and his mouth twisted with the effort of containing an explosion of self-defense. To her surprise, though, he said nothing, at least not right away. Instead he sat staring at her, his eyes boring into her as if he meant to scale every layer away until he could see into her mind and her heart.

"You believe that?" he finally said, his voice hoarse. "You believe it's my fault that Aidan stayed behind?"

"I *know* it's your fault!" Vangie pushed herself up on her elbows, facing him. "I also know that even if we had stayed in Ireland, Aidan would have left us. Our son is a man grown, but you insisted on treating him like a disobedient schoolboy. You never once gave him credit for anything he did, Conn! All you ever did was criticize him for not doing it your way!"

Vangie stopped to catch a breath, but she wasn't finished. Her nausea had subsided, but now the anger and resentment and bitterness that had built up for months came pouring out of her like poison out of a newly lanced abscess. "Perhaps if you had just once admitted to yourself that Aidan was a *man* and entitled to live his own life, he wouldn't have been half so eager to get away from us. From *you!* And even now, knowing the pain his absence has brought upon me — and don't think I haven't seen your own pain — you *still* won't give over and mend your differences with the boy. You won't even *try!*"

Even as the words ripped out of her, Vangie knew she wasn't being altogether fair. Aidan was every bit as stubborn as his father, and just as headstrong and rebellious as was common to a lad his age. But she had kept her churning feelings to herself too long and was now consumed by the need to make Conn face the fact that he wasn't entirely blameless for the troubles between himself and their son.

Still, when she saw his heavy shoulders sag, his features go slack, she wished she had been less venomous in her attack.

"Why haven't you brought this up before now?" he said, his tone as wounded as his eyes.

Vangie held his gaze, saw the pain ravaging his face, but would not allow herself to soften. "What good would it have done?" she countered. "You'd only accuse me of being 'overwrought' because I'm in the family way."

He frowned, his mouth set in a stubborn line, but Vangie could tell she'd struck a nerve.

"What more could I have done, then?" he said, his expression bleak. "Didn't I try to talk him out of his lunacy, even up to the time we were ready to board? Didn't I try to stop him from staying behind?"

"You did, Conn. But it was too late. Too much had passed between the two of you to undo it in a few moments. By then, Aidan was full to bursting with the need to get away and be on his own, where we wouldn't always be so close at hand, ordering his life."

"Where *I* wouldn't be so close at hand, is what you mean."

"Aye, that *is* what I mean. But even after we came across, didn't I beg you to write to the boy and try to make peace? It just might have made a difference, had a letter come from your hand instead of always being written in mine."

"If he was as set against me as you claim, I can't think a letter would have made any difference at all."

"But you could have *tried*, Conn! You could have *tried!* I don't know if I can ever forgive you for not *trying!*"

Her words came out as a wail, and Vangie cringed both at the sound of her own voice, and at the agonized look on Conn's features. But didn't the great oaf have some of this coming at last?

Yet, when he gazed at her so, his face lined with old sorrows and the slow dawning of a new wisdom, when she met his eyes and saw nothing there but regret and love — love for *her* — Vangie found it exceedingly difficult to stay angry with the man.

He got to his feet and stood looking down

at her as if trying to decide what to say next. Fortunately, they were no longer bellowing at each other when Renny Magee banged upon the bedroom door and called out to them.

At Conn's grudging, "Come," the girl crashed into the room, waving an envelope.

"The post just came!" she announced, her voice shrill with excitement. "There's a letter! Miss Fallon said I should bring it to you."

"A letter?" Vangie repeated.

Conn reached for it, but Renny Magee charged toward the bed and thrust the letter directly at Vangie. The girl stood there then, clearly bent on learning, if not the contents of the letter, at least the identity of its sender.

Conn shot a dark look at the girl, but Vangie ignored the both of them.

"*Aidan!*" she choked out. " 'Tis from Aidan!"

She scarcely noticed when Conn hauled himself to his feet and with a jab of his thumb motioned for Renny Magee to follow him out of the room.

Well, let him go, then. If he was so stubborn that he wouldn't read a letter from his own son — the son they hadn't heard from in months — then let him just go and sulk.

Her heart pounding with anticipation, Vangie propped her pillow behind her, opened the letter with trembling hands, and began to read.

Minutes later, when Conn came back into the room, she had not moved, but sat clasping the letter with both hands against her heart as she wept.

"Why didn't you tell me?" she choked out. "All this time I've begged you to write to him — and you never said a word! Why? Why didn't you tell me you *had* written to him?"

Conn sat down beside her. "I thought it would be cruel to raise your hopes." He paused, his eyes going to the letter still clutched in her hands. "What does he say, then?"

Watching him, Vangie handed him the letter. "You read it," she told him. "I want to hear it again, and if you read it, it will be almost like hearing it from himself."

Conn looked at her, then took the letter and began to read.

Dear Mother,

I suppose by now you know that Da wrote to me some time past. In truth, I was relieved to hear from him, for I hated having the hard feelings between us.

I have missed all of you more than I would have thought possible, and now that I know Da is not still set against me, I am making plans for my own journey to America. I have been working, and soon I will be able to pay my own way across.

I cannot tell you exactly when I will come, for I still have to make arrangements to leave my job, and there are some other matters I must attend to. But it should be soon.

No doubt the twin terrors have found new mischief to get themselves into, and I expect Baby Emma is getting big. Has Nell Grace caught herself a fellow yet? Tell them all I am truly anxious to see them, and that includes Da.

And tell them I am coming soon. Just as soon as I can.

> *Your devoted son,*
> *Aidan MacGovern*

By the time Conn finished reading the letter, Vangie was weeping again.

"Oh, Conn," she said, grasping his arm, "he's coming! Aidan is truly coming! Finally, we'll all be together again!"

Conn patted her hand. "Aye, love. We'll

all be together again. Will that make you happy then, Vangie?"

She leaned toward him. "I can't think of anything that would make me happier!" She paused. "Conn . . . the things I said to you —"

He shook his head. "Never mind that. We both know I deserved to hear everything you had to say."

"No, that's not true." She studied him, and to his surprise a faint smile appeared, though the tears were still streaming down her face. "Perhaps you deserved . . . *some* of it. But not all."

She opened her arms to him then, and with a long, shaky sigh of relief, Conn gathered her to him and buried his face in her hair.

"Oh, Conn," she murmured against his shoulder. "Now we'll have our family together at last. Aidan, our new babe — all our children — under our roof again. That's how things are supposed to be."

Aye, that's how things were supposed to be, Conn thought. And this was how things were supposed to be between him and Vangie. This was how things should *always* be.

He understood, perhaps better than she thought he did, how difficult, how agonizing, this situation had been for Vangie. As a child, her father had deserted them, and after the death of her mother from heart failure, Vangie and her three sisters — all of them but wee girls — had been separated and passed around to different relatives to raise, none of whom wanted an extra mouth to feed. Her early years had been years of fear and abandonment, years of never feeling "whole" because of the way her family had been torn apart. When she was grown and agreed to marry Conn, she had made him promise that they would have a large family, and that, no matter what, nothing would ever divide them.

Conn had done his best to keep his word; staying behind had been Aidan's idea, after all. But as time passed and he saw the way Aidan's absence was tearing at her heart, he knew he had to do something — whatever it took — to reunite them.

As he held her, he tried to convince himself that he was grateful for the joy Aidan's letter had brought Vangie. And *him*. He, too, was happy the boy was coming across. He tried to put down the vague uneasiness gnawing at the back of his mind, but something about the boy's letter nagged at him. In truth, he hadn't expected it to be this easy. All along, he'd worried that Aidan would either ignore the "peace offering" Conn's letter was meant to be and not reply at all, or else he would make his father beg — and Conn wasn't at all sure he had it in him to beg his eldest son, not even for Vangie's sake.

But here was the reply, and it had come fairly quickly at that — seemingly a genuine response that held an olive branch of its own. And here was his wife, happy and content in his arms. So why was he acting like a fool, instead of making the most of the moment?

With one finger under her chin, he tipped her face up to his. "And so I am forgiven, then?" he said, only half-teasing. "Great *amadan* that I am?"

Her eyes still glistened with tears, but these were new tears, tears of happiness. "I don't think you're an *amadan* at all," Vangie said softly. "I think you're a good man and a wonderful husband. And as for forgiveness, I should be asking yours, Conn MacGovern."

Conn frowned. "For what, love?"

"For keeping the announcement of our new babe from you. It was a terrible cruel thing to do."

He kissed her — carefully, for he was already feeling the need to protect her. "You are forgiven, Evangeline MacGovern. And now, seeing that we're both forgiven, do you think I might have a bite to eat? 'Tis starving I am."

To his dismay, Vangie turned a pale shade of gray. "Oh, did you have to mention food, Conn MacGovern?"

Before he could help her stand, she was out of the bed and on her way to the back door, not even stopping in the kitchen to tell their lasses the big news.

There were times, it did seem, when a husband could do nothing right.

A STEP TOWARD TRUST

> I do not ask for any crown
> But that which all may win;
> Nor try to conquer any world
> Except the one within.
> Be Thou my guide until I find
> Led by a tender hand,
> The happy kingdom in myself
> And dare to take command.

LOUISA MAY ALCOTT

Frustrated that there had not been an opportunity to make a thorough apology to Michael after the night of her birthday, Susanna was determined to seek him out before any more time had transpired. After three days, she finally summoned the courage to approach him.

Finding the opportunity, however, was another matter. He had stayed in the city the two days following her birthday, returning so late last night that Susanna and the rest of the household had already retired. He made an unusually brief appearance at breakfast this morning, only long enough to talk briefly with Caterina while he hurried through a few bites of food. Although he had been painstakingly polite to Susanna, they exchanged only two or three sentences before he excused himself.

Apparently, he was going to be at home tonight. Earlier that morning, Paul had mentioned that he would be taking the evening rehearsal in Michael's place. If she were going to speak with him — and Susanna was feeling an increasing urgency to do so — this evening might be her best chance.

It had been a busy day — busier than usual. In addition to her everyday responsibilities with Caterina, Susanna was overseeing the preparation of one of the guest rooms, making a final check of the medications and other supplies Dr. Carmichael had suggested, and tending to other details in anticipation of their new guest's arrival.

The child, Maylee, would be coming just before Christmas, and Susanna wanted everything to be ready for her.

She had not met Maylee yet, but Michael's accounting of the poor child's condition wrenched Susanna's heart and made her eager to see the girl settled here at Bantry Hill, where she could have as much attention and care as she needed. Caterina was excited about having "a new friend" on the premises, although Michael had cautioned that Maylee would not likely have the stamina to be a playmate.

To Caterina's credit, she had taken this to heart and then made a remarkable observation: "Well, I'm happy that she's coming anyway, because she will probably feel better here, since she'll get lots of love and good food."

The only one who seemed less than happy about having a new child around the house was Moira Dempsey, but then Susanna was beginning to think that Moira was content only when she had something to complain about.

As the day wore on, Susanna sensed that Michael was deliberately avoiding her. After his usual morning ride, he retreated to his office, taking his midday meal there as well. He worked through the rest of the afternoon until supper, after which he told Susanna he would see to Caterina's bedtime.

By nine that night Susanna had had enough. She *would* talk with him — now, tonight, before he had a chance to start the same routine over again the next day.

She was headed downstairs on her way to Michael's office when she stopped outside the kitchen to pick up a piece of cookie. A deposit, no doubt, from Caterina or even the wolfhound, since they tended to travel as a pair. The kitchen door was partially open, and a voice from inside arrested her. She was a little ashamed to be eavesdropping, but when she heard her own name, she couldn't bring herself to leave. She held her breath and pressed herself against the wall.

"She'll not be staying here; don't think for a minute she will." It was Moira, in her usual caustic tone.

Her husband answered, his voice gruff. "You don't know that."

"She might stay for now, if she has designs on him, as I suspect she does. But you watch. That'll change soon enough. Who's to say but what she's not the same turn as the sister, after all?"

Susanna cringed at the comparison with Deirdre. But to her surprise, Liam Dempsey came to her defense. "This one's not at all like the other. She seems a good enough sort. The wee wane dotes on her, and she turns a steady hand to her work. And doesn't the man have a right to a bit of happiness? The Lord knows he's had little enough of it these past years."

"Even if she means well, she's too young," Moira insisted. "A girl like that is not going to tie herself down with a blind man and a child for long! You mark my words, she'll not be staying! And there he'll be again."

" 'Tis none of our affair, woman!" Liam growled. "You worry too much!"

"And wasn't I right about the other one?" Moira shot back. "Didn't I tell you what *she* was, early on?"

"Aye. But I've been married to you long enough to know you're not right *all* the time, and this is one of those times, I'll wager."

Susanna stood staring at the kitchen door for a second or two more, then quickly turned and retraced her steps. She went into the library and stood at the window, fuming. How dare Moira Dempsey assume she was anything like Deirdre, simply because they were sisters! She had done nothing to earn the woman's suspicion and contempt. And yet . . .

The Dempseys *had* known Michael since he was a boy, and Moira obviously considered herself a surrogate mother to him. Not only had she been a part of his childhood, but she would have experienced the difficult years after his accident when he'd endured both blindness and a devastating marriage. She would have witnessed much of the anguish and humiliation Deirdre had brought upon him.

Even though Susanna was shocked at the animosity that apparently fueled Moira's disapproval, once she calmed, she had to concede that perhaps in the housekeeper's place she would have reacted the same. The woman did not know her, after all. How could she be expected to trust Susanna's motives or her actions where Michael was concerned? Nothing but time — most likely a great deal of time — would win Moira Dempsey over.

She left the library and went in search of Michael, still mulling over the conversation. She hated being the object of someone's distrust. More distressing still was the awareness that Moira's suspicion was based on nothing but the deceit of another person — in this case, Susanna's own sister.

And wasn't this very nearly the position in which she had placed Michael?

The realization slammed her like a hammer blow, and she stopped in the middle of the hallway. From the beginning she had been unable to trust Michael, and all because of Deirdre. Her own suspicions had been based entirely on what she'd been told by her sister — whose deceit had been monumental.

Down the hallway, she heard noises from the music room and started in that direction. Just as she reached the door, she heard a dissonant crash, like a cat jumping on the piano keys. Then a loud thud.

She found Michael on his knees near the piano. Manuscript pages were scattered everywhere, and he frowned and muttered to himself as he vainly tried to sort through them. He looked unusually disheveled, his hair tousled, his tie askew, his face flushed.

Rarely had Susanna seen a flare of the proverbial "artist's temperament" in Michael — that volatile emotionalism and passion of one completely consumed by his work, or the blistering flash of impatience when the work did not go well. For the most part, despite the limitations his blindness imposed on him, he almost always maintained an enviable calm, a reserve of self-control she never would have expected to find in so complicated and gifted a man.

She wasn't sure she really believed there *was* such a thing as the "artist's temperament," but if there was, Michael certainly didn't seem to fit the mold. This was one time, however, when his even disposition had clearly abandoned him.

She hesitated at the door, waiting for the right moment to enter.

His head came up. "Susanna?"

"Yes." She walked the rest of the way into the room. "Can I help?"

Without waiting for him to answer, she stooped down and began picking up random manuscript sheets from the floor, glancing at them to see what they were.

"*Grazie,*" he said. "I was foolish enough to think I could manage this without Paul."

"What sort of order do these belong in?"

He sighed. "I had two stacks and managed to drop them both. One section is partially coded — but not numbered. The rest is Paul's notation. Everything is out of order."

"Why don't you let me do this?" Susanna offered, already beginning to sort the pages numbered in Paul's neat hand from those coded in the New York Point for the blind, which Michael used for his personal reference. "I'll just separate the Braille sheets and put Paul's in order."

"Ah. *Grazie,*" he said again.

He pushed himself up to one knee, staying

there as if he could watch Susanna's progress. His closeness unnerved her and made her hurry even more.

"Was it terribly hard for you?" she asked, attempting to make conversation as a means of easing the awkwardness between them. "Learning to use Braille?"

He hesitated, then nodded. "It was not easy. I think for children, it is probably a little easier. Their reading and writing habits are not so well-formed yet. Becoming blind as an adult is much like beginning a new life."

He said it without so much as a trace of self-pity. Susanna looked at him. He seemed weary to the point of exhaustion, and in that instant she felt as if she might suffocate with love for him.

Love. How studiously she had avoided that word! Yet how easily it seemed to slip into her thoughts of late.

Flustered, she glanced away and finished scooping up the manuscript as quickly as she could.

"There," she said, "I think I've got it back together the way it should be."

They stood, and for a moment they faced each other, Michael's hand on her arm, his head bent low.

"Michael . . . I wonder if we could talk,"

Susanna ventured. "I . . . want to apologize for the other night. There hasn't been time —"

Unexpectedly, he lifted his hand as if he would touch her face, but didn't. "There is no need."

"There *is* a need," Susanna insisted. "Please, can't we just . . . talk?"

"Susanna —"

"Michael, I have something I need to tell you, but there's something else I need to say first. *Please,* just let me say it!"

He frowned in surprise at her outburst, but stood waiting, his features taut, as if he were apprehensive about what was coming.

"Can we —" Susanna glanced toward the settee in front of the fireplace. "Can we sit down?"

"*Sì.* Of course."

He was in his shirt sleeves but moved now to shrug into the jacket tossed on top of the piano before crossing the room. Susanna followed him, watching as he stooped to punch up the fire: his broad back, his great mane of dark hair, his easy movements. Emotion seized her again, and she had to look away.

He racked the poker and joined her on the small sofa. "So, then, what is it you wanted to tell me?"

"About the other night. I want to explain why I acted as I did —"

"You did explain," he broke in. "And I told you, I understand."

"Oh, Michael, will you please stop being so . . . *forgiving!*"

One dark eyebrow lifted, but he said nothing.

"You're always so . . . kind to me." Susanna's voice rose. "But I don't deserve your kindness this time, don't you see? I'm trying to tell you that I'm dreadfully sorry, really I am, about what happened. I've no idea why I jumped to the conclusion I did. I know you better than to think you'd deliberately deceive me. You wouldn't. It was foolish and unfair, and I still can't believe I acted as I did. You have every right to be upset with me —"

"But I'm *not* upset with you, Susanna."

"Well, you *should* be! I jumped to conclusions, I accused you of a perfectly awful thing. Can you forgive me? And please, don't just say you do! Don't be kind! I need to know you really *do* forgive me, if you can."

He sat utterly still, his expression thoughtful, as if he was choosing his words with deliberate care. "Of course, I forgive you, Susanna," he said softly. "But you're wrong in thinking it was all your fault. I should have told you about Christopher's accident before rehearsal. But I suspected you would accuse me of deliberately taking advantage —"

"And that's exactly what I *did* accuse you of! It probably wouldn't have made any difference *when* you told me, I would have —"

He lifted a hand to stop her. "But more than likely, you would not have been so quick to assume what you did if I had simply explained beforehand. That was my fault, not yours."

Finally, some of the tension began to seep out of Susanna and she managed a deep breath. "It should never have happened. I . . . don't really know why —"

"Is it so difficult for you to trust me, Susanna, even now?"

"Oh, Michael, no! I *do* trust you! It's so much easier, so natural, to trust —"

Susanna stopped, putting a hand to her mouth to stop the words she had almost blurted out: *"It's so much easier, so natural, to trust someone you love . . ."*

"I would like to believe that, Susanna. But I can't help wondering . . . why now?"

"I've changed," Susanna managed to say. "I can't explain, but I *have* changed. And there's something else —"

She stopped, trying to quell her nervousness. What was she letting herself in for? But she had promised herself — and God — that she was going to *try*.

"If you want, I'm willing to help with the concert. I'll . . . play the organ. If I can, that is. I'll at least try."

He leaned forward so suddenly the sofa pitched under his weight, and the smile that slowly spread over his features made Susanna feel as if she'd just handed him a rare and precious gift.

TWENTY-EIGHT

THROUGH THE EYES OF A CHILD

Truth cannot hide
from the eyes of a child.

ANONYMOUS

"So . . . what changed your mind?"

"It's not that I haven't *wanted* to help you, Michael. I *have*. I can't tell you how many times I've refused to do something I really wanted to do." Susanna paused. "Because I was always afraid. Afraid I'd fail."

She went on, struggling to explain about the safe place she had made for herself by always staying in the background, never undertaking anything beyond her capabilities, and the false humility she had birthed and nurtured through the years.

She *hated* being this honest with Michael, recoiled at letting him see just what a pitiful coward she had been . . . and perhaps still was, if truth were told. She would much rather have had his respect, even his admiration — but it seemed important that she make as honest an explanation as she could manage.

She thought it futile entirely to mention Deirdre's attempts to diminish her, so she didn't. Her sister's contempt had not created Susanna's inadequacies and fear of failure, after all, but had only added to the weaknesses already there. Only in letting slip the nickname Deirdre had given her — "Mouse" — did she hint at her sister's ongoing abasement. And when she saw Michael's countenance tighten, she hurried on, giving him no time to respond.

"It was Caterina, I suppose, who finally helped me come to realize what I had done to myself all these years."

"Cati?" he said with a look of surprise.

"Yes. When she brought up David and Goliath at the rehearsal, it triggered something in me, something that forced me to confront what I'd done to myself." She paused. "Children often have a way of . . . *mining* truth from a grownup's heart."

Michael smiled a little and nodded. "I,

too, have sometimes had to confront a truth because of one of my precocious daughter's incisive questions."

Caterina had flung one of those "incisive questions" at him only that evening, after he had heard her prayers and tucked her into bed.

He had bent over to kiss her good night when the question came. "Papa? Why are you unhappy with Aunt Susanna?"

"But I am *not* unhappy with Aunt Susanna. Where did you get such an idea, Cati?"

"You hardly talked to her today," Caterina had replied, her tone uncommonly solemn. "And when you did, Aunt Susanna looked . . . worried. And you sounded like you do with me sometimes when I've done something to make you unhappy."

He took her hand. "I've been very busy, Cati. Too busy. But I promise you, I'm not unhappy. Not with Aunt Susanna nor with anyone else."

A long sigh escaped her — a very *adult* sigh. "Do you like Aunt Susanna, Papa?"

"Such questions tonight! What is going on in that clever little head, eh? Of course, I like Aunt Susanna. I like her very much. Don't you?"

"I *love* her!" Caterina said fiercely. "I love her more than anyone else in the world except for you!"

"Good. I hope you have told her so. She would like hearing it, I know."

"Have *you* told her, Papa? Does she know you like her?"

"Well . . . it is . . . different for grownups," Michael stammered. "We do not always speak of such things."

"Why not? Don't you think Aunt Susanna would want to know you like her? She likes *you*. A lot. I can tell."

"And how is it that you know this, hmm?"

"When she looks at you, I can see it. I think Aunt Susanna likes you almost as much as I do."

Caterina was just a child, Michael reasoned. A child who loved her father and her Aunt Susanna with all her heart. Even so, her words made him lose his breath for an instant, wishing that *he* could see how Susanna looked at him.

Susanna watched Michael retreat and wondered where he'd gone. Michael was a man who needed quiet as much as food and water, and somehow he seemed to have carved out a place within himself where he could withdraw — even in the middle of a crowd or an ongoing conversation.

She had grown accustomed to his silences, but in light of what she'd been trying to tell him, she wished he hadn't picked *now* to turn inward.

"Michael?"

He straightened. "I'm sorry, Susanna. I was thinking about what you said. About Caterina. What else did you say?"

"Yes, well, I was saying that even though I'm familiar with most of the music you're doing for the Christmas concert, your arrangements will be altogether new to me. And there's so little time left — only a few days. I'd have to practice a great deal, but where? I can't very well go into the city every day and leave Caterina."

"That need not be a problem. Saint Catherine's has a fine organ. I'm sure Dermot would be more than happy for you to use it for your practice."

"Dermot?"

"Dermot Flynn. You met him your first evening here, remember? He's the priest at Saint Catherine's. It's close, not quite a mile away. And you needn't worry about Caterina. Moira will be here, even if Paul and I are gone. Perhaps Caterina could go with you sometimes. I'm sure she'd like that."

As Susanna listened, Michael proceeded to work everything out, precisely and thoroughly. And Susanna began to realize that she had lost any hope of a way out.

Perhaps this was God's way of making his will perfectly clear.

With a bit of help from Michael.

TWENTY-NINE

A NECESSARY FLAW

I have sought, but I seek it vainly,
That one lost chord divine,
That came from the soul
    of the Organ
And entered into mine.

ADELAIDE A. PROCTER

Only three days remained until the concert. In addition to spending hours at Saint Catherine's every day in practice, Susanna also had to help ready the house for Christmas. Decorations were constructed and put up; preliminary baking had begun, with Moira Dempsey feverishly supervising every move made in the kitchen; gifts were

348

prepared — some homemade, others purchased; and Caterina insisted on adding a new Christmas carol to her repertoire on a biweekly basis, which of course required extra instruction.

Susanna felt as if she were living in a whirlwind. By now it was difficult to believe there had ever been a time when a concert didn't loom like a waiting storm and every hour of the day wasn't filled with too much work to do.

The world outside might just as well have not existed, so frenzied and all-absorbing was life at Bantry Hill. Most of the news she managed to glean came through discussions between Michael and Paul about events going on in the city or her own random reading of the newspapers.

Apparently the Tilton-Beecher scandal still dominated the gossip circles, even though a mistrial had been declared the previous year and Henry Ward Beecher had been exonerated by his congregation. The famous Brooklyn preacher and brother of Harriet Beecher Stowe had been accused of adultery with the wife of one of his parishioners — a parishioner who also happened to be his closest friend. But then Mr. Beecher seemed to be the subject of more than one scandal. Apparently, there was much speculation that the clergyman was also involved in the rising spiritualism movement — especially with its women.

Susanna had the feeling there might be more to this story than what Michael and Paul discussed in her presence. She had read mention in the newspapers about the character of some of the women who participated in the spiritualist groups springing up all over New York State, and their reputations were questionable at best.

Indeed, scandal seemed to be the leading fodder for the newspaper mills these days. In addition to the tales about Beecher, there was also the recent news that the infamous "Boss" Tweed, the leading, albeit corrupt, political force in the city of New York for years, had escaped from jail and was on his way to Cuba.

Some journalists were having a field day exposing all manner of disgraceful tales from within the women's suffrage movement — everything from rumors of its members advocating "free love" to accusations that some were actively campaigning against marriage and motherhood.

Even President Grant and his administration weren't exempt from the rumors of scandal. So rampant were stories of debauchery and corruption that Susanna had almost resolved to simply give up reading the papers altogether. And she rather wished Paul would do the same before he inadvertently brought up one of the unsavory news reports in Caterina's hearing.

In truth, she had precious little time for leisure reading these days. As Liam drove her to Saint Catherine's for her afternoon practice, she spent most of the ride there ticking off all the things she still had to do afterward. She found herself feeling a great deal more harried and distracted since she'd agreed to take part in the Christmas concert.

So distracted, in fact, that she had to ask Liam to repeat himself as he deposited her at the walkway to the church.

"I said himself will be coming along with me when I return."

"Michael?"

"Aye. We've some errands to tend to, so we'll be stopping for you afterward."

Susanna nodded absently, already turning and starting for the front doors. She hoped Michael didn't show up early; she wasn't ready for him to hear her progress just yet. In fact, she was beginning to wonder just how much *progress* she was actually making. She had left the church yesterday altogether frustrated, keenly regretting all the months she'd gone without touching an organ. Her efforts to regain her former technique and agility seemed to be taking an inordinate length of time.

The music itself wasn't all that difficult. Even though Michael's arrangements were new to her, they were fairly easy to follow and blessedly practical in construction. But her legs ached from using muscles that hadn't been exercised in over a year, and her playing was still wooden, not merely in physical dexterity, but in emotion.

The organ at Saint Catherine's wasn't so grand as the one she'd be playing in the concert hall, but it was still daunting, even in its simplicity. An organ was a mighty, formidable instrument at the best of times. An exacting taskmaster. And, when the organist was not at her best, more foe than friend.

Much later in the afternoon, she was making her fifth — or was it her sixth? — pass through the "Hallelujah Chorus" and finding it every bit as stiff and as unemotional as her preceding attempts. Tired, discouraged, and demoralized, she uttered a cry of frustration and deliberately slammed the final chord in an angry thud. She ripped her music from the rack and sat pressing it to her chest, her head down, tears streaming from her eyes.

The fact that she was crying only served to heighten her self-disgust, for she had never by nature been a *weeper*. Even as a child she had always taken pride in maintaining her composure. But at the moment she was weary beyond words and furious with herself, that she had agreed to this — this impossible undertaking. She hated the organ. She hated the music. And she hated weeping. All of which only made the tears come even harder.

When a pair of strong hands clasped her shoulders, she whipped around, sending her music flying. "Michael! How long have you been here?"

She winced at the accusatory tone in her voice, but if he noticed, he gave no indication. "I came through the back," he said, evading her question about how long he'd been listening. "Why are you so upset?"

"I'm not."

"I see." He paused. "Then why are you so angry?"

Susanna stood, then stooped down to retrieve her music. "I am angry with *myself*," she said between clenched teeth, "because I've committed to do something of which I'm obviously incapable. And if you've been here very long, you know exactly what I'm talking about. I'm *never* going to be able to do justice to this music by the time of the concert."

She straightened to find him standing quietly, his head tilted to one side as if he was giving her his closest attention.

"I'm — it's as if I'm made of wood when I try to play. I don't understand it! The music isn't all that difficult, and yet I'm murdering it entirely!"

"Come, sit down."

Reluctantly, Susanna followed him to the front pew and sat down beside him. "Michael —"

"First, you are not . . . *murdering* the music, Susanna. You are placing too great a demand on yourself and creating an unreasonable tension. It is not the music that is thwarting you, but your own expectations. And perhaps a part of that is my fault."

"It's hardly your fault that I play like a clumsy schoolgirl!"

"You do not play like a clumsy schoolgirl. You play like a highly gifted young woman, even a professional — but one who has set for herself an impossible goal. A goal of nothing less than perfection."

He continued to speak, using his hands as much as his voice as he attempted to make his point. "Now that you have agreed to do this, you are determined to do it *perfectly*. But because the time in which you must achieve this self-imposed perfection is unrealistic, you're becoming tense and disillusioned with your own abilities. You will do just fine when the orchestra surrounds you and you can forget any limitations you now imagine — for they are negligible and will go completely unnoticed once you join the other musicians. You will see. God will then imbue your music with . . . *spirit* and power. He will enable it to soar."

Susanna sat staring at him. With her music tucked under one arm, she lifted her other hand to wipe away the dampness from her cheeks. "How can you know that?"

"I know." He shrugged. "No music is perfect. No performance is, either. I would not *allow* my people to perform the music without *some* imperfection, no matter how small."

"But your orchestra is *wonderful!* I've never heard the slightest mistake when they perform. Never."

"The fact that you have not heard a mistake doesn't mean it isn't there. There is always a flaw. A small dissonance somewhere, at least once. Always." He gave a cryptic smile. "I insist on it."

Susanna stared at him. "You insist on a *flaw?*"

"*Sì.* It is my way of reminding them — and myself — that no one and nothing is perfect except God." He stopped, his expression all seriousness as he added, "Of course, I allow for only *one* flaw. No more."

"Well," Susanna said dryly, "I expect you won't have to worry about anything being perfect as long as *I'm* a part of the orchestra."

He reached to touch her face. "If it were up to me, you would *always* be a part of the orchestra."

He stood then and helped her to her feet. "Remind me to tell Dermot he needs to heat his church. This sanctuary is unconscionably cold. Come now, let's go home and have a fire and something hot to drink."

Susanna took his arm but hesitated before starting up the aisle. "Michael . . . I want to be sure you know that I'm not trying to back out of the concert. I *want* to do this for you, really I do! But —"

He turned toward her. "No, Susanna. You must not do this for *me*. You must do it for *you*. Do you understand?"

The intensity in his voice surprised her. Before she could reply, he added, "This is between you and God. Like a covenant. Do this for him, and for yourself. He wants you to see that he has gifted you . . . and called you for this. He wants to show you that in spite of your fear and feelings of inadequacy, you can trust him to be faithful in helping you to fulfill that calling. No matter what."

"How can you know that?" The same question she had asked before.

He smiled, then gave the same reply as before.

"I *know.*"

BETWEEN GREATNESS
AND GRACE

Life's but a walking shadow, a poor player
That struts and frets his hour upon the
stage. . . .

WILLIAM SHAKESPEARE

Michael never held rehearsal the day before a concert. "Just as the music must have its silences, its rests," he said, "the musicians themselves must also rest."

But tonight, with the concert looming less than twenty-four hours away, Susanna did not feel rested. Instead, she stood at her bedroom window thinking with grim irony that Michael might as well have held rehearsal. A *long* rehearsal. She wouldn't be

358

getting any sleep tonight, and no doubt would feel even more lightheaded and queasy tomorrow.

She hadn't even bothered to change into her nightclothes. Earlier she had tried to read, but she could have been staring at a blank page for all the good it did. She did manage to write a letter to the Mahers, her former employers, but barely remembered what she'd written. She had checked on Caterina three times and found both her and the wolfhound sleeping soundly. Now, unable to think of anything else to do, she decided to go downstairs and fix some warm milk. She didn't particularly *like* warm milk, and wasn't at all convinced it encouraged sleep. Still, it was worth trying.

Besides, the kitchen was comfortable and inviting — when Moira wasn't there. It was certainly the warmest room in the house. Susanna usually kept her distance when the housekeeper was working. It would be nice, she decided, to have it all to herself for a change.

But when she approached, she was surprised to see the door open and light filtering out into the hallway. The Dempseys usually retired much earlier than this. Perhaps Moira was working on some special Christmas delicacy. Tentatively, she stepped into the room. It was softly lit by candles, and a cheerful fire blazed and crackled in the enormous stone fireplace.

Michael sat at the kitchen table. In front of him was a plate of bread and cheese, and he was drinking something from a cup. He pushed his chair back and stood the instant he heard her footsteps.

"Susanna?"

"Yes. Sit down, Michael. What are you doing?"

"Indulging myself." He smiled sheepishly, brushing the front of his sweater as if to dispel any crumbs. "You couldn't sleep either?"

"No. I didn't really expect to. But surely *you* don't get nervous the night before a concert?"

"Come in, please. Join me. I heated some milk — have some with me. And something to eat? Paul said you scarcely touched your supper."

"Paul is too observant for his own good." Susanna poured herself a cup of milk and went to sit down across the table from him.

"So . . . *do* you get nervous before a concert?"

He shook his head. "At the moment I am excited. I had a letter from my father today.

It seems he is finally coming to visit."

"Oh, Michael, that's wonderful! How long has it been since you've seen him?"

"A long time. Years. I have been trying to convince him to come here and stay, but he insists this will be only a visit. Perhaps once he is here I can change his mind."

"When is he coming?"

"Not until spring. Sometime around the end of March or early in April, I think. I haven't told Caterina yet. She will badger me incessantly once she knows."

"Well, I'm very happy for you. You'll have to tell me what you'd like me to do to help prepare for his visit."

"That is not your responsibility, Susanna," he said firmly. "You are not a part of the household *staff* — you are Caterina's aunt."

"But I *want* to help."

"Probably you can help most by keeping Caterina from driving all of us to lunacy once she learns the news. She has been wild to meet her grandpapa."

"They've never met? Then she *will* be thrilled. What a splendid opportunity for both of them."

He nodded. "But now I will answer your question. About the stage fright. I don't get nervous, no. I pray much about it, however," he added with a wry grin.

"I find it odd that you would be even the slightest bit tense," Susanna said. "You always look so completely calm when you're conducting." She took a sip of milk. "I'm terrified, of course. I suppose I'll be even worse tomorrow."

He nodded, although Susanna was quite sure he couldn't comprehend what she was feeling.

"You told me once that you understood about stage fright," she said. "But I can't imagine why."

He shrugged. "I don't have stage fright with the orchestra, because when we perform, I become one with them. But when I was still singing —" He raised his eyebrows. "I know about 'terrified,' I assure you."

"I certainly can't think *why*. Your success was legendary."

"The fear was as real to me as it is to you. It happened every time I went on stage. Sometimes I became physically ill and thought I could not possibly go on."

"But you always did . . ."

He nodded slightly. "But not always *willingly*."

"Is that why you quit singing? Or was it because of the blindness?"

He was about to take a sip of milk, but the

cup didn't quite make it to his mouth. It stopped in midair, and he frowned.

"Forgive me," Susanna said quickly. "That's really none of my business."

"*E'niente.*" He shrugged. "Actually, it was neither. God helped me to function in spite of the stage fright. That's why I can be so certain he will do the same for you. As for the blindness — I actually left the opera *before* the accident."

"*Before?* But *why?* I'd just assumed —" She stopped. "Deirdre?"

"It's not easy to explain."

"I shouldn't have asked —"

"No, no, it's all right." He tilted his head. "But are you sure you want to hear this?"

"Only if you want to tell me."

Slowly, he nodded, then clasped his hands on top of the table. "I know that Paul told you . . . about Deirdre and me."

Susanna hadn't expected him to bring up the subject of his marriage. "Michael, there's no need —"

He lifted a hand. "It's all right, Susanna."

She sank back against the chair, watching him. His face had grown taut, his expression intense. The creases at the corners of his eyes seemed more deeply drawn, his mouth tighter. His hands, always elegant and expressive, clenched, then unclenched and began to move as he spoke.

"To fail in one's marriage — this is a hard thing, a very hard thing for a man to live with. But the truth is that Deirdre was never happy with me. I was not a good husband for her. It was a mistake for us to marry. We barely knew each other. But she wanted it that way, and I . . . well, I was impulsive then, too. But from the beginning we were very different. Later, things changed even more. I changed. And so did Deirdre.

"She needed more, much more, than I could give her. Deirdre, I think, was driven," he said quietly. "She had a kind of hunger in her, a need, that nothing seemed to fill. She was always searching for more. And when she didn't find it, when she could not have what she thought she wanted, she would grow angry. Very angry. Ultimately, she wanted a much different kind of life from what we had, much different than I could endure.

"She loved the opera, you understand? More than anything, she loved the life of the theater: to perform, to be surrounded by people, to be adored. She had so much ambition, so great a passion, that at times she simply overwhelmed me. I felt as if I were drowning."

He brought his hands to his face, kneading his temples as if his head ached. "We were, as I said, very different. We believed in different things, wanted different things. But at the time, I tried to tell myself that we were *not* so different after all."

He got to his feet and went to stand with his back to the fire. His hair fell forward as he stood there, his head dipped low, his hands clasped behind his back. "I must tell you things about myself I would rather you not know," he said with a rueful smile. "I would prefer that you think the best of me. But —"

He shrugged, then went on. "For some years before Deirdre and I met — and during much of our marriage — I had . . . great success. And I enjoyed it; it was —" He made a circular motion with his hand. "It made my head spin. There was the money, of course. There was always much money. More than I needed, more than I could spend. And the celebrity — ah, the crowds! With every role I sang, every stage I walked onto, I felt more and more the adulation of the people, the audience. And the excitement of the lifestyle: travel, new experiences — this was important to me, especially as a young man. I was very restless, never satisfied. Much like Deirdre, no?"

Susanna noticed that the longer he spoke, the more pronounced became his accent — and the more strained his expression.

"So . . . I, too, was driven, you see. I possessed a different kind of hunger, but a hunger all the same. More than anything else, what drove me was the music. Always the music. Always, I searched for something I had heard — in my head, in my heart, when I was but a child. Something I knew I was meant to create, or discover, yet something always just out of reach.

"I later came to realize that as a child I had been given a kind of *vision*, a glimpse of God's plan for my life — I am almost embarrassed to tell you this, it sounds so presumptuous — but it is true, nevertheless. Then as I grew older and the success came, I allowed the vision to pale. For a time I was caught up in it all — the chaos and the excitement and the adoration of the crowds. Always somewhere to go, something to do, people demanding more and more from me. I suppose I grew to *need* it. Perhaps I even *fed* on it. It made me more *alive*, gave me that rush to the blood that can be a kind of . . . seduction. To my shame, I reached a place where the music no longer mattered nearly as much to me as what it could *provide* for me. Even my God, who *gave* me the music in the first place — he no longer mattered so much to me either.

"But eventually, something began to change. At first, it happened slowly, very slowly. At some point, I began to sense a need for something more important and fulfilling than the crowds and the fame and the money. The way I was living — the way *we* were living at that time — had become meaningless. Empty."

He stepped away from the fireplace and came back to his chair. Susanna couldn't take her eyes off him as he braced one hand on the table and let the other fall at his side. In that moment, with his tousled hair and commanding Mediterranean features, he seemed to belong to an older time, a different place. If he were to exchange his casual clothing for a cloak and a walking stick, he could easily be taken for an Italian prince from the remote past.

Perhaps Susanna should have been shocked at the things he was telling her. She could hear his voice, see his face, feel his pain — and his shame. And yet she took it all in as from a distance, all the while knowing that the man he *used* to be could never in any way diminish the man he had become.

The man she loved . . .

"There was much chaos in my life at that time, and in my marriage as well," he went on. "I almost became ill. Not physically, but in my mind and" — he touched his heart — "in my spirit. I could never seem to find a quiet place. I could never be alone. There was such confusion, such clamor all around me and inside me.

"And so I left. I went away." He shuddered. "I *ran* away."

THIRTY-ONE

A New Song

I cannot sing the old songs,
For me their charm is o'er
My earthly harp is laid aside,
I wake its chords no more.
The precious blood of Christ
   my Lord
Has cleansed and made me free,
And taught my heart a new song,
Of his great love to me.

FANNY CROSBY

"By now I was desperate," Michael said. "Desperate to find some peace, a quiet place. I needed to *think*. I needed to find God again."

He heard Susanna's sharp intake of

breath. "You went alone? Without Deirdre?"

"Deirdre would not have gone, even if I had asked. But I *didn't* ask. She became very angry with me. But I had such an urgency, such a need to get away — I felt I had no choice. I canceled my performances. All of them. And then I left."

Michael's back knotted with tension, and he straightened, easing his shoulders before going on. "As it happened, I ended up staying away for a long time — weeks. But it was the best thing, the most important thing, I could have done." He paused. "It changed my life.

"A friend — another singer and a man of great faith — allowed me the use of his cabin in Canada. I took nothing with me except a few clothes, some food, my Bible — too long unread — and a collection of Mr. Moody's teachings and sermons that my friend lent to me . . ."

As he went on, Michael forgot his present surroundings, forgot even Susanna's presence. He was back in the lonely cabin in the Canadian wilderness, back to the time when he had still been able to see . . . but only with his eyes, not with his heart.

It had been agony . . .

And it had been glory.

Alone in that cabin in the woods, he soon discovered that he had almost forgotten how to pray. He was like a child who had to learn his letters all over again. At last, when he did manage to break through the clutter of his mind and soul, when he finally began to pray — haltingly at first, but honestly — he found himself speaking to silent walls.

God's only response had been *no* response.

Drenched in self-pity, drowning in desperation, he begged and raged and wept. He learned what it meant to "storm heaven." At times his words were little more than the babble of lunacy, but still he went on praying, trying to break through the wall his own foolishness and sin had erected.

Only years later did he recognize how troubled and tormented he had been. And only with the perspective of time did he come to understand what God had wanted from him: total brokenness. Nothing less could release him from his past so that a new heart could be born in him, a new life begin in him.

Days turned into weeks until one morning, shattered and bitterly disillusioned, he faced himself in a soot-clouded mirror and saw a filthy, unkempt, unshaven *husk* of a man with wild eyes and streaks of silver in his hair. An empty man: empty of pride, his will crushed, his hope abandoned.

A man in total despair.

Only then did God speak. Not with a shout of judgment or angry rebuke, but in a whisper that pierced Michael's spirit and stitched his very soul to eternity. In that isolated, wind-battered cabin, Michael found his mind opened to truth, his soul flooded with the healing, all-encompassing love of his Savior.

He remembered the moment, remembered the Word: *"But what things were gain to me, those I counted loss for Christ. . . . What shall it profit a man, if he shall gain the whole world, and lose his own soul?"*

He also pored over the book his friend had lent him, the writings of the evangelist, D. L. Moody, a man known to despise the limelight. Moody repeatedly cautioned that one must *"sink the self"* and get rid of *"this man worship."* Man's desire, he wrote, is for *"the great and the mighty,"* but God's way is to use the *"foolish and despised things."*

One passage in particular reverberated in Michael. He read it over and over until finally it was seared into his memory forever. *"If we lift up ourselves and say we have got such great meetings and such crowds are coming, and get to thinking about crowds and about the people, and get our minds off from God, and are not constantly in communion with Him, lifting our hearts in prayer, this work will be a stupendous failure."*

That's what his work had become, Michael realized. That's what *he* had become. *A stupendous failure . . .*

And in the realization, Michael found new hope. God had broken his heart only to fill it with his own presence, his truth, and his love. At times, Michael thought he would surely die of the outpouring of such wondrous love.

A few days later, he went home: a new man, with a new heart, and a new life.

As Michael went on speaking, Susanna realized that he was not so much recounting the past as *reliving* it. She could see it in the tension of his hands, the tightening of his mouth, the disjointed frame of his words.

She could also sense what this was costing him. The pain of the account was chipping away like a sculptor's chisel at his reserve and composure. Once she was tempted to save him from the agony, to tell him he needn't go on. But her need to hear the rest — to hear *everything* — was too compelling. He was opening the door of his soul to her, and she had no intention of standing outside.

So she sat in rigid silence, her breathing shallow, her mind scrambling to imagine what he had gone through — all the while wishing she dared to touch him, to put her arms around him and comfort him.

"I tried to explain to Deirdre what had happened to me," he finished. "And the changes I needed to make in my life — in *our* lives. Foolishly, I believed I could persuade her to want what I had found."

"And you never went back to the opera?"

He shook his head. "No. I knew before I left the cabin that I was finished with that life, that I would never again go seeking after the world's idea of greatness. I knew that I would never sing again in public except to praise my Creator — and only then if God specifically led me to do so."

He grew still for a moment. "I think it might have been much like this for the great Jenny Lind. You know of her?"

"Yes, of course."

"She, too, left the stage at the height of her success and never returned. It is said that her reason for doing so was because her career had begun to draw her attention and her loyalty away from God. She feared it would consume her and eventually separate her from him entirely. So she gave it up."

"But wasn't it nearly impossible to abandon all that? Your voice — it's such an incredible gift —"

"I still sing," he said before she could finish. "I simply sing a new song. The orchestra is my voice now, and the music I write — this is my song. A song from my own pen, from my heart — and from God's heart, of course."

Susanna gazed at him with dawning understanding. She couldn't begin to comprehend everything he had relinquished, even though she stood in awe of his willingness to surrender it. But she could see for herself that what he had renounced was nothing compared to what he had gained.

Michael had exchanged a crown for a Cross; the crown of celebrity for the Cross of Christ.

There was no doubting the serenity she saw in his face, the undercurrent of peace that emanated from him, even when life was at its most chaotic. The strength of his character and the power of his genius were tempered only by his submission to the God who had gifted him.

The life he lived was a victory, a tribute, a rare and continual blessing to everyone who knew him. Michael himself was a gift.

Finally, Susanna realized, she had met the man behind the music.

When he had completed his story, Michael's mood seemed to change. He rose, facing her. "Well, I've kept you long enough."

"Oh, no, Michael! I'm so grateful you told me. All this time I've wondered why . . ."

She stood, feeling the need to say more, to say something . . . meaningful. Instead, she was able to manage only a question. "Michael, will you ever sing again? In public?"

He seemed to frame his words with great care. "Only if I knew it was what God wanted."

"But how would you know?"

"I would know," he said after a moment, "because I would not be able to *not* sing. It would be . . . that I could not contain the joy, and so I would have to give it voice."

Susanna studied him. "Tonight, for the first time," she said, "I finally feel as if I know you."

"*Sì?* And now that you know me, Susanna, I wonder — do you *like* me?"

"What? Of course, I —" She broke off. "What do you mean?"

He started around the table, then paused, a ghost of a smile touching his lips. "It's something Caterina said just the other day. She informed me that she loved you better than anyone else in the world — with the exception of her papa, of course."

Susanna warmed to his words. "Thank you for telling me that, Michael."

"And then," he went on, "she asked me if *I* liked Aunt Susanna. Naturally I assured her that I . . . like Aunt Susanna very much."

Susanna found it nearly impossible to swallow.

He drew closer.

"She also asked if you are *aware* of how much I like you, and pointed out that I should make my feelings known to you, lest there be any doubt."

"*Did* she?" Susanna fought for breath.

"Oh, yes. Cati was very firm about that."

He came the rest of the way around the table and took Susanna's hands in his.

"Since I will most surely never hear the end of it if I don't act upon my daughter's advice, allow me to reiterate what I said to Caterina."

He squeezed her hands a little. "I like Aunt Susanna very much," he said, his voice scarcely more than a whisper. "Very much indeed."

Susanna's heart turned over as she saw the uncertainty in his expression and heard the tenderness in his voice.

"Cati also said that when you look at me, she can tell you like me, too."

Susanna inhaled sharply. "Did she? Precocious child, Caterina." She had intended to assume a light tone, but her voice wavered.

A look of surprise darted over his face. "Ah," he said. "Is it true, then?"

Susanna swallowed against the lump in her throat. "Yes . . . it's true."

When he opened his arms to her, it felt like the most natural thing in the world to step into his embrace and let his warm strength enfold her. And when he eased back enough to pass a hand over her cheek, not quite touching her but hovering as if he *wanted* to, Susanna had the strangest feeling that he could *see* her, that he was looking deep inside her.

She drew his head down to hers, closed her eyes, and with both hands began to trace the lines of his face with her fingertips, just as he had done the night he had first "looked" at her. He let out a long, shaky breath as she continued to mold his face with her fingers.

When she stopped, he touched his forehead to her forehead, then his lips to her lips. "Susanna?"

Again, Susanna squeezed her eyes shut, reveling in the sound of her name on his lips.

"Susanna," he repeated, "do you think you could ever come to love a hopelessly stubborn blind man who is probably too old for you and is given to long bouts of silence?"

Susanna framed his face between her hands. "I thought you knew," she said softly. "I already love such a man."

His smile was slow in coming, but infinitely tender. "And . . . do you know how I feel about you?"

"I think I should make certain, don't you? Caterina wouldn't want me to have any doubts."

"That's true. Ah . . . let me think: how do the Irish say it? 'I love you . . . more than anything.' "

"*Everything,*" Susanna corrected. " 'I love you more than *everything.*' "

"*Sì!* And I love *you* more than everything!"

He swept her into a dizzying embrace and kissed her again. And again.

"Do I make myself clear?" he asked.

"Perfectly," Susanna replied.

THE GIFT, THE GIVER, AND THE GLORY

That Voice that broke
  the world's blind dream
Of gain, the stronger hand may win,
For things that are 'gainst
  things that seem
Pleaded, the Kingdom is within.

PERCY CLOUGH AINSWORTH

New York City
A week before Christmas

Backstage in the rehearsal room, a few minutes before the concert, Michael put his arm around Susanna and drew her aside. "How are you doing?"

"I'm . . . ill. Yes, I'm definitely ill. I'd really like to leave and go home now, please."

380

Susanna kept her tone light, but there was some truth in her reply. At the moment, she would rather be anywhere else than here, preparing to go onstage.

He smiled and clucked his tongue at her. "You're going to be fine, *cara*." He turned his head as if listening. "Are we alone?"

Susanna glanced around. "Yes, but I don't —"

"So, then — tell me again what you're going to remember if you get nervous."

"Michael, I'm more than nervous! I'm terrified!"

He lifted an eyebrow. "*Tell* me."

"Oh, all right! The *Gift*, the *Giver*, and the *Glory*."

"And explain."

Susanna glared at him. "I must remember that my gift is no greater — and no smaller — than any of God's other gifts." She paused, her voice a little stronger as she went on. "In playing the organ, I offer it back to the Giver of all gifts, who makes it shine with glory."

Michael lifted a hand to graze her cheek. "Tonight God will make your gift . . . *all* our gifts . . . shine with glory. You will see, *cara*."

He leaned down to kiss her — a gentle but lingering kiss.

"Ahem."

Susanna turned. Paul Santi was standing there, his face the color of ripe beets. "*Scusi,* Michael, Susanna. It is time."

The lights dimmed. The velvet curtains opened. The audience vigorously applauded the orchestra, then waited amid rustling and murmuring.

Relieved that she'd actually made it to the organ without tripping, Susanna sat staring at the manuals. The stops. The music. Her hands.

There had been so little time, so few rehearsals.

She stared at the backs of the musicians and choir members. They were ready. Confident. At ease. Again she glanced at her trembling hands, then wiped them down both sides of her dress.

Paul stood with his violin and gave the musicians their note of A. He waited until the cacophany of tuning swelled and finally died away. Then he left the stage to get Michael.

Susanna forced herself to search the audience, her gaze traveling upward to Michael's private box where Caterina and Rosa Navaro were seated. Caterina saw her and waved, and Rosa smiled. Buoyed a little by the sight of them, Susanna took two or three deep breaths and wiped her hands again. Downstairs, in orchestra seating, she found Dr. Cole and Dr. Carmichael — newly betrothed, both their faces aglow. Beside them sat Miss Fanny Crosby, beaming in the direction of the orchestra.

A hush fell over the concert hall as Paul escorted Michael onto the stage, followed by an outburst of applause. A rush of pride and love swept over Susanna as she watched Michael acknowledge the audience's welcome with a small bow. Did others see him as she did — as elegant, as regal as a prince, achingly handsome in his black tails and snowy white stock?

He turned to the orchestra, touching his toe to the metal strip at the podium, the marker he used while conducting. Unexpectedly, he lifted his head and aimed a knowing smile in Susanna's direction, nodding ever so slightly, as if to reassure her.

And then it was time. Michael gave a light tap of the baton, squared his shoulders, and cued the organ's robust introduction to "Adeste Fideles."

A rich blast of sound rumbled through the concert hall as the mighty organ, the full orchestra, and three choirs announced to the audience that a celebration of joy had begun.

"O come, all ye faithful . . ."

What a glorious sound! Susanna had to remind herself that the music emanated not only from the organ, but from her, pouring out from the depths of her spirit and powered by the gift that had been given to her. Even so, she had to struggle to retain control and harness the power of the massive instrument she so precariously commanded.

She gave only an occasional glance at the music in front of her. Instead, she watched Michael: not the manuals or the stops or even her own hands, but Michael. She watched him so closely — every movement, every facial twitch, every lift of his head or sweep of his baton — that gradually she began to feel herself being melded into the orchestra, absorbed into the choirs. Under Michael's leadership, she became one with the musicians and the music.

So immersed was she in this festival of praise that she lost sight of her fears and inadequacies, forgot about notes and chords and arpeggios, no longer thought about crescendos and diminuendos or even stops and manuals. It was all a gift, and she was only one of the many givers.

Michael sensed the very instant when

Susanna's panic gave way to command, her self-doubt to excitement, her fear to freedom. He knew, exactly to the beat, when she wrested control of the organ and conquered it.

It happened long before the children's lighthearted selections and the traditional carol singing had come to an end. The gate of her spirit opened wide, freeing her gift to rise above the concert hall, to soar beyond her self-limitations — even beyond his own expectations for her.

From the first impromptu passage through the unexpected improvisations, the angelic winging of the descants, the elegant, inspired transpositions — he knew the fire that fueled her brilliance was *holy* fire. Her fear was gone.

By the time they reached the "Hallelujah Chorus," Michael himself was on fire, and the audience with him. The "Chorus" was, in his estimation, the greatest, most divinely inspired piece of music ever written.

Handel's servants had often found the composer in tears and exultation as he composed the *Messiah*, a miracle of music. He became a captive of its creation, writing in solitary frenzy, never leaving his house, day or night, until the work was completed — in an unbelievable twenty-four days. And when the final triumphant note had been penned, Handel himself had proclaimed that he had seen "all Heaven before me, and the Great God himself."

Of all tonight's selections, Michael knew that Susanna dreaded this one the most. She believed that in performing this incomparable work, one simply could not be anything less than brilliant, for fear of disappointing God himself.

Michael, too, was feeling the pressure, despite the fact that he had conducted the "Chorus" numerous times. He heard the crowd stir, but he gave the musicians a few seconds to ready themselves for the coming effort before turning and prompting the audience to stand. Then he lifted his shoulders, drew in a long, steadying breath, and inclined his head slightly in Susanna's direction to indicate that she should lead them onward.

Susanna had thought she would have to call upon every ounce of strength and skill available to her just to do an acceptable rendering of this greatest of all choruses. Instead, she found herself lifted almost from the beginning, empowered with an ease, an agility, and a depth of emotion she could never have imagined.

It seemed she could do no wrong. Her hands had never held such power; her fingers and feet seemed to fly. She felt as if she were riding on the wind, and thought her heart would surely explode with pure elation before this was finished.

She caught the look on Michael's face — pure, unmeasured joy — and only then did she realize she was seeing him through a glaze of tears. For the first time, Susanna understood, at least in part, what Handel meant when he insisted that God had "visited" him in the creation of this greatest of all music.

And then, as they arrived at the final measures, she heard the glorious, incredible voice that had once thrilled thousands on a different kind of stage now rise above the other voices to fill the entire concert hall.

Michael was singing.

Susanna's gaze swept the sea of faces before her. All through the audience, people wept for joy as they lifted and clasped their hands in adoration. The hall vibrated with this thundering outpouring of music and praise and power.

Her eyes went back to Michael, and his beloved face filled her vision. He would sing in public again, he had told her, only when God called him to do so. Only when he could not contain the joy . . .

> *And He shall reign forever and ever.*
> *King of Kings, and Lord of Lords,*
> *Hallelujah!*

The *Gift* . . . the *Giver* . . . and the
Glory . . .
Oh, the glory!